ONCE UPON A PHOTO BOOTH

INDIGO BAY BOOK 2

TERESA YEA

Visit me at teresayea.com
Sign up for my newsletter

ALSO BY TERESA YEA

Indigo Bay Series (Romantic Comedy)

Pixely Ever After (#1)

Once Upon a Photo Booth (#2)

Symphony in the Snow (#3) (coming October 2021)

Golden Age of Monsters (Dark Fantasy Romance)

Love in a Time of Monsters (#1)

Empire of Sand (prequel)

Gothic Horror

Black Heart, Red Ruby (standalone)

1

—————

ELYSE DARROW JUGGLED her laptop and latte, finding a precarious balance on a table no wider than her lap. With a backlog of wedding photos to retouch, she'd been airbrushing a bride's face for the better part of an hour. When she was in her creative zone, her surroundings ceased to exist. She was blind to the toddler waddling toward her. Her noise-cancelling headphones drowned out the stomping of his pudgy feet.

"Goo!"

Disaster in the snap of a finger.

The toddler's hand seized her tablecloth and yanked. Her latte was in her mug one second—her lap the next.

"Argh!" Letting out a pirate-like growl, Elyse bolted from her seat. Her thighs were on fire, her amorphous gray shirtdress soaked with steaming coffee.

Chaos followed to the tune of a wailing toddler and a frazzled though apologetic mother.

The barista swooped in with a damp dishtowel and dabbed the hem of her dress.

"Not to worry," he said, smiling up at her, "I'll have you cleaned up in no time."

His Aussie accent sent a thrill up her spine, conjuring up cinematic images of the land down under:

Majestic kangaroo courts hopping across the outback. Drovers in dusty bush hats tossing another shrimp on the barbie. Hugh Jackman and the Hemsworth brothers. Okay. Her idea of Australia was pretty cliche, but she was a small-town girl who'd watched a few too many movies.

"Thank you, Roger," she said, her teeth clenching as the dishrag touched her tender thigh. "Guess I should have ordered the cold brew."

Elyse sat back in her seat and let Roger attend to her spill. She eyed his tattooed forearm, admiring his toned bicep as he cleaned up. She'd been a frequent customer at The Coffee Haus since it opened in downtown Indigo Bay.

As an artist, she considered herself a connoisseur of quality:

Gourmet coffee imported from the jungles of Tanzania.

A cafe decorated in a minimalism meets Southern rustic decor of reclaimed wood tables, tiny succulents in mason jars, and painted brick walls.

Aussie exchange students in tight jeans with even tighter asses...

Such were the perks of forking over fifteen bucks for a cup of coffee.

Roger wiped up the trickles of coffee on her knee without breaking eye contact; the dishtowel disappeared beneath her skirt. His fingertips grazed her inner thigh, sending another rush of heat through her body.

Elyse's brows arched in surprise.

"Steady there, cowboy," she said, catching his wrist before his hand traveled any further. "I think you got it."

"Just making sure I get every drop," he said. "That latte was mighty hot."

No, *you* are mighty hot.

Elyse thought he looked like a delicious hipster. Dirty blond hair slicked back and tied into a tidy man-bun. Cheeks covered in groomed stubble. Roger could pass for the fourth Hemsworth brother. Definitely bad for her self-control.

Elyse's lips curled into a sardonic smile. "So you wanted to make extra sure I didn't burn my vagina?"

Shock registered across Roger's face. The toddler's mother, who'd been pelting Elyse with apologies fell into a stunned silence.

Elyse propped her elbow on the back of her chair, basking in the mother's disapproval. Growing up in a town as oppressive as Indigo Bay, she took great pleasure in shock and scandal. A firm believer in her First Amendment rights, she spoke as free as she pleased.

"Well I never! Come on, Billy." Scooping up her snotty kid, the mother shot Elyse a dirty look and stomped out of the cafe.

"I know her," Elyse said, watching the glass door slam shut. "Attends my mother's church. I predict there's a phone call from Mama in my future." She cringed, thinking of the reprimanding to come.

Roger rested his arms against her bare knees. "Do you make it a habit of shouting 'vagina' in front of children?"

Elyse rolled her eyes. "Billy the baby doesn't understand. And I didn't shout," she said, though her mama had criticized her in the past for her lack of an indoor voice. Not to mention her unladylike vocabulary.

"What if his first word is 'vagina'?"

"There are dirtier words for 'vagina,'" Elyse said, checking her nails. "Speaking of which, thank you for trying to save mine from a horrible scalding."

"I didn't want a lawsuit on my hands. What would that do to our Yelp rating?" he added with a wink.

Elyse did a double take. She was trying to make him uncomfortable, but Roger took to her flirting like a pro. "I bet you are."

Roger smiled at her from underneath his lashes. His voice

3

lowered into a seductive rasp. "It's in my best interest to make your vagina happy."

"You dirty dog," Elyse said in her best imitation of a cheeky Southern belle. The coffee had cooled, but her thighs were still flushed with heat. She leaned forward until they were nose to nose. "Whatever am I to do with a scoundrel like you?"

"I break in five." Roger reached out and wound a strand of her lavender hair around his finger. "I have a few ideas."

———

SPRAWLED ON HER BACK, Elyse stared up at the whispering canopy of crepe myrtle, pondering her life choices. She was waiting for Roger to slip on the condom and frankly he was taking a long time. Her fingers drummed against the soft grass. What was the problem? Were condoms packaged differently in Australia? How could someone so deft at making cold-brew be so clumsy with his equipment? The long wait between third base and home run was killing her mood.

Elyse raised herself on her elbows and watched him struggle. He looked a little foolish with his distressed jeans bunched around his thighs. "Need help?"

"I've got it," he assured her.

"You sure?"

Roger looked up and narrowed his eyes. "Yeah."

"Tear along the perforated line."

"I know," came his terse reply. "I don't wear condoms. Why don't we skip this part?" he asked, coming toward her. "It feels better anyway."

"Whoa," Elyse rolled away. "Holster that gun before you come near me."

"Fine." Roger sighed, then added, "Though I don't know what the big deal is..."

"Listen, do you want to do this or not?" Elyse snapped.

"Okay, okay. Don't rush me," Roger grumbled under his breath. "I can't stand bossy women."

"What's that?"

"Nothing."

Flopping on her stomach, Elyse thought about all her neglected client work. She reconsidered this romp by the millpond with Roger. It seemed like such a good idea. She was seizing the day, taking what she wanted while she could still get it, casting off the shackles of her oppressive upbringing and empowering herself as a modern woman. Her mother's disapproving face swirled into mind, slut shaming her with a purse of her genteel lips. Rebellion surged through Elyse, mandating she see the task through—not for her own pleasure, but to prove that she was in control. Fucking for feminism. It made perfect sense at the cafe.

She eyed Roger and another trickle of doubt cooled the flames of rebellion. Bathed in the fading evening light, he looked less delicious and more ridiculous. His man bun, now untidy because of their heavy make-out session, was more stringy than she realized. It hung down his face in greasy pro-wrestler strands, killing her Chris Hemsworth fantasy and replacing it with an unwanted Hulk Hogan stand-in. The flood of heat she'd experienced at the cafe was fading into regret. Elyse also considered suggesting that they run to the drugstore for another box of condoms as King Size was far too generous for what Roger was packing.

Ding.

Elyse snatched her phone from her purse.

A text from her roommate Olive Peale.

"At the grocery. There's a buy one get one half off deal on milk. You in?"

Elyse's thumbed a reply. "What kind of milk? 2%? Low fat? Soy?"

"Does it matter?"

"Hell yeah it matters!"

"Whole."

"Don't buy it," Elyse wrote. "Get the soy."

"But it's a great deal! And I have coupons!"

"We don't need two gallons of whole milk just because there's a deal. You don't even like milk."

No reply.

"Olive? I know you read my message."

Silence.

Elyse sighed. She'd find two gallons of whole milk in the fridge when she got home. It was hard maintaining a minimalistic lifestyle when your roommate was a collector. Since Olive moved in after the death of her dad, Elyse's loft had become uninhabitable. She couldn't turn around without knocking into a Funko Pop tower or stubbing her toe on a Star Wars action figure. They were both twenty-three, but sometimes Elyse felt like she was living with a five-year-old. It didn't help matters that Olive was dating her former wedding venue rival, Wesley Belmont, king of excess.

"Ha! Got it," Roger said. "Here's Johnny!"

Elyse shut off her phone. "Who's Johnny?" she asked, then her eyes traveled downward and grimaced. "You call your dick 'Johnny'?"

Roger pounced on her and nudged her legs apart with his knee. "A great sword needs a great name."

"I think you're being over generous with yourself," she said with a shake of her head.

His mouth crushed hers before she could say more. The kiss was all tongue, no finesse, and the longer it went on, the more Elyse thought she would choke. She could taste the garlic on his breath and the unpleasant aroma of Italian sausage from his lunch.

"You know something funny?" she asked, breaking the sloppy kiss. "I don't even know your last name."

"Elton-Smith," Roger said, mashing his mouth against hers again. They rolled around the grass. Elyse came out on top, straddling him with her long, Pilates-toned legs.

She had so many questions. "Don't you want to know my last name? I realize it's too late for introductions, but it feels like something we should know about each other. Is your name hyphenated? If I ever marry, I plan for my future husband to take my last name."

Roger squeezed her small breasts and with a twist, he was on top of her again, pushing against her with a jerky thrust of his hips. After rearranging her legs, he was inside her and pumping. Elyse laid beneath him, a little underwhelmed.

"Oh yeah Sheila. Does that feel good?" he asked, looming over her. His face was red and veiny. He looked strained... like he was about to take a massive dump.

Elyse grimaced, wishing she could prop a paper bag over his head. "It feels okay...Ow."

"What's wrong?"

"There's a twig poking me in the ass."

She tried to clear her mind of all distractions, but a million thoughts whizzed through her head. Did she remove that pimple on the groom's chin? Did she highlight the bride's cheekbones enough? What kind other useless junk would Olive end up buying? Takeout or leftovers for dinner tonight? She wished he would hurry so she could tackle the rest of her tasks for the day.

Over Roger's goat-like grunts and the din of her thoughts, she heard a crunch of footsteps on dry leaves. A whimper sounded from somewhere near by.

"Roger?" She pressed her hand against his chest. "Did you hear that?"

"Nope."

Raising herself up on her elbows, she checked over her shoulder. The sunset caught the gleam of the waters' surface, drenching the grassy embankment beside the old millpond with ambient orange light. A swirl of dust hovered above the deserted bike trails and the early autumn air was crisp, spiced with falling leaves and the promise of Halloween.

"Stop it!" Elyse seized his shoulder. "I heard a sound."

Roger groaned. "We're in the middle of bloody nature."

A breeze rustled the cattails, conjuring up the ominous soundtrack of an '80's slasher flick.

Elyse swatted the side of his head. "You know something? I don't like your attitude. Get out of me. I don't know about you, but I'm not going to be butchered with my panties around my ankles."

"Butchered? What is this nonsense?"

"It's not nonsense, I heard—"

Roger silenced her with a deep and searing kiss that dissolved some of her fears.

"Back in Melbourne," he began, cradling her face between his hands, "our yard was alive with noises. Wombat flies, pythons, cane toads, rodents of all shapes and sizes. They were everywhere, but none of them were deadly." A brief pause. "Well, the python might kill you, but that didn't stop us from living life and having a bit of fun," he said, flipping her on her stomach and covering her body with his. "Am I right?"

The tension dissipated from Elyse's body. "I guess."

As he dragged his bristled chin against the back of her neck, Elyse closed her eyes, trying to shut off her mind. Roger trailed kisses across her bare shoulders, licking the curve of her spine. Urgent fingers kneaded her buttocks, between her legs, urging her to lift her hips for re-entry. Elyse felt a twig probe against her ass. Underwhelming.

A lone howl echoed in the marshes beyond her head.

"There it is again!" Elyse scrambled out from underneath him.

Roger's forehead drooped to the grass, shoulders slumping. "You're making a big deal out of nothing!"

"You may not value your life," Elyse slapped the grass blades from her naked bottom and slipped on her gray dress, "but I have work to do and I'd rather not die a gristly death at the hands of a serial killer."

She peered into the thicket of cattails. Sure enough, something small and furry darted between the reeds. A bark pierced the quiet evening. Within moments, a runty terrier darted out from the cattails. The dog was no larger than a possum, its patchy midnight fur sprinkled with nettles and caked with mud. As it skulked about Elyse's feet, pausing now and then to sniff her ankles, she noticed that its tongue, a tad too long for its mouth, drooped at its side.

"Well, hello," Elyse said, squatting on her haunches to pet the terrier's matted fur. "Aren't you the most pathetic little thing? What's your name, honey? What's a sad little thing like you doing out here all alone?"

She earned a peppy bark and a lick on the wrist. The dog's tongue felt like sandpaper. Poor thing, it was probably dying of thirst.

"Where's your mama?" Elyse asked, scratching the stray behind the ears. The dog squinted at her with its one good eye; the other eye twitched and had a milky blue film over the iris. Its face was adorably ugly and looked mildly deranged.

"Look at you. Hey," she called over her shoulder to Roger, "don't you think he resembles Edgar Allan Poe?"

"That's nice." Roger had already slipped on his black Coffee Haus T-shirt and jeans. He was checking his phone.

Elyse rolled her eyes, all the heat for him earlier now turning tepid. What was she thinking?

As Elyse searched the dog's neck for a collar, the stray shivered beneath her fingertips.

In place of a collar, Elyse found a dirty length of rope, the frayed end dangling past the terrier's emaciated ribs. Frowning, Elyse sifted through its fur and discovered bleeding, broken skin around its neck.

9

Her entire body shook with murderous rage. "Poor little Edgar Allan Poe," Elyse cooed, scooping the dog into her arms. Its body was feather-light and its fur gave off a musky stench with every petting. "No one will harm you. I've got you now."

The nameless terrier, henceforth known as Poe, panted, his crusty tongue lolling out the side of his mouth. His stumpy tail wagged and Poe fired a series of excited barks. A line of drool made its way down Elyse's forearm and her heart melted. A self-proclaimed cynic, Elyse never believed in love at first sight. Until now. She was already making plans, adding doggie beds and kiblets to her Amazon shopping cart.

She stomped up to Roger and slapped him on the arm. "Look what this dog's owner did to him."

"Ow." Roger rubbed his arm.

"Look how malnourished and abused little Poe is!"

"Poe? Who the hell is Poe?" Roger, asked, glancing longingly at their romping spot in the grass.

Elyse hoisted the dog up. "I just named him," she said, parting the fur around Poe's neck. "Just look!"

"Whoa!" Roger held up his hands and backed away. "I don't need to see that."

"I suspect he might also have worms. To the vet! Stat!" Elyse checked her wristwatch. She lived across the street from Aiden Hines' pet clinic and knew Aiden closed at 5 pm. "It's four thirty. We need to haul ass."

"Listen, babe," Roger said, walking toward her with the speed of a snail. "Work calls."

"You're not going with me?" Elyse clasped Poe against her chest in a last-ditch attempt to garner his sympathy. "Look at this face."

"That's some face," he said, trying to hide his grimace. "But artisanal coffee isn't going to make itself."

Having said his piece, Roger idled around her Honda until

Elyse remembered that they'd only taken one car and he was expecting a ride back to The Coffee Haus.

"Fine." Fishing for her keys, Elyse yanked open the driver's side door. "Whoa, whoa, whoa. What are you doing?"

Roger was already sitting shotgun. "What?" he asked, buckling his seatbelt.

"Get your ass out of that seat. Poe gets to sit up front."

"Seriously?"

Elyse leveled him a 'don't mess with me' look.

Rolling his eyes, Roger snapped open his seatbelt and made a big dramatic gesture of flinging the door open. As Elyse revved up the engine, she heard him mutter something from the backseat. It sounded like "Nasty woman."

She glared at him in the rearview mirror. "*What* did you say to me?"

Roger glanced down at his lap. "Nothing."

———

AFTER DUMPING Roger off at The Coffee Haus, Elyse hightailed it to the town's one and only pet clinic. She stood beneath the awning, irritated.

Her history with the owner was... complicated.

Aiden Hines was Indigo Bay's darling. Respected veterinarian. Heir to his grandfather's barbecue sauce conglomerate, Hines & Sons. Boy next door turned most eligible bachelor. The guy you'd loved to have a beer with. The friend you called when you needed someone to help you move or drive you to the airport.

When he was fourteen, he made the front page of the Indigo Bay Observer when he rushed into a burning house to rescue Mrs. McCafferty's kitten. The major had given him the key to the city.

When the Cagney farm reported that someone had

kidnapped their prize turkey, it was Aiden who cracked the case, tracking down Mr. Gobbles to the local college. He'd stormed the frat house, fought off the pledges with a folding chair, and tucked Mr. Gobbles under his arm like a football.

According to the local news, Aiden, 16, administered first aid to Mr. Gobbles, who was molting, tipsy, and in a state of shock. In appreciation for his heroic efforts, the town erected a statue of a boy and a turkey on Main Street. The statue was ridiculous. Teenage Aiden, wearing a raccoon hat and armed with a musket, shielded his eyes from the sun as he surveyed the town from atop his vista. Mr. Gobble's feathers were ruffled by a mighty gale. They gazed—Lewis & Clark style—at a distant point beyond the horizon.

Whenever Elyse and her mother passed by that statue, Mama was fond of saying, "Aiden is a good boy to have around in a sticky spot." Then Mama would glare at Elyse, "His mother must be so proud."

Aiden became a veterinarian and opened a practice next to his statue. Elyse was still bitter. She was glad to see that a pigeon had taken a mighty dump on Aiden's raccoon hat.

The list of Mr. Perfect's many accomplishments were never-ending.To hear the locals fawn over him, one would think he was a superhero as opposed to the square Elyse knew him to be. In fact, everything about Aiden was square, from the shape of his jaw to his fashion sense to his by-the-book lifestyle. It seemed as if he had a vendetta against fun.

Elyse gazed around the empty waiting room in shock.

"Where's Aiden?" she asked, approaching the counter where Viannie Hines, Aiden's baby sister, was practicing her selfie.

"Gone." Viannie fluffed up her bleached blonde hair and struck another pose. *Snap. Snap.*

"What do you mean gone?" Dumping Poe on the counter, Elyse eyed the clock above the front desk, then peered into the hallway leading into the exam rooms. "It's fifteen till closing.

Where the hell's Aiden?" she asked, baffled that he should not be here.

Her photography studio, Once Upon a Photo Booth, was directly across the street from Aiden's practice. From her loft above the studio, she had an eagle's eye view of the practice's foot traffic. Locals, tourists with pet emergencies, even folks from the next beach town over brought their dogs, cats, birds, ferrets, snakes, and hamsters from nine to five, Monday through Friday. While Aiden was a square in every aspect of his life, he was flexible about his schedule, never turning away an animal in need of care even if it meant staying overtime. It helped that he didn't have a life outside of work.

"The doctor's out of the office," Viannie said, not taking her eyes off her phone.

"Seriously," Elyse laughed, "where is he?"

"Are you deaf? Aiden's out." Viannie fluttered her falsies, annoyed. "And thank God. All day long, it's 'File this, order that, see to this, bill that.' We had three surgeries scheduled in the morning. A three-legged dog, an obese cat, and a duck who had been mauled by a goose. What a freak show. Long story short, we're closing early and I'm heading home to look for another job," she said, rising from her swivel chair. Only then did she notice the terrier on the counter. "Goddamn that's an ugly dog!"

"Woof!" Poe wagged his tail in agreement.

Viannie sidestepped Elyse and made a beeline for the lights, dousing the office in darkness.

"I found him by the millpond," Elyse said, scooping Poe up in her arms. "He's in bad shape."

"Yeah... he needs a lot of work. Consider putting him down."

Elyse covered Poe's lopsided ears, suppressing the urge to slap Viannie. "Aiden needs to see him right away," she said, following the girl out the door.

"Well, too bad. Aiden's on a date."

"A date?" Her brows knitted into a frown. Figuring Viannie was trying to get rid of her, Elyse scoffed. "Be serious."

"I am serious."

Elyse peered into Viannie's face and found no trace of face-tiousness. She scratched Poe's stomach and received a yap which brought her a small measure of comfort from the unexpected nip of jealousy. "But, but... Aiden doesn't date!"

"I'm just as blown away as you. Hey, off topic," Viannie said, shoving her phone under Elyse's face. "What do you think of this picture? I'm thinking about using it for my LinkedIn profile page."

Elyse scanned Viannie's selfie. Tousled sex hair, heavy on the eyeliner. Blouse unbuttoned, cleavage abounding. Elyse shook her head. "Wrong. All wrong," she said, but her mind latched onto Aiden's mystery woman. "Who is she? What does she look like? Do I know her?" A pause. "For the record, I could give two shits about who he sees. It's just... *Aiden on a date*, I can't," her fingers burrowed into her lavender hair, "I can't even."

When she finished, Viannie was studying her with a strange expression. "I can see how much you don't care."

"I don't," she repeated.

"Her name is Lisa something or other. She's tall and blonde and gorgeous. Big juicy knockers."

"Good for him. Great." Elyse gave a noncommittal shrug. "Did he tell you where they were going?"

"Knowing my brother, dinner at Applebee's. Red Lobster if he's feeling fancy."

That brought a smile to both their lips. Aiden was thirty, going on eighty. Having grown up next door to him, Elyse had concluded long ago that Aiden had never been young. Even as a boy, he was studious and serious, never a scraped knee or a crooked tie. Somehow, recalling Aiden's inability to have any fun made Elyse feel better about this new window into his social life.

"Then again," Viannie added, eyeing Elyse up and down, "he

mentioned that he was taking her to his Charleston condo afterward."

"Wait! He owns a condo?" Elyse shook her head, baffled. "When did this happen? How come nobody told me?"

"Maybe because it's none of your business?"

The two exchanged venomous smiles.

"He hosts an Airbnb. On the off-chance there's no booking, he makes himself comfortable... if you know what I mean," Viannie said, enjoying being the deliverer of bad news.

Elyse's hands bunched into fists. Staying over the weekend implied sex and the thought of Aiden having sex didn't sit well with her. Especially when she needed... when Poe needed him.

"This is so selfish of him," Elyse blurted out. "Who'll look after my dog?"

"So come back tomorrow."

"I can't wait until tomorrow." She held Poe up so his stumpy legs dangled in the air. "What if Poe doesn't make it till tomorrow? What's Aiden's address?"

"Are you crazy? I can't tell you that. He'll kill me." Viannie headed for her parked car.

"Wait! Viannie! Give me your phone."

"What?" the girl turned around.

Elyse snatched the phone from Viannie's hand. She set Poe down and swiped through the camera roll. "Your selfies are all wrong. See? This photo has 'bitch face' written all over it. Stand here, shoulders back, chin down. Try smiling. Yes, better. No, not that wide." She snapped a series of shots and flipped the phone around. The photos were a vast improvement.

"These are fantastic!" Viannie gazed at her picture in awe. "I look hot yet responsible."

"That's why I get paid the big bucks, kid. You're much prettier when you're not posing. Natural smile, natural lighting. Got it?"

Viannie nodded. "Yeah."

"Good," she slapped her hands together, "come on, Poe. I

guess we'll come back tomorrow. Meanwhile, you'll just have to suffer overnight, but you're used to suffering aren't you, boy? Let's hope you don't die before Aiden has a chance to look at you."

As if on cue, Poe whimpered and covered his good eye with his paw.

Viannie looked to Elyse and her pathetic dog. She sighed. "135 Waterfront Park," she said, detaching a silver key from her keyring. "Here."

"What's this?"

"Key to Aiden's condo."

"How did you—?"

"I made a copy so Mason and I could have a weekend getaway away from all this small town scandal." A proud shrug. "We totally did it in his bed."

Elyse held up her hand. "Too much information. So why are you giving it to me?"

"I figure it'll piss him off if you make yourself at home. So be my guest, make yourself at home."

Elyse hesitated, then snatched up the key. Her lips curled in a mirror image of Viannie's mischievous smile.

Despite their differences, there was one thing they could both agree upon: Aiden needed his perfect feathers ruffled.

And no one was better for the job than Elyse.

2

A THUNDERSTORM DESCENDED UPON CHARLESTON, ushering in an unexpected downpour. Soaked to the bone, Elyse let herself into Aiden's condo. She kicked off her soggy shoes and left them by the Welcome Mat.

Poe whimpered, shaking off his wet fur.

"Promise you'll be quiet?" Elyse picked the dog up, her eyes roving around the living room.

"Woof!"

She received an agreeable lick on the cheek and grimaced, making a mental note to get Poe something for his breath.

A table lamp gave her enough light to see by.

Clutching Poe to her chest, Elyse tiptoed toward the couch.

The living room was spacious. A dark cherry dining table. A couch upholstered in deep navy fabric.

She plucked a pair of sheer lace panties from an armchair and wrinkled her nose. She didn't know what unsettled her most: Aiden getting action or Aiden getting more action than her.

"Disgusting." With a roll of her eyes, Elyse dropped the panties and followed the trail of discarded clothes. In the hallway, she sidestepped a peep toe pump and Aiden's brown oxford.

Her heart thumped faster the closer she crept toward the master bedroom. Raindrops pattered the window pane. The downpour against the roof echoed in her ears. A thunderclap lit the dark hallway in a flash of white.

Elyse halted beside the door, counting on the shadows to disguise her presence. Poe had mercifully fallen asleep in her arms, his legs jerking in the throes of a squirrel-chasing dream. On the other side, Aiden's "date," Lisa What's-Her-Face sounded like she was having one hell of a good time.

"Oh, oh, oh, God, Aiden..."

"Oh come on." Elyse flushed from head to toe and, despite her discomfort, she felt a sudden shot of heat between her legs.

This was awkward. Then again, what did she expect barging into Aiden's condo in the middle of his 'date'? A part of her expected to catch them playing Settlers of Catan, a board game he'd brought over on more than one occasion to the delight of her roommate Olive.

Her stomach grumbled. Realizing that she'd skipped dinner, Elyse glanced at the tidy kitchen with its marble counters and stainless steel fridge. The practical thing to do would be to make herself a sandwich and wait.

Elyse pressed her ear to the door. They didn't sound close to finished. After listening to Lisa *ooh* and *aaah*, Elyse deduced that Aiden was a master of foreplay. At this rate, it could be hours before he got down to business and who knew what his stamina was like. Knowing Aiden's tendency to excel at everything, it was probably outstanding.

Elyse swiped a damp swath of hair from her face and sighed. Her tumble with Roger was underwhelming, and this broad sounded like she was on the verge of the best orgasm of her life.

Elyse rolled her eyes as another moan escaped the bedroom.

"Enough of this." Patience was not her virtue. If she couldn't have good sex why should Aiden?

Taking a deep breath, Elyse shoved the door open.

A THUNDERCLAP ILLUMINATED THE SCENE: Rumpled bedsheets. The scent of sex. A gorgeous woman sprawled on her back, black evening dress bunched around her hips.

And Aiden's face.

Buried between her long legs.

Within that bubble of white light, Aiden looked up, his eyes squinted into slits, widening when recognition struck. "Elyse? What the hell are you doing here?"

The room faded to black. Elyse's heart dropped, her emotions flip flopping between malicious glee at catching Aiden with his pants down and discomfort.

Discomfort bordering on rage.

Except...

What did she have to be mad about?

"How dare you!" The words burst from her mouth before she had the chance to think it through. A wild idea struck. The opportunity for mischief was too delicious to pass up.

"Aiden?" Lisa propped herself on her elbows. "What's going on? Who's this?"

Rolling with her fictitious drama, Elyse stomped into the room and swatted a bewildered Aiden upside the head. She pelted him with vicious albeit harmless swats to the shoulders and back. "You ungrateful turd! I come home after a long hard day of waiting tables—" *Slap. Slap.* "—to help you pay off your vet school tuition. And this is how you repay me?—" *Slap. Slap.* "—by eating another woman's pussy?"

Aiden, no doubt more confused than he'd ever been in his life, shielded his face from her blows. "What are you talking about?" He turned to Lisa. "I don't know what she's talking about." To Elyse: "You're insane!" To Lisa: "She's insane!"

Poe, now awake, filled the room with rapid fire yapping.

Lisa scrambled off the bed and yanked down her black dress. "You're married?"

"No!" Aiden waved his hands in surrender. "No, no, no!"

Elyse couldn't help herself. "We've been married for three years!"

"You lying piece of—— " Lisa clocked him across the jaw with a vicious *thwack*.

Stunned, Aiden stumbled and collided against Elyse, who continued to pummel him. "Stop hitting me!" He grabbed for Lisa. "Calm down, I can explain. If you'll only listen."

"Don't touch me!" Snatching her pumps from the floor, Lisa whirled on her bare feet. "And don't you dare call me!"

"Lisa! Wait, Lisa!" Shooting Elyse a murderous glare, Aiden chased after his date.

Left alone, Elyse clamped a hand over her mouth, her shoulders shaking with mischievous laughter. "I can't believe I did that," she said to Poe.

"Woof!"

Aiden disappeared for so long that Elyse began to worry. Suppose he'd ran out in the street and right into the path of a car? She enjoyed riling Aiden up, but she didn't want his untimely death on her conscience. Wringing her hands, Elyse wandered to the kitchen. She grabbed a cereal bowl from the cabinet, filled it with tap water, and set it on the upholstery.

"Here, Poe," she whistled.

The terrier's toenails tapped across the hardwood at the sound of her call. Poe lapped the water, his stunted tail wagging back and forth.

Elyse ruffled his fur. "What are you so happy about?"

"Yip Yip!" Poe looked content. After draining his bowl, Poe trotted over to the leg of Aiden's couch and lifted his stubby hind leg. A stream of urine sprayed the expensive leather.

"Poe!"

ELYSE WAS in the middle of slicing her roast beef sandwich in half when the front door burst opened.

A shadow spilled across the floor.

Elyse glanced up, grateful she had a knife.

Aiden was back. He lingered at the entryway, his arms braced against the threshold, his chest rising and falling as he tried to catch his breath. Elyse assumed he'd been running after Lisa.

He was drenched from head to toe, his hair plastered to his forehead in shiny dark-blond ribbons. His eyes scanned the living room and settled on her, pinning her with a homicidal gaze.

She gulped.

Elyse took a step back.

She'd known Aiden all her life, but this was the first time she felt afraid of him.

His presence filled the room: bigger, taller, and more imposing. His white dress shirt was plastered to his body, outlining the hard slope of his biceps and the chiseled V of his torso.

Elyse's attention dipped lower. His fly was halfway unzipped, his trousers tented around the crotch. She averted her eyes and, looking for any means of distraction, took a big bite of her meaty sandwich.

Aiden came toward her, his steps slow and deliberate, predatory and feral. The rye stuck to the roof of Elyse's mouth.

Reaching the kitchen, he flattened his palms on the granite countertop, his eyes burning like a pair of searing coals. One by one, his knuckles popped. A big vein throbbed at his temple.

"What. Are. You. Doing?" he asked, his words a murderous growl.

Elyse considered making a run for it but as she studied him, she remembered who she was dealing with. This was Aiden, rescuer of kittens and turkeys, eagle scout and professional goodie two shoes.

Growing up, her family's McMansion shared a pecan grove with the vast Hines' estate and now their respective small businesses shared the same street. She'd seen Aiden Hines each day, every day since she was born.

At six, she'd stuffed an entire slice of lemon meringue pie into one of his sneakers. At thirteen, she'd sideswiped his car with her bike. He'd bandaged her knee when she fell out of a tree. Once, out of a favor to her mother and to the mortification of her fourteen-year-old self, Aiden had driven Elyse and her date to the junior high's Sadie Hawkins dance.

He was a permanent fixture in her life, much like an older brother whose existence you didn't bother to acknowledge but you liked having around if only to annoy. She knew all about his rigid upbringing, his antiquated views of the world. She was never really in danger. Not from a guy who bandaged puppies for a living.

"I repeat," he said, "what are you doing?"

"Eating a sandwich." She held up the other half. "I see you've already eaten," Elyse grinned, "but may I interest you in a roast —Hey!"

Aiden ripped the sandwich from her hand and flung it across the kitchen. The sandwich smacked against the window and flopped in the sink. A sad slab of roast beef clung to the faucet. Horseradish streaked the window pane.

Elyse propped her hand on her hip. "I think you're over-reacting."

"Overreacting," he repeated in that same subdued whisper.

Aiden took one step forward.

Uh oh.

Elyse backtracked.

Six feet of enraged male shadowed her view of the exit. All memories of Aiden, the turkey rescuer of Indigo Bay, disappeared from her mind.

"How'd you get in here?" he asked.

Elyse held up the silver key. "That Viannie," she shook her head, "she's a troublemaker, that one. I didn't ask for the key or the address, she forced it upon me. Here, you can have it back."

Without tearing his eyes off hers, Aiden snatched the key from her fingers and chucked it over his shoulder. Metal clinked against marble.

"Oh, okay," Elyse said with a strained smile, "you're just going to throw it."

"Why?"

"You sound exactly like Batman right now. Christian Bale's Batman. Not that lame Ben Affleck Batman."

His demeanor was terrifying, the calm before a storm. "Speak."

Her hands fluttered like nervous birds. "There it is again! The resemblance is blowing my mind."

As Aiden advanced, Elyse bumped against the fridge. Cold steel chilled her damp back. Her muscles tensed; her heart drumming to the beat of her anticipation. What did she expect to happen? What did she *want* to happen? She imagined her legs wrapped around his waist, her bare ass thumping against the fridge's door as he took out his sexual frustration on her.

Flustered, Elyse eyed her dog. "Poe," she spoke out the side of her mouth. "Poe. Come save me."

"Woof!" Poe scampered away, seeking refuge beneath the kitchen table.

"Useless," Elyse muttered, her attention back on Aiden. "He's the reason —"

BAM!

Aiden slammed the flat of his hand against fridge.

Elyse jumped. "Okay, enough of this intimidation game. If you think you can scare me, think again. I'm here because that dog needs immediate medical care and you're the best vet I know—the only vet I know—"

BAM!

His other palm slammed against the fridge, bracketing her between his arms. Elyse's legs turned into wet noodles. He filled her field of vision, forcing an intimate awareness with the intensity of his eyes and the heat of his body, inches away from her own. He smelled of rain and the cool outside; a droplet still clung to the end of his nose.

She was scantily clad herself: braless by personal choice, pantiless thanks to Roger, and sopping wet. Her jersey dress outlined what little curves she had and clung to crevices she shouldn't flash in public. Aiden's gaze seared a trail down her body, lingering on her chest. Her nipples were as hard as marbles. Elyse gave her dress a conscious tug. This was like a set up for porn?

Oh sir, I came for shelter from the rain. Whatever will I do?

For a heartbeat, he leaned forward as if he were to bury his face in her hair. His breath brushed her temple.

"You broke into my home," Aiden said.

Are you saying I've been bad? Very, very bad?

Blushing to the tips of her ears, Elyse snorted. "Well, who's fault is that?"

"Are you implying that it's *my* fault you broke into my home and ruined my date?"

"Yes," she said, nonplused. "I found Poe by the millpond and took him straight to your office. Viannie said you left early. You never leave early," she glared at him, the accusation heavy in her voice, "you stay over for everyone else, then skip town when I need you. Are we becoming lax in our professionalism?"

"So I'm not allowed to have a life?"

"Not when I need you," Elyse fired back.

"When do you *not* need me?" His hand flexed against the fridge, opening and closing into a claw. "I hadn't had sex in over a year..." His eyes swept over her face. "*A year.*"

"Well, don't look at me," she croaked, her mouth turning to cotton. Elyse licked her lips, drawing his attention.

His eyes, now returning to the innocent color of warm mocha, never left her face. "You're the last thing I'd ever look at."

"You hate me now, don't you?" Elyse glanced up at him with big innocent eyes. "If you want me to go, I'll go. I'll even call What's-Her-Face and straighten things out, only please don't hate me. And please don't take it out on Poe."

As if on cue, the terrier trotted up to them. "Yip! Yip!"

Aiden turned his head and stared at Poe, who whimpered and shivered yet stood his ground.

"Look at that face," Elyse said. "Isn't he the cutest and ugliest thing you've ever seen?"

"Yip! Yip!"

Aiden turned to Elyse. She could see the struggle in his face to remain cold and knew she'd won. At last, Aiden's head drooped, his forehead inches away from her own.

"So we've been 'married for three years?'" he asked.

"White lie. It worked, didn't it?"

"You know you're psychotic, right?"

Elyse broke into a big smile. "I get things done."

"Don't look so smug about it," he said, bending down to pet the dog.

"Yip!" Poe bared his sharp white teeth. His pointy ears stood on end, poised for attack.

"Calm down, big guy. We know you're tough." Stroking Poe's nape, Aiden whispered a few gentle words and the dog relaxed, its scrawny body limp with supplication. Poe rolled onto his back and drew up his paws, shamelessly inviting a belly rub.

Elyse watched Aiden's fingers pause over the rope welts on Poe's collar. He glanced up at her, eyebrow raised in a quizzical arch.

"See?" she asked, kneeling beside him. "I wasn't kidding when I said he needed you. His former owner abused and neglected him." She took over the belly rubs and Poe's tongue lolled out of his mouth in doggie ecstasy. Feeling Aiden's eyes on her, she added, "Didn't you dedicate your life to saving poor, defenseless animals?"

"Within reasonable office hours." He paused and glanced toward the living room. "He peed on my carpet, didn't he?"

Elyse lowered her eyes. "He got a little excited."

With a frown, Aiden inspected a patch of raised scars beneath the dog's ribs. He turned Poe over and found a mass of bruises on its shoulder. "I have a stash of spare medical supplies in the hall closet..."

Elyse's face lit up. "You mean you will help him?"

His shoulders lifted in a sigh. "Whatever Elyse wants, Elyse gets."

"That's the spirit!" Overcome by gratitude, Elyse flung her arms around Aiden and pecked him on the cheek.

Aiden's eyes widened in surprise.

His skin imprinted heat on her lips. She wiped away the kiss and swatted him between the shoulder blades.

"You're the most dependable guy I know," Elyse said, rising to her feet.

"That's the problem." He sounded grim though she couldn't fathom why. As she ran to the hallway for the medical supplies, Elyse glanced over her shoulder. Aiden was still where she'd left him, sitting cross-legged on the floor, sullenly rubbing his cheek.

3

"How long does he need to keep it on?" Elyse asked, watching Aiden secure a cone of shame behind Poe's neck. "What's it for, anyway?"

Scribbling a note in Poe's chart, Aiden glanced up. His lab coat was pristine, the collar stiff. The side part of his honey-blond hair called to mind a '40's matinee idol or 'Captain America' as her nerdy roommate Olive dubbed it. He was all business today. Calm and collected, the consummate healthcare professional.

But Elyse recalled a different Aiden. Sopping wet and shaking with unspent lust. She liked that Aiden better—that Aiden was trouble while this one was as neutered as the canines in his waiting room.

"Poe has a rash on his left flank and several lesions because of self-inflicted gnawing," he explained. "I'd give it about two to three weeks until the lesions heal." Aiden pried open Poe's jaw and peered inside with a silver pen light. "Why?" he asked. "You have something against buster collars now?"

Elyse's mouth crinkled in distaste. "It offends my aesthetics. Can I take it off before Halloween? I have plans for Poe." Enshrouded in the cone, Poe looked more feeble than ever, and not at all fashionable. She tilted her head to the side, trying to get used to taking care of a handicapped dog.

"I'm afraid to ask," Aiden said. "What do you plan to do to the poor guy?"

"How do you feel about a silver stripe down his back? I've ordered a special doggie dye—"

"No." He shook his head. "Just no."

Elyse propped her elbows on the examination table. A strap of her oversized black cami slipped off her shoulder. She let it hang. Her wardrobe malfunction caught Aiden's attention, and in one fluid motion, he righted the fallen strap.

Their eyes met.

Last night's drama flashed between them.

Aiden clicked his ballpoint pen and frowned at Poe's chart. "Do you need to borrow a jacket?" he asked, the tips of his ears redder than usual. "I have a spare in my office."

"Nope. I'm perfectly comfortable. Just soaking in the last of the summer sun before the cold sets in."

He cleared his throat. "You should really think about wearing a bra."

"I never wear a bra. Don't believe in them. Besides, A-cups should be exempt from wearing anything that binding."

They'd had this argument before. Aiden had a real problem with her wardrobe—or lack thereof. Today it was about her braless choices, yesterday it was about her minimalist closet: a sea of gray with the occasional white and black pieces thrown in when she wanted to mix things up.

Elyse leaned even further on the table so the neck of her already low camisole dipped lower.

Aiden brought a hand over her dog's eyes. "Look away, Poe."

"What? I don't even have breasts. They're just nipples. Men show their nipples all the time," she said, snapping a finger in his face. "Aiden, look at me."

"No." He turned away, blushing from his neck to hairline.

"There are nude beaches all over Europe. It's no big deal."

"I don't know about Europe," Aiden said.

"You sound like my mother." Elyse gazed around the exam room. The faded cabbage rose wallpaper and nondescript water-color landscape of the low country wetlands reminded her of her grandmother's Thomas Kinkade collection. The waiting room was no better with its framed posters of cats and dogs. Aiden was working in a geriatric design nightmare. He wouldn't understand the importance of making over Poe, which would do wonders for the stray's self-esteem. As it stood, she suspected her dog was depressed.

Elyse gazed upon Poe's limp tail with concern. "I also bought him an autumn romper. Do you think it'll work with the cone?"

"Absolutely not. We want to let the rash breath." Slamming the chart shut, Aiden cast her skeptical glance. "I suggest you lose the romper. Dogs aren't meant to wear clothes."

"Sure they are," she said, knowing such logic would only rile him up. "Dogs freeze in the winter too."

"They have fur to keep them warm."

"I bet they prefer flannels."

Aiden narrowed his eyes. "I suggest you buy yourself a set of flannels and leave Poe alone."

Elyse plucked Poe from the table.

"Yip! Yip!" Poe's barks echoed from within the cone.

"Wait until you see his new sneakers," Elyse said as Aiden ushered her out of the exam room.

"No shoes."

"But I got him a pair—quad—" Elyse checked her math. "I got him *shoes* for every season. You'll dig his Halloween Doc Martin platforms."

Aiden pinched the spot between his eyes. "Spare the dog some dignity."

At the reception counter, Aiden handed Elyse a prescription for a topical rash ointment. "He's also blind in his left eye," he said, ripping off another page from his pad. "I want you to give him drops twice a day."

"What's this?" Elyse asked, overwhelmed from all the prescriptions.

"Anti-fungal ointment for his infected toenail, which," Aiden shot her a pointed look, "won't be helped by shoes. Let his paws breathe, wash often with a mild soap."

Elyse juggled Poe in her arms. "Poor boy, no wonder you're depressed." She turned to Aiden. "What's this lump on his back?"

"Lipoma."

She frowned. "What's that?"

"A tumor caused by an excess of fatty cells. Benign," Aiden added after Elyse's eyes widened at the mention of 'tumor.'

Her hand hovered over the golf-ball sized lump. "Is he in pain?"

"He feels nothing, I assure you. His tongue, however..."

"His tongue? What about his tongue?"

"Is too big for his mouth. I recommend you spray it with a quick spritz of water to avoid desiccation," he said.

Poe was nine, about sixty in doggie years. Elyse's head swarmed. His medical care was overwhelming. She wasn't sure she was responsible enough to look after her succulent collection (most of which are now dead) let alone an aging dog with a host of health issues.

Leaning over the counter, Aiden told his sister, "Schedule Poe for an X-ray next week. We'll take a closer look at his hips."

With a roll of her eyes, Viannie's fingers pecked away at her keyboard. "Anything else, boss?"

"His hips?" Elyse asked, studying Poe, who glanced up at her with his one good eye. "What's wrong with his hips?"

"He's having a hard time walking on his hind legs so he compensates by placing his weight on his forelegs," Aiden explained. "Ossification in the hip joints is common in senior dogs."

Elyse planted a kiss on the top of Poe's humpback. "So he's in pain every time he walks?"

"No worries," Aiden said, seeing her concern. "Minor surgery can correct that, but we'll cross that bridge when we get there."

Stroking Poe's fur, Elyse pondered these new medical expenses. Her wedding photography business was stable, her custom photo booth rentals were taking off, but she wasn't exactly flush with cash. Taking Poe to the pound wasn't an option. In just a few days, Poe had become her shadow. He slept in her bed, cuddled up next to her leg as she brushed her teeth, and even tagged along on her photo shoots.

"How much is all this going to cost?" she asked.

"Don't worry about it," Aiden muttered.

Elyse blinked in surprise. "No, really. I can pay," she offered, not wanting him to treat her like a charity case. She exchanged a quizzical look with his sister. Viannie swiveled to her monitor, a 'this is between you two' gesture if Elyse had ever seen one.

"We'll talk about the bill later." Aiden averted his eyes as he ripped off the last of Poe's prescriptions and handed it to Elyse. "That takes care of it. X-ray appointment scheduled, Viannie?"

"Sure thing, Cap," Viannie said, scrolling through Buzzfeed.

"Why does everyone call me Cap? Is there some joke I'm not aware of?" When no one answered, Aiden tossed Poe's file on top of a growing stack of manila folders his sister had yet to file. "Never mind, I don't want to know," he said. "Viannie, if you're not too busy, how's my afternoon schedule?"

"Mrs. Sawyer's Siamese at two. The Halladay kid's iguana at four," Viannie said with her back to her brother. She ditched her Buzzfeed browse and began filling out a job application. "Anything else?"

Aiden glared at the back of his sister's head. At last, he stripped off his lab coat. "Guess I'm off to lunch."

Viannie swiveled around. "Nice cami, Elyse. Where did you get it?"

"Thanks," Elyse smiled. "Ansley Mills. It's a British online retailer specializing in simple yet quality clothing." Elyse plucked at the transparent material. "This is part of the 'Kate Moss Circa '94 collection. I've got a discount code if you're interested. I'm a brand ambassador."

Viannie brightened up. "Yes, please." Then she glanced down at her bountiful rack. "But I'll probably have to wear a bra. I don't have that heroin chic thing you've got going for you."

Elyse dashed away Viannie's concern with a wave of her hand. "You don't have to wear a bra if you don't want to."

"Yes she does." Aiden stepped in front of her, blocking Viannie from view. He yanked the glass door open. "Come on, out you go."

"When I bring Poe back for his X-ray, I'll tell you all about European beaches," Elyse shouted over Aiden's shoulder.

"No you won't," Aiden said. "Don't listen to her, Viannie."

"I like her," Elyse said, as Aiden ushered her outside. "Despite what everyone says, she's a girl who knows what she wants. And I think she likes me."

Aiden shook his head. "Don't corrupt my sister."

"Liberate, Cap. I'm liberating your sister."

"Stop calling me that."

"Hey," she swatted him across the midsection, "cheer up. How about I treat you to lunch? It's the least I could do after all you've done for Poe."

"The least you could do is pay your vet bills," Viannie added from the doorway.

Both Aiden and his sister turned to Elyse.

Elyse flashed Aiden her most charismatic smile. "Lunch sounds like a better idea."

4

Elyse kicked a stray piece of gravel from the sidewalk. A pumpkin spiced latte-scented breeze caressed her cheek. She glanced at The Coffee Haus. Roger was wiping down the outdoor tables, hair slicked back, his man bun tidy once again.

Roger froze at the sight of her, then his gaze fell upon Aiden. He pulled his shoulders back, clenching his jaw as he eyed Aiden up and down.

Elyse turned away, her cheeks burning. She hadn't spoken to Roger since their interrupted tumble a week ago. No doubt there was bad blood between them. She picked up the pace.

"That guy is really checking you out," Aiden said, matching her harried steps as she lit down Main Street. "Someone you know?"

"I had a thing with him," Elyse mumbled.

"What kind of a thing?"

She shrugged, fixing her eyes straight ahead. "Just a thing."

"But it's over now?" Aiden asked, studying her stoic profile.

They passed Aiden's famous statue. She was disappointed to see that the town had cleaned up the pigeon poop and polished both boy and turkey to a shine.

"Oh *hell* yeah," she said. "And now I'm having major coffee withdrawals. Last time I shit where I drink."

Glancing over his shoulder, Aiden squinted at the cafe's sign. "So artisanal coffee, eh?" He squared his shoulders. "I'm a Folger's man myself."

Elyse sighed. "Of course you are."

She pointed at their final destination. "There it is," she said louder than usual. "Wesley and the girls should be waiting for us. It's barbecue. Right up your alley."

Aiden frowned. "I didn't know this was a group lunch."

"It wasn't," Elyse said, rapidly texting. "It is now."

The Pig Bar was nestled between the artisanal ice cream parlor, Icy Cauldron, and a men's hat shop, Bowler Alley.

Aiden raised a skeptical brow at The Pig Bar's facade, a mixed media marriage between chrome and distressed wood. A vertical herb garden divided the eatery from the ice cream parlor.

He gave a 'hmmm' of disapproval and glanced at his watch. "I'm jonesing for some Applebee's."

"I did *not* just hear you say that." A horrifying possibility dawned on Elyse. "Don't tell me you've never tried any of the new restaurants around Main Street?"

"I don't know about this hipster food. I'm a steak and potatoes kind of guy. Applebee's has a mean salad bar. I eat with my patients—well, their owners that is. Mrs. McCafferty, Mr. Bled-soe, Major Davis," he said, ticking off their names on his fingers, "we always get the corner booth on account of Mrs. McCafferty's walker."

Elyse blinked. Did she hear him right? "Those are your lunch buddies? Each of them are like ninety years old!"

"Only Mrs. McCafferty. She turns ninety-six this October and is still as sharp as a whip. Major Davis is a cool seventy."

"Oh dear God." She ran a hand through her lavender hair. "You're more hopeless than I thought!"

"What?" Aiden frowned. "I like what I like."

"And like what you know." Elyse shook her head and glanced down at Poe. "Ya hear that, boy?"

"Yip!" It was a judgmental bark.

"What do you talk about with your friends? Arthritis?"

Aiden nodded, ignoring the slight. "Arthritis comes up more often than not, but what can you do? Major Davis has tales about 'Nam. Mr. Bledsoe shows me his grandchildren's pictures and I helped him figure out how to use his new iPad. Mrs. McCafferty used to be a Rockette at Radio City Music Hall and tried to teach me how to tap dance. She says I have good posture, but two left feet."

Elyse couldn't hear another word. It was just too sad. "Oh Aiden, my mission is clear. You need to hang out with people your own age *and* expand your palate. Hang with me, kid, I'll teach you how to be cool," she said, hooking her arm through Aiden's and dragging him across the street. "Your family is in the barbecue business. If you had an inkling of financial savvy, Hines & Sons would be Pig Bar's main supplier."

Aiden snorted at the suggestion. "We're fine as we are."

"Change is good."

"Depends on what kind of change."

"Don't you want to rock the boat?" Elyse pinched her thumb and forefinger together. "Just a little."

"No," he said flatly. He gestured to the lamppost. "Do you want me to tie Poe's leash here?"

"Oh no," Elyse waved off his offer, "Poe's coming with us."

Aiden grimaced. "You're bringing him inside?"

"This is a dog friendly restaurant." Elyse set Poe down and he immediately sniffed the sidewalk, the edges of his cone scraping concrete. She looked Aiden up and down, noting his discomfort. "Don't tell me Applebee's doesn't allow dogs inside?"

Aiden narrowed his eyes at the health grade card on The Pig Bar's window. "'A', huh?" He squared his shoulders. "We'll see about that."

A BLAST of chilly air greeted them inside. Rows of long, distressed wood tables comprised the dining floor. Exposed air vents ran across the walls and ceiling. Concrete floors. Slaughterhouse vibes.

Elyse thought it was awesome, but one glance at Aiden and she knew she had her work cut out for her.

"Looks like a cafeteria," he said, scanning the decor.

"I like the canteen ambiance," Elyse said.

Aiden grimaced as he studied the daily specials on the chalkboard menu. She hoped he noticed the minimal yet multicolored script and the doodle of a pig with a waxed mustache.

Elyse whispered in his ears, "I did that."

"You mean you drew the picture of the pig?"

"And the lettering too." She rocked back on her heels, beaming with pride. "Yup, I'm a chalkboard artist. Freelance, of course."

"I didn't know 'chalkboard artist' was a job."

"It's not. It's a hustle."

Aiden narrowed his eyes at the chalkboard. "Why does the pig have a mustache?"

"It's ironic."

"I don't get the irony. It looks serious and yet it's also a pig so for 'irony' to apply is to say pigs are not serious. I've treated many pigs in my day and I have to attest that they are enterprising animals and very serious about their rooting and foraging."

Elyse clenched her teeth and rolled her eyes heavenward. "You're killing me, Hines!"

"Pig hoof marinated in a cilantro sake sauce," he read, meeting her eye. "I don't know about this."

"Live a little."

"Yip!" Poe said, seconding her advice.

"Elyse!"

Elyse whirled at the sound of her name.

"Over here!" Lucie Teegarden motioned her over from the corner table. Across from her, Elyse's roommate, Olive, had her arms hooked around the neck of her boyfriend, Wesley Belmont.

Dressed in a white sundress speckled with red poppies, Lucie was giving her side of the table a thorough wipe down with lemon-scented bleach wipes.

"Hope we're not late," Elyse said, approaching her friends with Poe in tow.

Making a face, Lucie pushed a tin tray containing a sampling of barbeque sauces to the side. "I had to wait fifteen minutes with those two," she said, jerking her head toward Wesley, who was nibbling on Olive's ear as she perused the menu. "You owe me big."

Three months ago, Olive and Wesley were locked in a war of wedding venues. All summer long, it was 'I loathe Wesley' and 'I will crush him.' But after the death of her dad, Olive surprised them all by selling Cottage on the Green to Wesley and now the two were a make-out away from committing a public sex act. Apparently they had been romancing each other online in some role playing game long before they ever met in person. Wesley and Olive engaged in some seriously kinky cosplay when they thought they were alone. Elyse had seen things that no roommate should ever see.

"Break it up." Elyse grabbed Olive by the elbow and dragged her from Wesley's lap. The last thing she wanted was an encore performance.

"Yes, mommy," Olive said, swiping a swath of bright auburn hair from her forehead.

"You're so cute when you do that," Wesley said, propping his chin in the palm of his hand. His midnight black hair was in artful anime-esque disarray. Elyse thought it sweet that he couldn't keep his eyes off his girlfriend. Sweet and sickening.

Olive blushed. "And you're so cute when you do that chin in palm thing."

"Come here," Wesley said.

As if pulled by some unseen magnetic force, Olive was in his arms again and the two made out like there was no tomorrow.

Shouldering the two apart, Elyse sandwiched herself between them. "Aiden, you sit here," she motioned to the spot beside Lucie. "Keep an eye on them."

Aiden tied Poe's leash to the leg of the table. Sedated from doggie antibiotics, the terrier fell fast asleep on the concrete floor, his cone of shame askew.

"Hey man." Reaching across the table, Wesley exchanged a fist pump with Aiden. "What are you doing here? Applebee's closed early today?"

Wesley was Aiden's only age-appropriate friend. They were old veterinary school classmates, but whereas Aiden graduated with honors, Wesley dropped out to become a professional poker player.

"He's being adventurous." Elyse said. "Aren't you, Aiden?"

"Seems like I didn't have a choice," he said, sitting down just as the server handed him a tiny clipboard with a slip of paper.

"I'll give you a minute," the server said.

Aiden studied the minimalistic menu, his lips pressed in a thin line of doubt. "Hmmm."

Elyse sipped her water. "What's the matter now, Hines?"

He scanned the menu. "Tripe in ponzu sauce. Kale salad with pig's ear and quail eggs. Grilled gizzard on a stick." Looking up from the clipboard, he said, "These are all parts of the pig that you feed your dogs. Are you sure this isn't some dog cafe? This is a travesty to barbeque."

Elyse tapped her temple. "Open mind, remember?"

"So long as my lunch doesn't open up my bowels." He turned the menu around. "Why is the menu so tiny? What is the purpose of this clipboard when they already have a chalkboard menu?"

Elyse, Lucie, and Olive erupted into giggles.

"What?" Aiden asked.

The menu made its way around the table and got a swipe from Lucie's bleach wipe. Wesley grabbed the sanitized clipboard and passed it to Olive, his fingers grazing hers a little too long.

The server returned with a pitcher of blackberry infused sweet tea.

"I'll have the cilantro sake hoofs," Elyse said. "And he'll have the pig's ear salad—extra quail eggs." She leaned over to Aiden. "Trust me, it's the chef's signature dish. The ears were the scraps of the pig back when you were young, but now they're elevated dish. Very delicious, I assure you. Right, Lucie?"

Lucie held up her hands in self-defense. "I'm just having a grapefruit salad. I don't eat meat."

"See?" Elyse took a swig of her iced tea. "Even Lucie is more adventurous than you. You're thirty—"

"Twenty-nine."

"Sorry, twenty-nine going on eighty. Why not live a little? Surely this is cooler than Applebee's."

Aiden remained silent until the server set his pig ear salad in front of him. He ate the kale, picked at the quail eggs, and probed the pig's ear with his fork.

Elyse kicked his shin. "Carpe diem, remember?"

Upon her insistence, Aiden lifted the tiniest piece of pig's ear to his mouth. He chewed and chewed. Paused. And chewed some more.

After an eternity, Aiden reached straight for his iced tea.

Elyse waited until he downed the entire glass. "That wasn't so bad, was it? Better than what you've been eating."

Wiping his mouth on his sleeve, Aiden looked for the server. "Refill, please...."

Elyse gestured to her plate. "Want a bite of my trotter?"

"I'll pass," he said.

Elyse forked a grapefruit from Lucie's salad and received a

scowl from Lucie. "I didn't lick my fork," she said, and licked the tines of her fork. "May I have another?"

"Ugh." Lucie pushed her salad away.

Olive frowned. "Stop tormenting her."

"You're so cute when you say that," Wesley said.

Olive smiled. "No, you are."

Elyse turned to Lucie. "If sharing food makes you sicker than these two, you've got to get your priorities in order."

"I agree," Aiden said, snatching a biscuit from the communal basket. "These two really are too much."

Suppressing a grin, Elyse glanced down at her phone. "Viola's late."

"Oh, she's not coming," Olive said. "Her co-worker called in sick so Viola had to cover her shift."

"She doesn't get a lunch?" Elyse thought about the fourth member of their group: quiet Viola de Roet, who worked in the dusty vinyl record store down the street. Viola was already tiny, probably malnourished, and shouldn't be missing any meals. Elyse caught the server before he moved on to the next table. "I'll have an order of ribs to go."

"Wait," Aiden blinked. "They serve ribs here?"

"Secret menu."

The gang was halfway through lunch when a voice that sounded like nails on a chalkboard screeched from the entrance.

"Olive!" Coralee Davis, the mayor's daughter, waved. Gaudy gold bangles clinked down her wrist. "Hope ya'll didn't start without me!" Her pumps clicked as she wiggled across the restaurant. She wore black tights and a skin-tight pink off-the-shoulder blouse. Her blonde hair was styled in fresh beach waves.

Elyse whirled on Olive. "You invited her?"

Olive gave Coralee a half-hearted wave. Next to her, Wesley heaved a long-suffering sigh.

"She found out we were all having lunch and invited herself,"

Olive said. "I couldn't very well say no. Not after everything she's been through."

Coralee's ill-fated wedding to the sheriff's son, Mason Cole, had rocked Indigo Bay with more drama than a daytime soap opera. Not only had Mason cheated on Coralee throughout their engagement (with barely legal Viannie, no less), he'd been caught with his pants down on the big day—literally.

Coralee pecked Olive on the cheek. "Is there room for one more?" she asked, squeezing herself into the already crowded bench.

Before her public breakup with Mason, Coralee wouldn't be caught dead with Olive or any member of their nerd herd. Now Coralee was as clingy to her former wedding coordinator as molasses to a spoon on a cold winter's night.

"What did I miss?" Coralee asked, slapping her hands together.

———

MUCH TO ELYSE'S CHAGRIN, Coralee talked, nonstop through the second half of lunch.

"... I looked into the mirror and said, 'Coralee, *who* are you? Why did you let Mason walk all over you?'" She poked herself in the chest. "And then I had an epiphany. How could I expect Mason to love me if I can't love myself?"

"Wow," Olive said.

Coralee smiled. "You may have noticed that my arms look exceptionally toned today." She flexed. "Yoga. Three hours every morning. You too can look like me. This year is all about personal healing..."

Elyse rubbed her temples. No one brought on a migraine faster than Coralee.

"Anyway, let me tell you about my grocery store run this morning. I was torn between what type of milk to buy. Whole. Fat free. 2%. Almond. Coconut. Cashew. Soy. There are just so many to choose from."

Elyse picked at her gelatinous hoof and leaned toward Olive. "I hold you personally responsible for bringing her here to torment us," she whispered.

Elbowing Elyse in the ribs, Olive nodded along with Coralee's mundane tale of her trip to the grocery, a polite smile plastered on her face.

Elyse glanced around the table.

Lucie, the baker amongst the group, was sampling the fruit tart and completely lost in her private confectionery world.

Wesley's thumbs moved across his phone. Seconds later, Olive's phone dinged. Olive glanced down at her screen and her ears turned pink.

Across the table, Aiden glanced at his watch, probably longing for the salad bar at Applebee's.

"Oh Elyse," Coralee touched the back of her hand. "Your blouse is so..." she eyed Elyse's oversized camisole in pity. "I didn't realize business was so slow for you that you had to resort to wearing lingerie in public. But things will pick up. In the meantime, you don't have to wear these poor rags." Her blue eyes lit up in an *Eureka!* moment. "What do you say you and I go on a shopping spree and get you out of that ratty thing? My treat."

Elyse gave Coralee a tight smile. "Tempting." She cast around for the server. "Check please."

"I'll text you about setting up a shopping date," Coralee said, helping her unwind Poe's leash.

"Oh, well..." Elyse arranged Poe's plastic cone. "I'll consult my schedule."

Aiden stood up. "Sorry to run. Work calls."

Taking care of the check for everyone, he followed her out the door with the speed of someone who had a fire lit under his ass. One last glance behind them and Elyse could see that Coralee had launched into another self-improvement story. Lucie was stuffing her bleach wipes inside her wicker tote, but Olive and Wesley were fenced in by Coralee. Elyse pitied them until she remembered all the great sex they were going to have later, then her pity dissipated.

"I can't stand Coralee," Elyse said, jaywalking across Main Street to Whispering Vinyl. "Now that she's single, she won't leave us alone."

"Maybe she's just lonely," Aiden said.

"She's got her own friends."

"You never know who your friends are until a crisis happens. Looks like her sorority sisters never stuck around after her breakup with Mason, but Olive did."

"Look at you, waxing philosophical. Don't you have to get back to work?"

Aiden was in no hurry to be anywhere. "Ten minutes to spare," he said, glancing up at Whispering Vinyl's neon pink sign. "Besides, I've never been inside this record shop. Heck, I didn't even know people bought records anymore."

"They've made a comeback in a big way."

"That's a trend I can get behind."

Elyse thought it strange and oddly endearing that he'd spend the remaining ten minutes of his lunch with her. "Do my ears deceive me? Are you trying something new?"

"Records are not new," Aiden said, opening the door for her.

Out of the corner of her eye, she saw him smile.

Cool air conditioning greeted them as they stepped inside. By design, the shop was an updated replica of an old warehouse. They wandered down the aisles and rummaged through wooden bins filled with old records. The decor was a mash-up of old and new. Classic albums pinned all over the walls; music piped through blue tooth speakers. Branches of string lights bathed the aisles in a golden ambiance.

In all her days shopping at Whispering Vinyl, Elyse was hard pressed to find a more tranquil store. Its chief shopgirl, Viola de

Roet, was an enthusiast for soft rock and folk, and kept the volume level down to a whisper. Today, however, the closer Elyse and Aiden got to the cashier's counter, the more their ears rang with the rantings of an irate customer.

A lady with an unfortunate perm slammed a stack of records on the counter. "I demand a refund!"

"I'm sorry but you purchased these a year ago." Viola shrank behind the counter. Her cheeks flushed crimson. "It's past our refund policy."

"What's that?" the lady cupped her ear. "Speak up, I can't hear you."

"We can't refund—"

Elyse expected Viola to recover, but her friend never got her bearings. Furling her hands into fists, Elyse took a step forward.

Aiden placed a hand on her shoulder, stopping her in her tracks. "It's none of your business."

"But..." Elyse gestured to her helpless friend.

"She's worked here for over five years. Why not try to have a little faith?"

"You don't know Viola," she said. "She's like a frightened little rabbit. In fact, we took an online quiz and her spirit animal literally is a rabbit."

"Have you considered that she may be braver than you think?"

Elyse arched her eyebrow. "This is Viola we're talking about here."

"This is nonsense! The customer is always right." The lady's voice reached meltdown mode. "Do you think I have time to stand here and watch this idiot mumble? Where's your manager? Let me speak to your manager!"

Viola wrung her hands. "I can't. He's not..."

Seeing her friend on the verge of tears tipped Elyse over the boiling point.

"Elyse," Aiden said between clenched teeth. "Don't meddle!"

"Get off me." She yanked her arm from his grasp and stormed into the fray.

Grabbing the pile of records, Elyse shoved the stack into the woman's arms. "She said 'no refund' so do yourself a favor and leave this store before we kick you out."

The woman's nostrils flared. "Who the hell are you?"

Viola's manager, a squirrelly man with buggy eyes and a thin waxed mustache, peered down from the loft. "What seems to be the problem here?" he asked, descending the staircase.

"Your customer service is a disgrace," the woman chucked the records to the floor and pointed at Elyse, "And this purple-haired hooligan attacked me."

"We're terribly sorry. I'm mortified. Don't worry, we'll refund you in full and I will have a talk with my employee. And as for the purple hair—I don't even know her. You there! Get out." The manager snapped his finger, a more offensive gesture Elyse never saw. "Come here, Viola."

She expected Viola to react appropriately, which, in Elyse's book would be to give this snapping weasel a piece of her mind, but Viola scuttled to his call.

"Did you see how he disrespected her?" Elyse spoke out of the side of her mouth. "I'm offended."

"What do you have to be offended about?" Aiden asked. "He didn't snap at you."

"I'm offended on her behalf. This is workplace chauvinism at its worst. I ought to report him to the labor bureau."

Aiden gave her a quelling look. "What are you even talking about?"

"Justice," she said, watching Viola huddle in the shadow of her manager.

The manager's volume was far from a whisper. "Viola, did we learn nothing? The customer is always right. What is wrong with you?"

"I-I- She- We-" Viola's bottom lip trembled. A tear dribbled down her cheek as she swiped away the wispy blonde hairs from her eyes.

The manager sighed and did a face palm. "Use your brain for once. Sometimes I wonder if you have a brain."

Elyse had heard rumors that Viola's manager was a tool, but this was the first time she'd witness the weasel in action. The more he talked, the taller he stood and the more Viola shrank into herself. It was too much. Viola's tears. The woman's smug face. The manager's bullying.

"That's enough!" Elyse marched behind the counter.

The manager's eyes widened. "Who are you? What are you doing? This area is for employees only."

Elyse stepped in front of Viola. "Don't you dare disrespect her like that," she said, squinting at his nametag, "Todd. Do you even know who you're talking to? This girl is a musical prodigy. Like Mozart and Beethoven and Eames Fawkes."

"Who's Eames Fawkes?" Todd asked.

Elyse clicked her tongue. "Only the best DJ in the EDM scene."

"What's 'EDM?'" the woman interrupted.

"Electronic dance music."

The woman gave a skeptical snort. "I don't like the sound of that."

Elyse locked eyes with Aiden. "Funny, you remind me of someone I know. Anyway, *you,*" she whirled on the manager, "are an asshole and Viola doesn't need this job."

Viola hiccuped. "I don't?" she asked, wiping the tears from her cheeks.

"Damn right you don't."

"Elyse." Aiden leveled her a warning stare. "Shut up..."

Todd glanced over Elyse's shoulder to Viola. "Are you saying you're too good to work here?"

Viola was a deer in the headlights. "I—"

Elyse stepped forward, blocking Viola from view. "Of course

she is! Even an idiot can see that. Come on, Viola," she said, seizing her friend by the hand and dragging her toward the door. "Your soul has been crushed long enough. Let's blow this popsicle stand."

"Wait," the manager called. "Viola! You're quitting?"

"You bet your ass she is!" Elyse called over her shoulder. "You can take this job and shove it up your—"

"Viola's not quitting," Aiden said. "Give us a moment," he glared at Elyse, "I'll have everything all sorted out."

"Don't put words in her mouth, Aiden. Viola's been under-paid and unappreciated long enough. Say goodbye Viola."

Viola gave her former manager a pathetic wave.

"If you walk out that door Viola," Todd called after them, "don't bother coming back."

Shooing Viola out the door, Elyse poked her head back inside. "Don't worry, she wouldn't come back to your shitty little store, anyway."

Aiden seized her elbow, yanking her outside.

5

"Look alive, Vi," Elyse said, noting the droop of Viola's head. "This is the first day of the rest of your life."

Poe scurried ahead, sniffing at a branch, lifting his leg to whiz on the trunk of a cypress tree. A lone seagull cawed overhead.

"Please don't make this any worse than you already have," Aiden said.

Elyse whirled on him. "*I've* made things worse?"

Aiden placed a gentle hand on Viola's shoulder, his face softening with sympathy. "There's still time to get your job back. Anyone can see it was the purple-haired hooligan's fault."

Elyse propped a hand on her hip. "Huh."

"Go back and apologize before she has a chance to do real damage."

Viola took a hasty step toward the record store.

Elyse couldn't believe her ears. "Apologize?! Viola, don't you dare move!"

Viola halted dead in her tracks, her eyes darting between the two. Elyse planted her feet apart. Aiden's jaw twitched, anger radiating off him in waves. Poe chased a flock of pigeons by the fountain. The birds scattered, landing on the fountain lip. One brave pigeon found a perch on Poe's cone of shame.

"Yip! Yip! Yip!" Poe ran in circles, trying to dislodge his new friend.

"Viola..." Elyse kept her eyes on Aiden. "Do you like working at Whispering Vinyl?"

Viola wrung her hands together. "Not really?"

"What would you rather do instead?"

"Um, I don't know."

Elyse turned to her friend. "Wouldn't you like to be a famous violinist? Or a celebrated country singer? Or both?"

"I—that would be nice." Viola's big doe eyes swam with dreamy possibility. Suddenly her shoulders slumped. "I'm not sure how I'd like being famous. I don't think I can sing in front of an audience."

"You don't have to be sure. I'm sure. The first time I heard you play the violin—"

"Fiddle," Viola interrupted.

"Whatever," Elyse said with a wave of her hand. "You moved me to tears! Classical music isn't my thing, but your rendition was like a religious experience. And your voice...what a voice. Eerie, ethereal, shy and innocent, it's, it's," she snapped her finger, "haunting. You're the entire package."

"I am?" Viola asked.

"Which is why I can't stand back and watch you squander your talent in some dinky little record store pushing artists who don't have half your talent. We're going to make your musical dreams come true. We're going to make it happen. Hashtag make it happen," she added, earning a groan from Aiden, who truly hated it when she inserted hashtags into everyday speech.

Viola gazed upon Elyse with awe. "We are?"

"You bet your ass! From this day forward, your life is going to change." Elyse seized hold of Poe's leash as he trotted back to her, his dessicated tongue lolling in triumph at having dislodged the pigeon from his cone. "What you need is a mentor to nurture your creativity, sort of like an artistic spirit guide. I will be that guide."

Viola's eyes widened into the size of saucers. "Ooh."

With every promise, the tick in Aiden's jaw intensified. "Viola, if you'll excuse us, I want to have a word with Elyse." He leveled another one of those pointed looks at Elyse. "Alone."

Elyse handed Poe's leash over to Viola along with the keys to her studio. "Help yourself to my gluten free muffins and go wild on the juice press."

"I don't know how to work the juice press," Viola said. "I'll just have milk."

"Well, we have an entire dairy in the fridge thanks to Olive. I'll meet you in a few."

Aiden rubbed the spot between his eyes, waiting for Viola to cross the street. Then, without another word, he began walking.

"Should I follow you?" Elyse asked.

No answer.

"I guess that's a 'yes'?" Elyse followed him behind the succulent shop and stopped before a mixed media wall made of wood and chrome. Another vertical garden, comprised of mini succulents, provided welcome shade. She pinched one of the waxy leaves between her thumb and forefinger.

"Okay, Hines," she said. "Reprimand me."

"What is wrong with you?" he exploded. "What *was* that?"

Elyse folded her arms across her chest, affronted. "Me helping a friend realize her dream."

"Helping? You call that helping? Harming is more like it." He shook his head. "What is her dream?"

"Fame. Fortune. Appreciation for her God given talents. If you ask me, she'll be much happier doing what comes naturally rather than waste her time toiling at some soul-crushing job."

"Fame? Viola is afraid of her own shadow. She could barely speak!"

Elyse tipped her chin up. "That's just a problem we'll have to overcome."

"Look," Aiden took a deep breath, "I think it's admirable that you're looking out for your friend, but this job is good for her. It's a steady paycheck, she's surrounded by music, the manager amuses her by keeping things quiet."

"It's prison," Elyse said. "And I'm breaking her out. I'm shocked that you're okay with her staying in that shithole. You battle drunken frat boys to save that turkey yet you don't lift a finger to rescue Viola."

Aiden raised a finger, his mouth partway open. "The day I walk into that record store and catch Viola's manager plucking her feathers and force-feeding her moonshine mash, then I will have cause to be concerned. As it stands, an unreasonable customer and unfair manager are all part and parcel of retail life."

"Well," Elyse folded her arms across her chest, "I don't accept it." She knew she sounded like a petulant child, but the injustice Viola had to endure was too much for Elyse to handle.

After a long and drawn out temple rubbing session, Aiden heaved a big sigh. "Listen, I want what's best for Viola just like you. But the reality is, she's twenty-three, has a high school diploma—"

"Working on her bachelor's," Elyse pointed out.

"For the past 5 years? She's still '2nd year status.'"

"Don't judge. Some people have to work to pay for their tuition. Not all of us are lucky enough be born a Hines."

"Need I mention your parents are board members of Hines & Sons," Aiden said, calling her out. "And you live in a big comfy McMansion, neighbor."

"I've moved out," she muttered.

"How much is your rent?"

She turned her head from his inquisitive gaze. Though her loft was tiny, the price of living in Downtown Indigo Bay was higher than she wanted to admit. Must be the ocean view.

"Why are we talking about me all of a sudden?" Elyse snapped. "If you're going to play the rich guilt card, it's not working. I have my own business. I pay my own way."

"Yeah?" Leaning back against the mixed media wall, Aiden tipped his head at a skeptical angle. "By taking over your mom's photography studio? Let me ask you this: did you have to buy it out from under her or did she gift it to you?"

Elyse frowned. "Your point?"

"You can't expect Viola to follow your path. You were born with advantages, Viola just..." he shook his head.

"Just what?" Elyse pressed.

"Someone like Viola just gets by," Aiden said. "She still lives at home. She didn't come from old money. Her dad is not an orthopedic surgeon. It's a wonder he hasn't drunken himself to death already."

Elyse fell silent. If Viola's father, scourge of the neighborhood, drank himself to death, all of Indigo Bay would throw a celebration.

"Have you stopped to consider what her father will do to her when he discovers she's quit her job?" he asked.

She gnawed on her inner cheek. No, the idea hadn't crossed her mind. Now that he brought it up, she couldn't think of anything else. Poor Viola, always so on edge and desperate to please everybody.

Out of all her friends, Elyse was the most protective over Viola. Olive had a loving dad and her jujitsu training to guide her through the wilderness of life. After her dad's death, Wesley Belmont was there to love and support her.

Elyse never worried about Lucie, who was so dead set on having things go her way she bent everyone to her will. Lucie was rife with flaws, crippling perfectionism being the chief offender, but she was an ambitious entrepreneur with a thriving catering business.

What did Viola have? An abrasive father, two brothers who

didn't even know she was alive, and a gig playing in a wedding string band for starvation wages. Viola was so lost, so unformed, so in need of rescuing that Elyse couldn't stand by and watch the real world crush her friend.

"All the more reason to lift her out of her sad little life," she said, her resolve to step in stronger than ever.

"You don't care about Viola at all," Aiden said. "You're doing this to feed your own hungry ego. Play with your dolls if you must. Don't play with Viola's life."

"How can you say that?" she snapped. "I care about Viola the most."

Throwing his hands in the air, Aiden stomped toward his office.

"You take that back," she called after him.

Aiden didn't even have the decency to turn around.

Left fuming by the mixed media wall, Elyse balled her hand into a fist and punched the chrome. "Owwww!"

6

_____

YOU'RE DOING this to feed your own ego.

Aiden's parting remarks plagued Elyse all week and loomed in the back of her mind as she hammered away at her custom photo booth.

Strangely enough, the project was commissioned by the Hines & Sons board of trustees for the company's 60th anniversary barbecue. Housing a network of mirrors and LEDs, the booth was meant to simulate the infinity of space and time. You shed away your identity once you step inside and float in a cosmos of blinking stars. Her vision was going to be spectacular and deeper than a company like Hines & Sons could comprehend.

What a conceptual art installation had to do with traditional southern barbecue was anyone's guess. Elyse suspected Mama called in a few favors on her behalf. With only three days before the big event, the booth looked more like a port-a-potty than the statement piece Elyse was aiming for.

"Diagonal strokes are more efficient," Olive said, trying to direct the others. "The shortest distance between two points is a straight line." A glob of black paint splattered the tarp-covered studio.

"Eeek! Watch it!" Lucie jumped back to avoid the splatter. Decked out in a full body jumpsuit, gloves, and respirator, she was dressed for chemical warfare. Her side of the booth was pristine, not a speck of paint on the tarp beneath her feet. Goggles obscured her eyes so one couldn't see her displeasure as she scrutinized her work. "I need to redo it."

"What are you talking about?" Elyse said, standing behind her. "It's perfect."

Lucie propped a hand on her hip. "There's an uneven patch here."

"Whaaa!" Olive's trademark whine echoed from the other side. Moments later, Olive's head peeked around the corner, her auburn hair bunched into a messy bun. "She's doing it again!"

Olive helped Lucie bake a batch of soufflés once and had still not recovered from the experience. Was it possible to have PTSD from an afternoon with Lucie?

Well, this was Elyse's project, and she called the shots. "It's good enough."

Lucie made a dash for the paint thinner.

"Touch that and I'll tackle you to the ground," Elyse's voice bounced off the walls of the empty studio. "Then you'll get some of this..." she cleared her throat, making sure she sounded extra mucus-y.

Lucie's hands flew up in surrender at the threat of a spitball. "That's biological warfare!"

"So it is. Step away from the booth," Elyse said, scouting the other side in search of Viola, who had been noticeably quiet for the entire afternoon. Viola wore a baggy aquamarine sweater over tights, her blonde hair gathered in a ballet bun.

While Lucie and Olive traded quips, Viola swiped at her side of the booth with short, timid brush strokes. Her workmanship was just as meticulous as Lucie's, though Viola didn't advertise it as loudly.

Elyse sighed. "What's wrong, Viola?"

Viola shook her head and kept her eyes trained on her work.

"Did you tell dad about quitting your job?"

Viola's paint brush froze mid-swipe. "I was going to," she said, her features pinched with worry. "I chickened out. I pay most—if not all— of the bills."

Lucie stepped forward. "Wait, in addition to doing *all* the chores, you pay *all* the bills too?"

Viola's dad, an able-bodied man on permanent disability, wasn't going to contribute anything to the running of the de Roet household.

"What the hell are Caleb and Conrad doing?" Elyse asked.

"After Mama left, the chores just fell to me." Viola apologized on behalf of her twin brothers. "They were little boys then. We couldn't expect them to cook or clean."

"But they're seventeen now!" Elyse said, disgusted.

"They've got school to worry about," Viola gave her a nervous smile. "They help with Hearts on a String."

"Let's be honest," Lucie folded her arms across her chest, "you carry that band. Half the time, I don't even know what they're doing. Caleb just stands there and I'd rather listen to someone bathe a cat than sit through one minute of Conrad's guitar solo. And none of them can sing worth a damn."

Observing Viola's discomfort, Elyse asked, "When are you planning to tell your dad?"

"Never," Viola said, rubbing her forearms.

"What's the worst that could happen?" Olive stepped out from behind Elyse.

As if the consequences were too horrible to contemplate, Viola shook her head, her fingernails leaving a trail of red across her soft skin.

"What's he going to do?" Elyse asked. "Ground you? You're twenty-three."

Viola glanced at her shoes. "I don't want to talk about this anymore."

Elyse's anger mounted. It wasn't all that surprising that Mr. de Roet never heard of sparing the rod.

Aiden's smug face swirled before her, reminding Elyse that her meddling would harm Viola in the end.

You don't care about Viola.

Of course she cared about Viola. How could he even suggest otherwise? His words cut her deep. How dare he doubt her intentions, question her character, and hurt her feelings! She'd prove him wrong. She'd turn Viola's life around. Before the first snowfall, she'd transform this wilting violet into a happy, fully rounded, confident woman.

Just you wait, Aiden Hines. You're about to eat a mouthful of crow.

"That's it," Elyse said. "You're moving out of that backwoods prison and in with me."

Her three friends stared at her, stunned.

Olive, current roommate, cleared her throat. "But how will she fit? I have a lot of stuff."

"It wouldn't hurt if you cull your Funko Pop collection," Elyse said.

Olive paled. "Whaaaa! My Funko Pops!"

"You have two Captain Americas."

Olive took a step back. "One is a special edition."

"We'll get bunk beds," Elyse added.

"Bunk beds?" Olive chewed her inner cheek. "Do I get dibs on top bunk?"

"Maybe." Elyse turned to Viola. "You *do* want to move out, don't you?"

"I do..." Viola frowned. "But—"

"But what?"

"Now that I'm unemployed, I don't know how I'll be able to help with the rent and—"

"Oh is that all?" Elyse dashed away Viola's concern with a wave of her hand. "Consider yourself hired as my new photography assistant."

Olive frowned. "I thought *I* was your photography assistant! Are you firing me? Am I fired?"

Elyse rolled her eyes. "Oh please, don't act as if you need the money. You're dating Wesley-Goldfinger-Belmont and you're flush with video game money," she said, referring to the recent success of Wedding Tycoon, an indie wedding planner simulation game Olive developed while mourning her father. "I can afford two assistants and maybe one of them will actually do her job."

Olive turned to Viola. "Work for her at your own peril."

"Girls," Elyse slapped her hands together. "My work is clear. Don't you see? Viola is living this sad, Cinderella-existence. No offense, Viola."

Viola waved off the insult.

"I personally see myself as your fairy godmother," Elyse continued.

Lucie arched her brow. "I bet you do."

Ignoring her, Elyse said to Viola. "How do you feel about being my new project?"

Viola's eyes shifted to Olive and Lucie for answers. "Okay, I guess..."

Elyse beamed. "That settles it," she said, thumping Viola between the shoulder blades. "Viola de Roet, welcome to the first day of the rest of your life."

"What do we do first?" Viola clutched her head, looking like she'd been swept up by a tornado.

Elyse was already halfway up the spiral staircase. "We start by cleaning out Olive's Funko Pop collection to make room for you, of course!"

Olive gave Viola a tight smile. "Excuse me..." She disappeared in a flash, 'Whaaaing' up the stairs. "Don't you dare touch my Funko Pops!"

7

THE NEXT DAY, they gathered at the window seat of Lucie's bedroom. The room was fit for a princess, complete with a queen-sized four-poster bed and an antique vanity. Black and white prints of Parisian street scenes decorated the Tiffany blue walls. On her bookshelf, Lucie had a 'Live Laugh Love' sign smothered in fairy lights.

Upon hearing what Elyse had planned, Viola pinched her wrinkled prairie skirt. "But I like the way I dress."

Elyse and Lucie exchanged a long suffering look.

"Viola, Viola, Viola." Lucie shook her head, her chestnut curls bouncing against her shoulder. "Don't resist. This is for your own good."

Elyse took Viola's lacy collar between her fingertips. "This screams porcelain doll goes to barn hootenanny."

Viola glanced down at her blouse. "It does?"

"Which is fine for Indigo Bay," Lucie said. "But this Easter Sunday look isn't going to fly in the music world."

Sprawled on the settee with her laptop, Olive was multitasking to the max: color correcting Elyse's backlog of wedding photos, coding updates for her Wedding Tycoon game, and contributing to Viola's makeover.

"I don't think she looks so bad," Olive chimed in.

Lucie rolled her eyes. "So says the girl with a Tardis on her T-shirt," she said, taking Viola by the hand and leading her inside her walk-in wardrobe.

For what seemed like an eternity, Lucie picked through racks packed with floral dresses and circle skirts, all in shades of candy-colored pastels.

Lucie picked up a mint dress and held it under Viola's chin. Musical notes on the skirt, ruffles around the sleeves.

"Here," she beamed, "perfect for your musical endeavors."

Viola's lips stretched into a polite smile.

Elyse said, "Urgh."

Olive wrinkled her nose.

"What's wrong?" Lucie asked.

"She'll look like Little Bo Peep on crack," Elyse said.

Lucie tipped her nose in the air. "This is the perfect wardrobe for a budding performer. It's romantic and ladylike—exactly what Dolly Parton would've worn on the stage of the Grand Ole Opry. What do you say, Viola?"

"Yes, what do *you* think, Viola?" Elyse asked.

Viola examined the mint skirt. "Um... I like the color?"

"Come on, Vi," Elyse folded her arms over her chest, "let's hear your opinion."

"Try it on, Vi," Lucie said, foisting the dress on Viola.

Viola shut the wardrobe behind her. A moment later, the doors opened. Viola stepped out in a dress that swamped her tiny frame. Beneath the stiff skirt, her legs resembled stumpy matchsticks.

Frowning, Lucie tapped a finger to her chin. "So it needs a bit of tailoring. What do you think, Vi?"

Viola's face was grim at best.

Elyse locked eyes with Olive. "No," they said in unison.

Olive stepped forward and handed Viola a tote bag stuffed with clothes. "Try my picks."

In the closet Viola went. Out she came wearing a skin tight bodysuit.

Seeing poor Viola in white pleather made Elyse's head hurt. "I don't know what to say."

Olive nodded in approval. "Doesn't that just scream celebrity?"

Lucie circled Viola as if she were the star attraction of a freak show. "It screams insanity." She whirled on Olive. "I thought she was your friend. I wouldn't wish this on my worst enemy."

Viola shifted from foot to foot, shrinking under the attention. Bending down, Elyse studied the piano keys printed on both sides of the bodysuit.

"Lift your arms, Vi." She brushed a hand under the white fringes, then glared at Olive. "What did you do? Recycle an Elvis costume from Wesley's Vegas venue?"

Lowering her head, Olive toed a run in the rug. "I think she looks good..."

Elyse rolled up her sleeves. "My turn," she said, snatching up her bag. "Viola, are you ready to look like a star?"

Lucie and Olive peeked inside the bag. Elyse yanked out her pick with a flourish.

"Oh no!" Lucie and Olive groaned.

"You're not going to make her wear one of your sacks, are you?" Lucie asked.

"I see what you're doing!" Olive pointed an accusatory finger at her. "You're trying to turn Vi into your dystopian Mini-Me."

"Oh shut up, this is an Ansley Mills exclusive. I own the same one in a different shade of gray." Elyse held out the hem for her skeptics to feel. "Cashmere blend. Dystopian my ass, this dress is dry clean only."

"The quality is acceptable," Lucie said. "But it's so... gray."

"'Lavender Fog,'" Elyse said. "Let's get that straight."

"Right," Olive grinned. "Gray is such a pedestrian color."

Lucie shook her head. "You sure do spend a lot of money looking like a pauper."

"I'll pretend I didn't hear that," Elyse said. "Viola, try this on."

Viola seemed unconvinced. "I don't really like gray."

"Lavender Fog," Elyse reminded her. She held up the dress. "It can't be any worse than the Elvis suit you have on."

"Good point," Lucie agreed.

"Okay..." Viola disappeared inside the closet and reappeared, transformed.

Lucie blinked. "Wow."

Olive clasped her hand over her mouth. "Whaaa."

"Good whaaa or bad whaaa?" Lucie asked.

"Good whaaa."

'Lavender Fog' complemented Viola's rosy complexion to a T. The dress didn't look like much on the hanger, but on Viola's petite figure, the quality-made fabric enhanced her curves and showed off a pair of sexy legs no one knew she had.

Elyse crossed her arms over her chest, a smug grin spreading across her face. "Well, Vi? What do you think?"

"I love it!" Viola twirled around, the apples of her cheeks flushed with a burst of confidence. "I feel like an ultra mod princess!"

"A *minimalist* princess," Olive pointed out.

"I can't believe it," Lucie turned to Elyse, "you pulled it off."

"Was there ever any doubt?" Elyse said, propping a straw fedora on Viola's head at a rakish angle. "Clothes are just the first step. We still have our work cut out for us."

Viola stared up at her with wide, hero-worshiping eyes. "What's the next step?" she asked.

"We revamp your YouTube channel, of course."

"Revamp?" Viola glanced from one friend to the next. "Wait... I have a YouTube channel?"

8

"TELL your viewers about the ice cream, Vi," Elyse said, holding up her camera.

Viola glanced down at her shoes. "It's um, pumpkin spice latte?"

Elyse zoomed in on Viola's petrified face. "Lick it," she said, then paused for a beat. "Ignore the innuendo and lick."

Viola's hands shook as she brought the cone to her mouth. She took the tiniest of licks.

"Describe what it tastes like," Elyse asked, staring into her DSLR's screen.

"Tastes like coffee."

"And...?"

"A-a-and... pumpkins," Viola mumbled.

"And?" Elyse pressed.

"And I think I'm going to throw up." Without warning, Viola darted out of frame, scrambling down Main Street like a celebrity hounded by paparazzi.

Elyse gave Viola the benefit of the doubt. It wasn't every day you found out you had a YouTube channel. Especially one with ten thousand subscribers who adored your voice.

"Are you still mad I uploaded those videos?" Elyse asked, tracking her down the street.

She kept the camera rolling. What began as a stealth recording of Viola singing at Coralee Davis' wedding ballooned into a legit channel as the performance gained in popularity.

Viola kept walking. She glanced over her shoulder. "You could have at least told me," she said, sounding more hurt than angry.

"I did tell you."

"Three months later."

"I was a little out of line, but what was I supposed to do? You wouldn't have signed off on it in a million years and I needed to build your portfolio. I made it happen. If there's one thing you can learn from me, it's that life gives nothing to you. Not money, success, or fame. You *take* it. I took it for you."

Viola crossed her arms over her chest. Per Elyse's wardrobe advice, Viola looked chic in distressed skinny jeans, a simple black T-shirt, and black suede ankle boots. Her white-blonde hair was styled in loose beach waves. Elyse glanced down at her own wardrobe. She was dressed similarly, except her top was gray (Lavender Fog to be precise) and her hair was piled on top of her head in a messy bun. Together, they were prime subjects for any passing street fashion photographer. Too bad there were never any fashion photographers roaming Indigo Bay's cobblestone streets.

"Look," Elyse said, whipping out her phone. Viola's YouTube channel, Prodigy in the Rough, was already open. She scrolled through the video uploads. "This is one of you playing Ashokan's Farewell at old man Calhoun's funeral. Fifteen thousand views. Lindsey Stirling better watch her back because you're about to give her a run for her money. And look!" She scrolled to the channel's most popular video. "Everybody loves your voice. Over forty thousand likes. Nothing but praise in these comments—okay, this one guy with the topless anime character avatar is an asshole, don't pay attention to him—but everyone else adores you."

Viola peered down at the phone. "Then how come I have five hundred dislikes?" She pointed to a nasty comment. "This one says he's seen more talent in his bowel movements. This one says I have a face she wants to punch."

"Don't pay attention to those trolls," Elyse said, shutting off her phone. "You can't win them all. *Overall*, most viewers adore you. Doesn't that make you feel good?"

Puzzled, Viola licked the melting ice cream off her fingers. "People actually watch this?"

"Honey, they watch *you*," Elyse said, grabbing a napkin from her back pocket and dabbing a spot on Viola's chin. "You're the quintessential girl next door: nice, pretty, humble. That's important. You aren't annoying or divisive. You don't *offend*. You can sing *and* play the violin."

"Fiddle."

"Whatever." Elyse continued without taking a breath, "Between your talent and my cinematography prowess, I'm not surprised if you hit a million subscribers by Christmas. I don't want to brag, but everything I touch turns to gold. As in a gold YouTube play button."

A shy smile flickered across Viola's face. "Then why aren't you a YouTube celebrity?"

"Because I am anything but humble and all I do is *offend*. Now," she lifted her camera, "it's important that your fans get to know you outside of your art. We need some B-roll shots of your fabulous yet down-to-earth country girl lifestyle."

Viola batted away a swath of hair from her eyes. "But I don't have a fabulous lifestyle. I'm unemployed and I live in a trailer."

"*Lived* in a trailer. It's all part of your Springsteen-esque working-class heroine origin story. Keep this in mind: an artist is always working even when she's not working." Elyse licked her fingers and smoothed back Viola's unruly baby hairs. "Tell us about your delicious gourmet ice cream. Some name dropping would be appreciated since the kind folks at Icy Cauldron were generous enough to supply us free samples in exchange for the plug."

"Oh right," Viola glanced down at her melting prop. "This ice cream..."

Crickets.

"What does it taste like?"

"It's sweet?" Viola said.

"And?" Elyse motioned with her finger. "Tastes like..."

"Ice cream?" Viola squinted, unable to decode what Elyse was mouthing. "Auburn? Adam? Autumn? *Autumn!*" She paused, a frown creasing her brow. "How can something taste like autumn?"

Sighing, Elyse stopped recording. "Vi, Vi, Vi," she said with a shake of her head. "Now that we have your look down, we need to work on your poise, speech, and mannerisms."

"My mannerisms?" Viola whispered.

"How you walk, talk, the volume of your voice. How you portray yourself to the world," Elyse said, as they entered the veterinarian's office to collect Poe. The terrier was cooling it at the reception counter, perched comfortably in Viannie's lap. The waiting room was empty. Aiden, minus white lab coat, was slouched against the counter, chatting with his sister. His eyebrows rose at the sight of his city-chic visitors.

"... we're going to makeover your self-esteem," Elyse continued to speak as they approached the counter. "I won't rest until I've made you a confident woman... like me." Out of the corner of her eye, she caught Aiden shake his head. "Yes?"

Aiden gestured toward their matching outfits. "So the brain-washing has begun."

Elyse gasped in mock-affront. "Viola takes offense to that."

Viola waved her hands. "I'm okay."

"So you're not only forcing her to dress like you, but you're also speaking for her as well?" Aiden asked. Then his eyes narrowed at Elyse. "What's with the camera? Wait, are you recording?"

"It's for Viola's YouTube channel." Elyse zoomed into his face. "Say Hi!"

Aiden ducked out of frame.

Viannie waved Poe's paw and mugged for the camera. "I think they look great," she said, waving with Poe's limp paw. "Is this for Viola's YouTube channel?"

"The one and only," Elyse said.

Viannie turned to a still-confused Viola. "I'm a big fan. *Big* fan," she said, her hands fluttering to her heart. "Your voice got me through some hard times."

An uncertain smile ghosted Viola's lips. "Thank you?"

Aiden ran his fingers through his hair. His baffled gaze traveled between the three girls. "What's going on? What YouTube channel?"

Filling Aiden in on the bizarre circumstances in which Viola came to be an up-and-coming internet celebrity took up the better part of half an hour. He pelted Elyse with so many questions that she was ready to rip out her hair.

"Does it really matter how Viola came to have a channel so long as she has it and people like it?" Elyse asked as the Hines' siblings closed up the office.

Aiden waved goodbye to his sister. Poe clawed at Elyse's shin. She scooped him into her arms and received a lick across the jaw with his sandpapery tongue.

"Don't frown," she said to Aiden. "I can tell you're judging me again. What I'm doing for Vi is a good thing. Why can't you see that?"

She only wanted the best for Viola, but Aiden was hell-bent on believing Elyse cared only for herself. Why was it so hard for him to believe she only had the best intentions?

"How do you feel about all this, Vi?" he asked.

Elyse opened her mouth to answer.

"I asked Viola," Aiden said.

Elyse narrowed her eyes.

Viola clasped her hands in front of her and bowed her head. "It's fun?"

Aiden studied Viola's holey T-shirt and shredded jeans. "Yeah, she looks like she's having a lot of fun, dressed like she's been mauled by a wolf."

"Oh shut up, Aiden," Elyse snapped. "This shirt is from an exclusive French online boutique. Cashmere blend. Dry clean only." Faced with Aiden's skepticism, it was vital she pointed that out. "Viola adores her new make-over. Don't you Viola?"

Viola opened her mouth. "I—"

"There! See!" Elyse was aware she sounded like a petulant five-year-old, but she so dearly wanted to prove him wrong. "What do you have to say now?"

Aiden dug in his pocket for his car keys. "Consider buying yourself a doll if you want to play dress up and leave Viola alone. No offense, Viola."

Viola shook her hand. None taken.

Elyse had been in a great mood. Leave it to Aiden to rain on her parade. "We have to go," she said, walking off without a good-bye. She sensed Viola and Poe following on her heels.

"I'll see Poe back next week," Aiden called after her. "And remember to apply the cream three times a day. If he chews on his wound, the collar is going back on."

Elyse raised her arm, showing that she heard. She watched Aiden cross the street and head toward a parked BMW. A beautiful blonde waited in the driver's seat, her red fingernails rapping against the wheel.

Lisa.

Elyse spun around, her emotions going haywire. She high-tailed it down the sidewalk, her hands flexing into fists. "Urgh," she said, kicking a rock out of her way.

Taking charge of Poe's leash, Viola chased after Elyse. A squirrel darted across the courtyard and it was all she could do to keep Poe from chasing after it.

"Bad dog! Bad!" Elyse said, taking the leash from Viola.

Poe glared at her with beady, defiant eyes. "Yip!"

"Don't get sassy with me. Sit!"

"Yip!"

Elyse pointed at her disobedient dog. "You can kiss your gourmet kibble treats goodbye. Sit!"

Poe hunkered down on his haunches and covered his eyes with a paw.

"Are you mad at Aiden?" Viola asked.

Elyse rubbed her brow, feeling terrible for snapping at poor Poe. Aiden knew exactly which of her buttons to press and how to press them. "Let's not talk about him. I can't stand him."

"For someone you can't stand, you certainly hang around him a lot."

Elyse narrowed her eyes at Viola. "He's my vet."

"He's not the only vet in town," Viola said, trying to hide her smile.

"For someone who supposedly doesn't speak, you sure have a lot to say. Okay, let's refocus. Today's all about you. First, we work on your posture."

"My posture?"

"You're always slouching." She hunched forward in demonstration. "It's gives you a humpback and is very unattractive."

Viola wrinkled her nose. "Do I really do that?"

Elyse straightened her spine; Viola followed suit. "One of the few useful things I took away from cotillion is the importance of good posture," she said, imagining how proud her Mama would be if she could only hear her now. Horrible thought.

Viola lowered her eyes. "I do look horrible, don't I?"

"Nonsense. You're beautiful and don't let anyone—particularly yourself—tell you any different. That's your low self-esteem talking. When I'm done with you, you'll be a changed woman."

"I don't feel like a woman..."

"You will. Trust me." Elyse could tell that fighting off Viola's self-doubt was going to be an uphill battle. How does one build someone's self-esteem from the ground up? She led them to the fountain and gestured for Viola to sit on the lip. The old lilac tree provided some shade though the tree was no longer in bloom and most of the leaves had fallen to the ground.

"Now sit up. Take a deep relaxing breath. Inhale. Exhale. Good. Straighten your shoulders." Elyse tipped her finger under Viola's chin. "Keep your head up. Stop looking at your shoes."

"I feel more confident already," Viola said, staring straight ahead. "But my neck hurts."

"Beauty is pain." Elyse paced around the courtyard. Autumn leaves crunched beneath her shoes. "Now that we've covered posture, let's talk about your speech."

"What's wrong with the way I talk?" Viola asked.

"Meaning no offense," Elyse held up her hands, "you're a low talker. If I hadn't known you all my life, I would never be able to hear you. You whisper. You mumble your words."

Viola's gesture deflated with Elyse's every word. "I do, don't I?"

"You want to project." Elyse's voice echoed down deserted Main Street. "Howl. Roar. *Awwwooool!*"

Poe poked his head up and howled along with her. A flock of pigeons scattered from the fountain.

Amid the flapping of wings, Elyse said, "How else do you expect to be heard? Everyone talks all over you. You want to be loud. You want your words to resonate."

"You mean like Coralee? She talks all over me and she definitely has no trouble being heard."

"If by Coralee you mean whiny and unbearable— God no. Don't be like Coralee. You want to be confident and urbane, brash but elegant... I'm going to turn you into a tough broad like yours truly." Elyse delivered a saucy little bow. "Heck, if you're half as sassy as Poe here, I'd consider it a job well done."

Wagging his stubby tail, Poe sauntered to the trunk of the lilac tree, lifted his leg, and whizzed.

"Let's practice," Elyse slapped her hands together. "Repeat after me. 'The rain in Spain stays mainly on the plain.'"

Put on the spot, Viola fumbled a rendition of Rain in Spain.

"That was... not bad." Elyse sighed.

Turning shy Viola into a confident, multifaceted entertainer was going to take more than a magic wand and movie rhymes. She had her work cut out for her, but she was *not* a quitter and she'd be damned if she let Aiden see her fail. Elyse put on her biggest smile, confident in her ability to perform miracles. "Okay, let's try this. What's your favorite color, Vi?"

A moment of silence. "Yellow?"

"Your favorite food?"

Viola cautioned a glanced through a fan of blonde lashes. "Shrimp and grits?"

"Favorite song?" Elyse pressed.

"Music of the Night?"

For the second time that day, Elyse pinched the spot between her eyes. "No offense again..."

"Uh oh. When you preface things with 'no offense,' you usually mean to offend."

"Viola?" Elyse angled her body toward her pupil. Viola mimicked her body position. "Why do you talk like that?"

"Oh no," Viola whispered. "I'm sorry."

"Don't lower your head again. You did nothing wrong and for God's sake, stop saying you're sorry! I'm merely making an observation. You've spoken like that ever since I've known you."

"Like what?"

"When I asked you your favorite color, instead of simply stating 'Yellow,' you said 'Yellow?' Instead of 'shrimp and grits,' you said 'shrimp and grits?' You have a habit of adding question marks to the end of your sentences."

"Oh." Viola looked lost. "I'm sorry."

Elyse took a deep breath and glanced longingly at the glass face of The Coffee Haus. She stood up. "I need an espresso shot."

Inside the cafe, Roger was busy blending a bunch of vanilla frappes for a gaggle of high school girls.

As Elyse studied the chalkboard menu, Viola nudged her with an elbow.

"The barista's looking at you," Viola said.

Ripping her attention away from the menu, Elyse met Roger's eye. He raised his hand in an awkward wave. Elyse nodded, then resumed perusing the menu.

The high school girls, all conspicuously love-struck by the hot barista, were going to be awhile. Besides, Roger didn't deserve the privilege of her attention. She hadn't heard a word from him since that day at the millpond. And she didn't care for his attitude toward Poe.

"Do you know him?" Viola whispered.

"In passing," Elyse said, scraping the chipped nail polish off her thumb. "He's an Australian grad student. I forgot what he studied. Marine Biology." She tapped her chin. "Or was it Biochemistry?" She couldn't recall, having been distracted by his other assets.

"What's his name?" Viola asked.

Struck by the dreamy note in Viola's voice, Elyse paid closer attention to her friend. Along with the underage groupies, Viola seemed entranced by Roger's every movement. Roger was currently squirting whipped cream atop a caramel macchiato, flexing his biceps for all they were worth.

"Roger Elton-Smith," Elyse said.

Viola sighed. "What a lovely name."

Elyse frowned. "He's pretty cute, huh?"

"He's beautiful," Viola said.

As if on cue, Roger tugged his black Coffee Haus T-shirt up and wiped his nose sweat on the hem. A collective sigh rippled through the cafe at the six-pack sighting.

Viola turned beet red and looked like she was in danger of fainting. "I don't drink coffee, but I think I'm going to start."

Within earshot, one customer sighed, "He doesn't know what he's doing."

Elyse rolled her eyes and leaned forward. "Honey, he knows exactly what he's doing."

As they approached the counter, Elyse sensed Viola shaking with nerves. "Calm down, I can introduce you."

Viola shook her head violently.

"Elyse," Roger greeted her with a charismatic smile, "you kept the dog."

"Yup." Smile unreciprocated.

"How are you doing, Elyse?" he asked.

Her gaze swept right over him. "Tell me about the gluten-free muffin of the day."

"It's carrot cake with a lemon cream cheese frosting." He lowered his voice. "Hey, no hard feelings? I was going to text you later, but I've been swamped. Work. My master's thesis. I've got a lot going on here."

She honestly didn't care. Funny how adopting a dog could change one's dating perspective. Now that she had Poe to look after, she didn't want to waste time on a playboy barista. After their less than sexy tumble at the millpond, she'd sworn off one-night stands for good. Guess her nesting instincts were kicking in and she was thinking for two.

"All water under the bridge," she said with a casual shrug. "What's past is past, right?"

"Right." Roger cleared his throat, uncomfortable. "So who's your friend?" he asked, nodding over her shoulder. "She looks like she had the fright of her life."

Elyse glanced over her shoulder to find Viola cowering behind her. "Roger meet Viola. Viola, shake hands with Roger."

Viola held out a trembling hand. Her eyes widened as Roger leaned over the counter and planted a kiss on the back of her palm. Smiling, he winked at Elyse.

Elyse rolled her eyes. "Charmer from Down Under."

"Thanks, Sheila," Roger said, drawing a smile from Elyse. "So what do you do Viola?"

Seeing her friend struggle for the words, Elyse jumped in. "She's a musical prodigy and rising YouTube star."

Roger's eyebrows lifted. "Impressive."

"I used to work at Whispering Vinyl," Viola said, finding her voice. "But now I'm unemployed.

Elyse stared at Viola, aghast. The one time Viola remembered to use declarative sentences... "Oh Vi, you're too humble."

"No, I'm really unemployed."

Roger laughed. "You're funny." He turned to Elyse. "I like her." Leaning forward, he dropped his voice to a whisper. "Since this joker's with you, two coffees on the house. What do you say?"

Shocked but pleasantly surprised, Elyse put away her wallet. "Can't say no to free coffee."

Later, with two monster sized cups of coffee in hand, Elyse stepped onto the sidewalk with Viola by her side.

Viola glanced behind her shoulder. "Elyse," she whispered. "He's still looking at you. I think he's checking you out."

Elyse gave a nonchalant glance backward. Roger punched an order on his tablet, his attention fixed on the both of them. And then... to her delight and disbelief...his eyes shifted beyond Elyse.

"Vi," she whirled around. "He's checking *you* out."

Viola's face turned white. "No he's not!"

"He's waving at you. Wave back."

"I can't. I-" Viola flapped her hand.

In response, Roger broke into a big smile.

Elyse lifted her free drink in thanks, then nudged Viola's shoulder. They ran down the street toward Elyse's studio, collapsing in a breathless heap. Sensing their excitement, Poe ran in circles around their feet, then wore himself out and plodded to his doggie bed at the foot of the spiral staircase.

"Oh my god, Vi!" Elyse swatted Viola between the shoulder blades. "Why didn't you tell me you were such a big flirt?"

"I wasn't flirting." A wrinkle materialized between Viola's brow. She touched her crimson cheek. "At least I didn't think I was."

"Then you're a natural." Elyse held up her cup for a toast. Her mind buzzed with possibilities. From her experience, Roger had his flaws. He fell short in some areas, but she firmly believed he'd redeemed himself today. Just because her chemistry fizzled with him didn't mean she should deny Viola a shot at love.

"And I'll tell you something else, Vi, now he can't take his eyes off you. See what happens when you use declarative sentences? You seem more confident and multifaceted already."

Viola slumped into the settee reserved for Elyse's portrait clients. "I do? I mean," she cleared her throat and straightened her shoulders, "I do."

9

PERCHED ATOP A GIANT PUMPKIN, Olive leaned forward, her eyes rapt with attention. She stroked Poe's flannel-clad back. The terrier opened his jaw in a contented yawn. "Tell us again what Viola said."

"You're reading too much into it." Lucie's hands were covered in extra durable gardening gloves. She picked up a pumpkin with a huge nodule growing on its side and inspected every inch. "They only just met and you have them falling in love at first sight."

"Okay, Ye of Little Faith," Elyse said, setting her camera down. She had snapped her fill of lifestyle shots of her friends amid rows of pumpkins, scarecrows, and corn mazes. Taking a sip of her pumpkin spiced latte (gotta love October), Elyse counted on her fingers all the ways she smelled love in the air.

"One: he was bewitched by Viola's beauty. Two: he's charmed by her self-effacing sense of humor. So charmed, in fact, that he's been offering free drinks and upgrades to me every day this week, purely because I'm Viola's friend. If that doesn't spell crush, I don't know what does."

Lucie frowned. "I went to The Coffee Haus, and I didn't get a free drink."

"I accompanied Elyse," Olive said, taking a big gulp of her hot chocolate. "Who babbled about Viola. He gave me a drink upgrade and a bear claw. I'm a believer."

Lucie's lips pressed into a doubtful line. "Hm."

"Maybe you're not as charming as our Viola," Elyse said and smiled as Lucie crossed her arms in a huff.

"Where is the subject in question, anyway?" Lucie asked.

Olive glanced up from her phone. "One of her brothers clogged the toilet, so she's at Home Depot buying Drano."

"Wait? She's plumbing?" Lucie did a full body shiver. "How sad."

"She's actually an accomplished plumber," Olive said. "Between twin brothers and her good-for-nothing pa, she's up to elbows in shit."

"But why is their plumbing her problem?" Lucie asked. "She doesn't even live with them anymore."

"Yet they still hassle her 24/7," Olive explained. "The three of them can't boil water to save their lives."

"So Viola still returns to cook for them?" Lucie asked.

"And do their laundry and clean and pay the bills."

Lucie stood up, aghast. "Why that's indentured servitude!"

"Why doesn't she rebel?" Lucie asked.

"Ya'll know Viola can't say no to anybody. She lives to please," Elyse said. "When she tries to set her boundaries, her dad shames her for moving out. Says she takes after her mama for splitting on them all those years ago. Calls her selfish for putting herself above family and convinces her to hand over her paycheck, no questions asked. He spends it on beer and chew, she washes their dirty dishes and folds her brothers' socks. It's a vicious psychological cycle. Centuries of sexism at work."

"Urgh," Lucie clenched her hands into fists. "This makes me so mad I could... I could spit! I'm not going to because spitting is a disgusting habit, but if I ever come face to face with that nasty drunk I'll show him what's what."

"As much as you would terrify him, Lucie, it's more constructive if we band together and fix Viola. Break the cycle by building her confidence," Elyse said. "I'm setting up a private photo shoot with Viola this weekend. Publicity headshots for her channel. I dropped a mention to Roger, and he practically begged to come watch."

Lucie and Olive's eyes widened. "Oooh."

"Now full disclaimer..." Elyse set her drink atop a pumpkin and tried to find the most innocuous way to spill the not so glamorous truth. She decided not to mince words. "I slept with Roger."

"Ohhhhh!!!!" Chaos followed. Jumping. Screaming. Arm waving and hand flapping. Poe took a tumble off Olive's lap and landed on the ground.

"Yip!" he barked, baring his tiny bottom teeth in irritation.

Feeling like the mother of rambunctious sisters, Elyse seized Olive and Lucie by the arm and hissed in their ears. "Quiet! We don't want You-Know-Who to know."

The trio turned to where they last left Wesley. He'd been sidelined by a man while parking his Ferrari.

Now a group of men had gathered around his car, bombarding him with questions about mileage and transmission, asking to see the engine and the leather interior. Wesley was patient with his audience. A few minutes later, he glanced over his shoulder and locked eyes with Olive. "Help me," he mouthed.

"Wesley's not going to tell Viola," Olive said, letting her boyfriend fend for himself with the car enthusiasts. "He can barely talk to her as it is. Her silence makes him uncomfortable."

"But he's Aiden's best friend," Elyse pointed out. "The last thing I need is for Mr. Judgmental to get involved." Aiden already considered her villainess of the year. As much as she told herself she didn't care what he thought, she didn't want to add more fodder to his lowly opinion of her. So maybe she did care. Just a little.

"In any event," she continued, "it was hardly sex. It was like three pumps and I was texting Olive most of the time. It was *that* disappointing."

Olive screwed up her face in disgust. "Don't involve me!"

"How does it stand with you and Roger now?" Lucie asked.

Elyse thought about their last interaction at the cafe. A free latte upgrade care of her Viola connection, a noncommittal smile from Roger, and absolutely no mention of their one-night stand. The sex was probably so bad that Roger wanted to forget it too.

"That ship has long sailed," she said. "Our chemistry is non-existent."

Lucie lifted a skeptical brow. "Are you sure about that?"

"Of course," Elyse said with a little snort.

"How?"

"Not to toot my own horn, but I'm exceptionally perceptive when it comes to reading people. It's part of my job as a wedding photographer, which is why I'm confident that any feelings Roger had for me have all been transferred to Viola. She's prettier, more talented, and is a better person overall."

Lucie and Olive nodded in agreement.

Elyse glared at them, mildly annoyed. They didn't have to agree so fast. "I don't want Viola finding out I ever had a thing with Roger. It would be weird."

"Uh... yeah," Olive said.

"There's another problem. Viola doesn't have much sexual experience—if any." Elyse took a deep breath. "How do I tell her about his tiny little..." She scanned the pumpkin patch, then very discreetly wiggled her pinky finger.

Lucie and Olive blinked.

"It's tiny?" Lucie asked, meeting Olive's eye.

Olive leaned in. "How tiny is tiny?"

Elyse scanned her surroundings. "*Very.*"

"Well." Lucie fumbled words. "Viola is quite petite," she said, lifting her palms up in explanation.

Elyse propped her hand on her hip. "What are you getting at, Lucie?"

"Oh, I don't know. Small girl, small..."

"Vagina?" Olive asked.

"Did I hear someone say 'vagina'?" an irritating voice called from the other end of the row. Coralee strolled toward them with an armful of food. Her hair fell in fluffy blonde curls around a pink cashmere scarf.

Elyse leveled Olive with a pointed look.

"I might have checked into Hennigan Farms on Yelp," Olive whispered. "How am I supposed to know she checks my status?"

"I'm never inviting you to anything ever again," Elyse said between clenched teeth. But they both knew it was an empty threat. No group outing was complete without Olive. Wherever Olive went, Coralee was sure to follow. At least Coralee came with treats.

"Here you go," Coralee said, handing them each a cone of caramel popcorn. "So, I hear you were all talking about vaginas—my favorite topic."

"I thought 'you' were your favorite topic," Elyse said, stuffing a sticky popcorn cluster in her mouth.

Her comment drew a braying donkey-like laugh from Coralee.

Elyse jammed her pinky in her ear and wished she were deaf.

"You are such a jokester," Coralee said, punching Elyse in the arm.

"Ow." Rubbing her arm, Elyse narrowed her eyes at Coralee, who prattled as if nothing were amiss.

"Anyway, my cousin is a gynecologist and I worked at her practice three summers ago."

"You?" Elyse snorted. "Worked?"

"I like to work. On occasion," Coralee said, the insult flying right over her head. "I saw my share of hoo-has that summer." Then she added with a flip of her hair. "I consider myself an expert."

"Like a vaginaologist?" Olive asked.

Lucie held up an instructional finger. "The proper term is 'gynecologist.'"

"Exactly!" Coralee said.

Elyse had been holding her tongue, but such idiocy was too much for her to handle. "You need a medical degree to be a gynecologist."

"Details, details." Coralee dashed away Elyse's concern with a wave of her hand. "Let me tell you, the size of a woman has no bearing on the size of her vagina. Olive, you're tiny and weird. For all we know, you may have a huge vagina."

Olive blanched. "I'm feeling very uncomfortable."

"We had three sizes of speculums—small, medium, and large —and we kept all three on hand because you'll never know which one you might need. It was like playing Russian Roulette with reproductive organs. "

"I thought it was one size fits all," Olive said.

"My cousin likes to be prepared—for anything." Coralee pointed a manicured finger at Lucie. "You look like you have a large vagina."

"What the—" Lucie did a double take. "Excuse me?"

"You've got robust childbearing hips, but you could have a teeny tiny vag. We'll never know."

Lucie was on the verge of strangling Coralee. "You—"

Elyse stepped in front of Lucie to stop the carnage. "What about me?"

Coralee looked Elyse up and down. "I shouldn't."

"What?" Elyse frowned. "Why? You've assessed both of them. Come on," she took a step back, inviting Coralee to have at her. "I can take it. I won't be offended."

"On first glance?" Coralee sucked in her breath. "You'll definitely require the big speculum."

"That makes absolutely no sense," Elyse snapped. "I have no hips or curves whatsoever."

"High use," Coralee said.

"What the—"

"See? I knew you couldn't handle the truth."

Lucie folded her arms across her chest. "Are you calling me fat?"

"Why does everyone think I sleep around?" Elyse asked, yelling over Lucie. "It's because of my no-underwear phase, isn't it? I was letting the air circulate! It's like a living organism. You have to let it breathe!"

"But you were just telling us about your one-night stand," Lucie reminded her.

"It was barely even sex! Don't you dare slut shame me!"

Coralee's eyes lit up with interest. "Who did you sleep with?" she asked Elyse.

"Butt out, Coralee!"

"Stop it, you guys!" Flailing her arms, Olive shouted at the top of her lungs. "Don't you see? This vagina talk has divided us all!"

She suddenly clammed up as Wesley approached with two large pumpkins tucked beneath his arms. He froze at the word 'vagina,' and, looking like he'd stumbled upon no-man's-land, slowly backed away.

10

"AM I INTERRUPTING?" Roger poked his head into the private portrait corner.

Elyse had Viola posed in front of a slate blue backdrop and wearing a lacy white evening dress. Giant soft-boxes flanked the nervous subject.

Viola, already uncomfortable in front of the lens, turned white at the sight of Roger.

"Oh Roger, what a surprise! How nice of you to drop by." Avoiding Viola's questioning gaze, Elyse offered her cheek for him to kiss. She saw the gesture in a '60's New Wave French film and decided to infuse some culture into her life.

Roger overshot the target, his lips grazing the edge of her mouth. Elyse blinked, stunned, but with Roger acting so nonchalant she assumed it was an accident and gave him the benefit of the doubt.

"What are you doing here?" she asked, wiping her mouth on the back of her hand.

"I came to see the artist at work," Roger said, his gaze lingering on Elyse.

Elyse gestured to Viola. "She's a natural in front of the camera, don't you think?

"Yeah," he said, lifting his hand in a brief acknowledgement of Viola's presence.

Viola's eyes dropped to the floor.

"So what are we doing?" Roger asked, sidling up behind Elyse for a gander at her viewfinder. The smell of coffee lingered in the fibers of his red and black flannel shirt. He palmed his jaw, rubbing the bristles of an impressive yet carefully groomed five o'clock shadow.

"Promo shots for Vi's social media." Elyse stepped away from him. Frankly, he was invading her personal space.

"Can I help?" Roger asked.

"Just lend us your moral support. Otherwise, I've got this." She nodded toward a corner stool. "Why don't you sit over there. We're just finishing up."

With Roger out of the way, Elyse concentrated on getting the perfect shot. Viola was not an easy subject and while the camera loved her natural beauty, Elyse captured bland shot after bland shot.

Snap. "Look over my shoulder." *Snap.* "My *right* shoulder." *Snap.* "Hold your hands like this." *Snap.* "Try not to clench your teeth when you smile." *Snap.* "Better. Now look up."

Try as she might to coax emotion her subject, Viola remained as stiff as a board. After twenty frames of the same strained pose and lifeless facial expression, Elyse lowered her camera, her body tense with fatigue. Getting a winning shot out of Viola felt like an uphill battle.

Roger jumped from his stool. "You're doing great," he said to Viola. "But you need something to do with your hands." He glanced toward the corner where a bouquet of yellow chrysanthemums decorated the coffee table. "Hang on."

Moments later, he handed her the bouquet and brushed a curl behind her ears. "One for the muse."

"Thanks," Viola smiled, afraid to meet his eye.

With a sly grin, Roger snatched a single flower for the bunch and handed one to Elyse. "One for the artist."

"Um, thanks," Elyse said, taking the flower and tossing it atop her equipment table. "Vi, try kneeling as if you're taking a bow. Look to the left. Good. Profile to me. Eyes down. Perfect! Now hold that pose!" Still fiddling with her focus, she asked Roger, "She's breathtaking, isn't she? Like a cross between a fairy-tale princess and Grace Kelly."

"Who's Grace Kelly?"

"Nicole Kidman then."

"Ah... Stunning," Roger said loud enough for Viola to hear.

In her viewfinder, Elyse saw a pleased smile cross Viola's lips. The moment was almost perfect. Elyse waited, finger on the button.

Viola tipped her head forward and sniffed the bouquet.

Snap.

Elyse had her shot. "That's a wrap!"

"My cue to go," Roger said, hopping off the stool and gathering his backpack. "Work calls."

"Did you enjoy yourself?" Elyse asked.

"It was everything I expected and more. I'll tell you what: once you've put the finishing touches on the picture, have one printed for me. Money's no object."

"Really?" Elyse locked eyes with Viola, who was as fidgety as a squirrel at Roger's interest in her photograph.

"This session opened my eyes," Roger said, plucking a chrysanthemum from Viola's bouquet. He sniffed the flower. "Let's just say I'm appreciating fine art more and more. Anyway," he said, tucking the flower into his shirt's pocket, "Late for work."

"You're serious about the print?" Elyse called after him.

"Extra large," he said, half-way out the door. "Matte finish. I'll have it framed."

As the door shut behind him, Elyse whirled on Viola. She was as dumbstruck as Elyse felt. Viola glanced at her bouquet, her hand caressing the yellow petals as if she were trying to tell herself this was real.

"Didn't I tell you, Vi?" Elyse asked, grasping her friend by the shoulder. "Can't you see he's smitten with you? I'm always right." Frowning, she took a closer glance at Viola. "You look pale. How do you feel?"

Viola tore her dreamy stare away from the flowers. "I think I'm going to be sick."

"That's wonderful," Elyse said, cupping Viola's face in her hands. "That means you're in love." Then she narrowed her eyes and examined Viola's face. Looks like...

Hives!

Elyse plucked the chrysanthemums from Viola's grasp. "On second thought, gimme these flowers."

11

"This is your mother," Elyse said, gripping her bathroom sink. In the mirror, her exhausted reflection stared back at her. Lavender hair riddled with knots. Dark circles beneath her eyes thanks to a night of tossing and turning.

She jogged in place, stretched to relieve the tension in her neck, threw a few air punches. "She's a harmless, middle-aged lady. You're just having lunch. Stay for one hour. What could happen in an hour?"

By the time lunch rolled around, Elyse was still jogging in place at the doorstep of her childhood home. She did a series of hamstring stretches while she tried to mentally prepare herself for one-on-one time with her mother.

The giant double French doors opened and Mama stood before her, four inches shorter and one hundred terrifying pounds of Southern etiquette. Chestnut brown hair pulled into a formal chignon. Meticulously ironed salmon-pink Jackie O sheath dress, a staple in her daily uniform. Matching kitten heels and an expensive French pedicure.

"Hello, Mama," Elyse swallowed a lump in her throat, her

resolve withering under the heat of Mama's assessing stare. "What? No white gloves?"

"Oh Elyse, darling..." Mama pecked her on the cheek. Elyse caught a familiar whiff of Liz Taylor's White Diamond perfume. "I didn't know you were doing so poorly."

Elyse rolled her eyes. "Here we go again."

Her mother's gold bracelets clinked as she held Elyse at arm's length for inspection. "Did you get this outfit from Goodwill? These holes in your jeans... how can you leave the house like this?"

Why did everyone assume she was poor? "I bought them ripped. These are artfully distressed acid washed denim."

Her mother shook her head. "Oh honey, if you want to go around town looking like a derelict, be my guest. Who am I to judge? Come, come, lunch awaits and you're already ten minutes late."

Elyse clenched her hands, her teeth, and every muscle in her body as she followed her mother inside the grand foyer of her home. Stepping beneath the swooping Italian marble staircase, Elyse gazed up at the series of commissioned family portraits. One of herself as a chubby toddler, dolled up in a lace frock, her pudgy legs encased in white stockings. Another stiff studio portrait at age nine, wearing a god awful red velvet Christmas dress and polished black dress shoes, a bouquet of holly in her hair.

Mama caught her grimacing at her own portrait. "Remember how you used to be so cute, darling?" She pursed her lips and scrutinized Elyse.

It was going to be a long afternoon.

Over a lunch of finger sandwiches, Mama grilled her about the family photography business. Elyse shifted in her rose-patterned cushioned seat and fingered the white-lace tablecloth.

"How's this quarter's revenue?" Mama asked, delicately stirring her tea.

Elyse slumped in her seat and blew the hair from her eyes. "Did you invite me over for lunch or a business meeting?"

"Elyse, dear, please sit up straight. Slouching is not good for your scoliosis. And cross your legs like a lady. You weren't raised in a barn."

Elyse raised a petulant brow and slumped even further. Why did every meeting with her mother turn into a battle of wills?

"Are you in financial trouble?" Mama pressed.

Frowning, Elyse snatched two mini cucumber sandwiches from the tea caddy and jammed both in her mouth. "We're doing just fine."

"Darling," Mama glared at her over the rim of her teacup. "One sandwich at a time."

"I'm hungry!"

"You wouldn't want word getting around town that you could cram all that in your mouth."

Narrowing her eyes, Elyse shoveled another sandwich into her mouth. Crumbs littered her oversized grey T-shirt. She downed her tea in one gulp and let out a massive burp.

"I hope you don't mind: I had Jean forward me the books." Jean was Once Upon a Photo Booth's trusty bookkeeper. "You barely scraped by with a profit during summer. Do you want my opinion about this fall's bookings?"

"No, but I'm sure you'll give it."

"Abysmal."

"Mama!" Elyse heaved a frustrated sigh. "I can't believe you! You swore you wouldn't butt in when you signed the studio over to me. Photo Booth is no longer your concern. Go enjoy your retirement."

"Elyse, dear, don't be bullheaded. I may not own the studio anymore, but I will not sit by and watch you sink my life's work. I've heard complaints. You're losing my clients." To prove her point, her mother grabbed her ancient iPad and pulled up Elyse's current portfolio.

A stark still life of a bridal bouquet resting atop a trash can. A tear-streaked bride sobbing into a tissue. The groom lounging on a couch, one arm draped across his eyes in mourning for his lost freedom. The broken heel of a Jimmy Choo pump. A wedding cake attacked by seagulls. The mayor's daughter, Coralee Davis, on her ill-fated wedding day, beating the cheating groom with her pump.

After her mother put her iPad to sleep, Elyse straightened her shoulders. This wasn't a mother-daughter lunch. This was an ambush.

"I don't approve of strong language," Mama said, gesturing to the controversial portfolio, "but what the *hell* is this?"

"These were taken during my deconstructionist phase," Elyse said, sitting taller. She was proud of her work and she'd be damned if she was going to let her mother bring her down.

Mama sighed. "Deconstructionist what?"

"It's art that portrays the raw, behind-the-scenes atmosphere of a traditional wedding day." A grin tugged at her lips. "I'm keeping it real."

"Keeping it real? Keeping it real?" Mama's voice got higher and shriller, her fair complexion hotter and redder until Elyse thought her mother's head would spontaneously combust. "This is a wedding photography business! There's nothing 'real' about what we do. We create happiness. We airbrush pimples. We Photoshop faces to make couples look like they're soul mates!"

Shaking her head, Elyse had a horrible flashback to all the ghastly wedding pictures her mother used to pass off as professional photography. Cliche shots of the bride and groom embracing at the beach. The stiff studio engagement portraits. Shadowy vignettes. Soft focus filters. Brides with crispy perms; grooms with mullets. The abominable pre-Photoshop imposition of the groom in the bride's soft-focus dreams. Sometimes Elyse couldn't decide if her mother was the world's most horrible photographer or just a victim of the '80's, '90's, and early 2000s.

Elyse was certain of one thing: it would be a cold day in hell before she embraced her mother's brand of photography.

"This pretty dead girls thing," Mama went on.

"Hashtag pretty dead girls," Elyse corrected.

"Elyse, I don't see what speaking a punctuation mark has to do with anything."

"'#prettydeadgirls,'" Elyse continued, "my wildly successful Instagram photo series is raking in the dough. So how am I doing financially? Just fine. Companies are paying me a hefty licensing fee to use my pictures in their ads. I'm a brand ambassador for Ansley Mills."

"It's driving our loyal clientele away." Her mother held up a finger, silencing Elyse's protest. "Brides want to hire a photographer who will turn their special day into a fairy tale, not some derelict with a morbid obsession with death. Not someone who —" air quote "—'keeps it real.'"

Elyse scrubbed a hand over her face. "God, you make 'keeping it real' sound like a four letter word."

"Here in Indigo Bay, it practically is. I've also heard complaints from the nana of a potential bride that you're putting up these..." Mama's face took on a pinched expression "... porny pictures of yourself into the cyber."

Elyse buried her face in her hands. "Mama! Please don't call the internet 'the cyber' ever again. And I did not upload porn. These are tasteful and aesthetically pleasing self-nude-portraits. I'm proud of my body and I'm not afraid to show it."

"Be that as it may," Mama said, "the mothers of Indigo Bay are not going to hire some vulgar pornographer for their daughters' big day."

Somehow Elyse knew this luncheon would descend into an argument as all her get-togethers with her mother were destined to do.

She stood up, scraping the marble floor.

"I'm leaving," she said, grabbing as many finger sandwiches as she could fit into her tote bag.

"Don't be such a drama queen," her mother said, rushing into the kitchen for the Tupperware. "Put those in here."

"They're just fine in my bag," Elyse said, rushing toward the back door. Yanking it open, she found herself face to face with Aiden, his arm raised mid-knock.

"What are you doing here?" she blurted out.

Dressed in an ancient pair of jeans and a worn white T-shirt, Aiden held up a battered toolbox. "I'm here to fix your mother's car."

Elyse eyed him up and down; it was hard looking anywhere else. Aiden minus his stiff lab coat and starched collar was a work of art. Aiden in a tight T-shirt was a sin.

Gathering her wits, Elyse whirled on her mother. "Why didn't you tell me you were having car trouble? I could've fixed it for you."

"Elyse, please don't start. Come Aiden," she said, looping her arm through his and leading him outside toward her beige Cadillac. "Once you're done, I've got a nice lunch fixed up for you."

Elyse rolled her eyes. Like the rest of Indigo Bay, her mother adored Aiden. Growing up, every other word out of Mama's mouth was "Aiden this. Aiden that. Aiden's so kind to his mother. You'd never see Aiden getting busted for public drunkenness. Aiden passed that class with flying colors. Why can't you be more like Aiden?" One would think Aiden had sunbeams shooting out his ass. Even as an only child, Elyse never escaped the sting of sibling rivalry. Aiden Hines was the perfect older brother she never wanted, the ideal she could never live up to. It wasn't until fairly recently, when she took over Once Upon a Photo Booth, that she had begun to escape from under his shadow.

From the kitchen window, Elyse watched Aiden jack up the Caddy and slide underneath the car. The sight of him bending over in a pair of tight Levi's was not objectionable. Nor was the sight of him lifting the hood.

"What a view," Mama spoke in her ear, causing Elyse to jump.

Pressing her hand to her heart, Elyse shot her mother a dirty look. "I was listening to the engine. Sounds like you have a busted fan belt. You didn't need Aiden to fix that. Unless you invited him over to look at his ass." They both peered out the window just as Aiden slid out from the undercarriage, his T-shirt stained with grease and stretched tight across a rock-hard torso.

Mother and daughter tipped their head to the side. "Mmmm."

"There's been talk amongst my fellow directors," Mama whispered, "that the Hines & Son's barbecue sauce label is due for a modern facelift." The current label featured a grainy black and white of Aiden's grandfather with the whole country getup: white mustache and a ten-gallon hat.

"They'll need a photographer to re-shoot the label to attract a younger generation," her mother continued. "I nominated you."

Did her ears deceive her? Mama showing faith in her photography skills? Maybe Hell really did freeze over? She blinked at Mama, touched by the unexpected show of faith.

"Re-shoot the Hines & Sons label?" Elyse said. "Yes, please." If she snagged the commission, it would mean her chance to break away from the wedding photography business and punch straight into the commercial world. Just one problem. "I can't take it," she sighed, feeling her heart sink.

Her mother frowned. "You don't want the job?"

"Of course I want the job, Mama." Her voice broke. Although it would kill her to admit it, she was touched that her mother thought of her. "But this reeks of nepotism."

Mama arched a brow. "Well, don't count your chickens yet. I wrangled an almost unanimous 'yea' from the board."

"Almost unanimous?"

"Just one 'nay.'"

"Who?" Elyse asked, though she had a sinking feeling where

that dissenting vote came from. Her eyes shifted to the denim-clad legs beneath her mother's Cadillac.

Mama shrugged. "You'll have to convince him, not me."

"Well, who cares what he thinks! You don't need a unanimous vote."

"It is going to be *his* face on the label after all.

Elyse peeked out the window again. "Hold that thought," she said, brushing past her mother.

Aiden was still tinkering away beneath the car as she approached. She kicked his foot. "Nay? You 'nay-ed' me?"

The tinkering stopped. "We have several interested applicants," came his muffled voice. "It wouldn't be very fair if we just hired you, would it? You'll have to submit your portfolio like everyone else."

"You've seen my portfolio."

"I have," he said, sliding out from underneath the car. His thigh bumped against her ankle, causing her to jump aside.

Elyse leaned against the Caddy, unable to tear her gaze away from his biceps as he pulled himself up. His hands and forearms were filthy. A smudge of motor oil stained his jaw. The day was suddenly getting very hot.

She handed him a rag to wipe his hands. "So what do you think?"

Aiden pondered long and hard. At last, he jammed the rag in his back pocket. "Meh."

"Meh?!" She pushed him with all her might; he barely budged.

The corner of his mouth crinkled. He was enjoying every moment of this. "Hines & Sons has a family-friendly image. Your work may be a little too risqué for us."

"Are you referring to my self-nude-portrait series? Have you seen them?"

Aiden ducked his head, his cheeks burning with embarrassment. "I might have glanced at your slideshow."

"What do you think?" Elyse pressed.

"They're... nice." He cleared his throat.

"You'll sell a lot more bottles."

"Think clean. I assume you're capable of family-friendly photography?"

"Of course I am!" Elyse sniffed, insulted that he would question her skill. "I can do anything. I'll audition just like anyone else, though we both know I'll win, not because you know me, but because I'm better than everyone else."

"Overconfident as always," Aiden said, shutting the hood. "Which reminds me: how goes your little makeover project with Viola? Word on the street is that you're a matchmaker now." He paused. "Viola and the barista, huh?"

She couldn't help smirking. "His name is Roger, he's an Australian grad student, and a celebrated cricket or lacrosse player."

"Which one is it? Cricket or lacrosse?"

"Does it matter?"

"They *are* different sports."

"Whatever," Elyse said. "Anyway, my matchmaking, like all my endeavors, is a success. Viola and Roger are smitten with each other."

"This Roger," he began. "What do we know about him?"

Elyse laughed. "Listen to you." She lowered her voice in imitation of his. "Roger... Is he an honorable fellow? I don't know about him. I question everything and everyone."

Aiden frowned. "What do you really know about this Roger character other than a muddled understanding of lacrosse and cricket?"

"More than you think," Elyse said, chewing on her inner cheek. "If you're so concerned about my judgement, meet him yourself. We're all going to try Wesley and Olive's new escape room at One Enchanted Evening."

"Count me in." Aiden fell into a meditative silence. "What's an escape room?"

12

"Avast, Mateys!" Wesley Belmont said, squinting at his scroll. "The notorious pirate captain Raul Juarez thinks you and your fellow crew members have stolen his loot and has thrown you in the hold." Pausing, he winked at his fellow gamemaker.

Olive beamed from ear to ear. "You have one hour to find where the actual thief has hidden the gold and return it to the captain or it's the ole keel hauling with ye. Who's ready?"

"Exciting!" Elyse nudged her Plus One on the shoulder. "Isn't it, Aiden?"

Aiden eyed the double doors behind Wesley and Olive with a dubious stroke of his chin. "I can confidently say this is all new to me."

"I think..." Viola began. "It sounds thrilling?"

Elyse arched a pointed brow.

Viola squared her shoulders. "Thrilling," she corrected. "It sounds thrilling."

Elyse turned to Aiden with a smug smile. "She sounds like quite the confident lady, doesn't she?"

"Or a parrot," Aiden whispered in her ear. Before Elyse could retort, he glanced at his watch. "So where's this Roger? He's late."

"It's okay," Olive said. "We'll only start the clock once every-one's entered and locked in."

Elyse's phone dinged. "Lucie can't make it."

Olive frowned. "Did she say why?"

"I'll ask." Elyse paused a moment, waiting for Lucie's response. "It says she's read my text." She rolled her eyes. "Just like Lucie to blow us off without an explanation."

"I hope she's okay," Viola said.

"She's probably trapped in a bathroom." Making a face, Olive turned to Elyse. "Some people carry their escape rooms with them."

Wesley nodded. "That's very deep, Babe. And cute."

Olive wrinkled her nose. "You think so?"

"You look like a bunny rabbit when you do that," Wesley said, giving her an Eskimo kiss.

"Never have I wanted to kill two people more than I want to kill them," Elyse mumbled.

Aiden eyed the couple with a knot between his brow. "First time we agree on something."

Viola cleared her throat. "I think I'm going to be sick."

Elyse looked up in alarm. Last time Viola declared she was sick, she'd meant it literally.

Viola covered her mouth, her shoulders shaking from silent laughter. "It was a joke," she said. "That's funny, you didn't know I was joking."

Elyse glanced over at Aiden.

"Guess she got you," Aiden said, suppressing his laughter. Then he glanced at his watch. "Back in my day, time meant something."

"Back in your day?" Elyse nudged his shoulder. "What are you? Ninety?"

As the minutes ticked by and Roger still hadn't shown up, Aiden asked Olive, "So what inspired you to build an 'escape room'?"

"I don't like people," Olive said, matter-of-factly. "I mean, I like you guys, but after a summer of venue tours, it's become clear to me that ninety percent of the population are annoying. Most of them happen to be wedding guests. Boisterous aunts and uncles. Rowdy cousins. One's overbearing mother or grumpy father. There's got to be some way to corral them away from the happy couple. Out of sight, out of mind."

"Remember when you originally wanted to fence them in the gazebo?" Wesley asked with a dreamy smile.

"But you had the better idea of distracting them with the candy room." Olive pecked him on the cheek. "You're so smart."

Wesley nuzzled her neck. "No, you are."

Elyse poked Aiden in the ribs. "Stop them before they start that again."

"So the escape room?" Aiden asked.

"Ah yes," Olive said. "Since we fell in love over a game, what better way to bring opposing factions together than in a live role playing simulation right here at One Enchanted Evening?" She gestured to Wesley. "He's got the space."

"And the legacy of over-the-top entertainment," Wesley added. "Our escape room is still a prototype, so let us know if the puzzles are too difficult or not difficult enough. For your own safety, Olive and I will monitor you throughout the hour."

At the mention of the word 'safety,' Aiden stepped forward, prepared to grill them within an inch of their lives. Before the interrogation could begin, Roger yelled 'Hello' at the end of the hall.

"Sorry I'm late," Roger said, jogging toward them. "Couldn't get through the guard." He whacked Wesley on the chest. "Quite the place, mate." Then he swooped in and pecked Viola's cheek. "That's a nice dress. Orange looks good on you."

Viola turned the shade of a stewed tomato.

"It's 'canyon rose,'" Elyse corrected.

Roger's smile broadened as he turned to her. "There you are," he said, looking her up and down. She wore an oversized gray T-shirt with abstract triangles over ripped skinny jeans. Roger kissed his fingers bon appétit style. "You look good enough to eat."

"Thanks..." She paused. "I guess."

"That's a weird thing to say," Aiden mumbled.

"Aiden, this is Roger. Roger..." Elyse gestured toward Aiden, noting the tick in his jaw. His posture reminded her of Poe at his fiercest, limbs tensed, ears pulled back, ready to maim that squirrel. Any further introduction quickly lost steam.

Roger held out his hand. "G'day, mate."

Aiden stared at the pro-offered hand for a long time before finally grasping it. Standing between the two men, Elyse could see Roger's hand turn red, then white.

She glared at Aiden, surprised by the aggressive gesture.

Roger yanked his hand from Aiden's grasp. "That's quite the grip you've got there," he said, shaking the pain away.

Aiden replied with a hostile grunt. He turned to Elyse. "I don't like him."

"I can tell." She slapped her hands together. "Now that everyone's been introduced, let's get started."

As they shuffled into the room, an obnoxious voice bellowed from down the hall. Elyse's shoulders tensed.

"Oh God no..." She had an out-of-body experience in which she saw herself doing a slow motion turn, her facial muscles rigid with terror. Her karma couldn't be that bad. "What did I do to deserve this?"

"Wait for me! Wait!" Coralee jogged toward them in her bare feet, strappy heels dangling from her hands. "Sorry I'm late. I had to run through the lawn and the sprinklers came on." She turned to Wesley. "Your lawn is the size of a football field and very nicely trimmed but that is neither here nor there. Anyway," she paused and flashed a smile, "I made it. Who's excited to escape this room? I know I am. I don't really know what we're doing. To tell the truth, I'm very anxious but my therapist said it's good for me to try new things so here I am. La dee da! I don't know why I just said 'la dee da.' It came to me in a moment of inspiration."

Elyse touched her ticking left eye. "Coralee... I didn't know you were joining us." She cast a suspicious glance at Olive.

"Lucie asked me to take her place," Coralee said.

"Fun." Elyse felt like she was going to break her teeth smiling. One hour locked in a room with Coralee Davis was her idea of hell. All the more reason to beat the escape room. Fast.

"Okay, enough chit chat," Wesley said. "Gamemaker, your line."

Olive jumped at attention. She lowered her voice and got into character. "You have one hour. Find the treasure chest or face death by keelhauling." She and Wesley pushed the doors open. "Let the games begin."

———

THE DOORS SLAMMED. A bolt locked into place.

Once their eyes adjusted to the dark, they gawked in awe at the sheer attention to detail put into the room. The walls resembled the weathered wood of a ship's hold. Several cleverly hidden projectors simulated the ghostly ripples of waves from an imaginary sea. A running sound clip supplied the creaks and groans of an aged ship.

"Just goes to show that adults with money have the best toys," Elyse said, sidestepping an oak barrel. She weaved between one of three rope beds. The flickering wave-simulation tricked her mind into believing the floor was moving. She steadied herself against a barrel.

Roger pointed to the monitor mounted atop the barred entrance. "Fifty-nine minutes, three seconds left. We'd better get started," he said, his voice gaining a hint of panic.

Aiden motioned for them to huddle. Roger remained rooted to the spot, his eyes glued to the countdown screen.

"Okay, we need to find this chest of gold, so here's the battle plan," Aiden said, rolling his sleeves up over his strong forearms. Uncertain where to begin and befuddled over his role in an interactive role playing game, he was going to go all in. "The treasure will probably be locked, ergo—"

"We'll need a key!" Elyse said.

"We'll split up into two teams," Aiden continued. "Team One: find the chest. Team Two: locate the key. Ideally, both teams will find their object simultaneously."

Elyse couldn't help smiling. They were on the same page for once. Aiden didn't grumble or drag his heels. He was trying something new and giving the escape room his all. She was proud of him, but she'd never tell him that.

"Roger and Viola," he said, "you take care of the chest."

Elyse stepped forward. "Aiden and I will search for the key. Go! Go! Go!"

"What do I do?" Coralee asked. Before Elyse could assign her to a task, Coralee perked up. "I'll supervise."

"You—"

"Fifty-seven minutes," Roger announced, dragging his hands through his hair. "Twenty three—no—*twenty-two* seconds! Oh shit..."

"Roger," Aiden snapped. "Stop announcing the time and help us."

"Fifty-six minutes left."

"Roger," Elyse waved her arm. "Come help Viola search this oak barrel."

Roger hadn't budged.

"Where did you find this guy?" Aiden asked.

"Don't start. I've been to my share of escape rooms and there's a countdown fixator in every group."

"If he can't handle the pressure," Aiden shrugged, "maybe he should sit it out. Roger," he called over his shoulder, "hit the benches."

"Hey!" Elyse smacked him in the arm. "Who gave you the right to bench him? Don't pay attention to him Roger!" she called. "I'm the captain. I call the shots. Don't you dare move!"

Roger was in no danger of moving.

"*You're* the captain?!" Aiden's eyes widened. "I was a quarter-back in college. Three time division finals—"

"I know. Everybody here knows." Elyse said, blowing a strand of hair away from her eyes. "Your point is?"

"A team is a well-oiled machine, one weak cog will throw the game."

Elyse folded her arms across her chest. "Well this isn't football is it? This is an escape room. My turf."

"Technically Olive's turf," Aiden mumbled.

"I'd say he's in. Put that in your playbook and smoke it."

Aiden followed her, resigned. "Whatever you say, Cap. But I want to win."

"We'll win," she assured him.

He gave one last doubtful glance at Roger's back before following her to a wall plastered with the biggest world map they'd ever seen. A yardstick rested beside it with a message tied around it with a slip of rope.

"What's it say?" Coralee asked, peeking over Elyse's shoulder. "I found its twin underneath a hammock."

Viola ran up to them, waving an object in her hand. "I found this quill and inkpot hidden inside a book."

"Are we just grabbing random objects?" Elyse asked. "There's got to be a method to this madness."

Studying the map, Aiden stroked his chin. He leaned forward until his nose pressed against the weathered parchment. "Look! Do you see this? X marks the spot," he said, tapping the map.

Elyse peered at the spot. Sure enough, a microscopic X marked their seaside town. "That's Indigo Bay."

Aiden grabbed the yardstick from her and motioned for

Coralee to hand over the other. The two sticks fit together to form a cross. "What if the longitude and latitude are codes?"

"That's..." Elyse watched him trace the navigational coordinates with a ruler. "... brilliant," she finished, with a grudging admiration for Aiden's innovative leadership.

Aiden paused for a precious second, his eyes shifting to her in surprise.

"And look at the floor," Elyse continued. "It's a painted map." A large scale replica of the parchment.

"Forty-five minutes!" Roger announced.

A wry smile flickered across Aiden's lips. "You heard him."

"How could I not?" Elyse said.

After copying the numbers, the four team members, minus a useless Roger, discovered that the coordinates led the way to a corner bar. Elyse browsed shelves stocked with jugs of moonshine and bottles of Caribbean rum.

Her attention zeroed on an empty glass jug and snatched it from the shelf. "There's a key inside!" She shook the jug. The skeleton key rattled against the slender glass neck, almost touching the lip. She jammed her fingers inside and could just about touch the key, but it was a toss up between keeping the key from falling to the bottom and angling her hand just right.

"Pour rum inside," Coralee suggested.

"I don't see how."

"With enough liquid, the key will rise and you have to..." Faced with confused looks, Coralee snatched the jug from Elyse, grabbed a decanter, and poured. The key rose to the top. She jammed her fingers inside and grunted in frustration. "My hand is too big!"

"Give it a shot, Vi," Elyse suggested.

Viola came up to bat. "My hand won't fit either!"

"Why don't we break the jug?" Coralee suggested.

"Good point," Elyse said. "Give it a go, Vi."

Viola lifted it over her head. Before she could smash the jug to the ground, Olive's voice boomed on the loudspeaker. "Immediate disqualification for breaking anything inside the room."

"That's not part of the rules," Coralee shouted, searching for the hidden surveillance camera.

"It is now," Olive said. "I'm not cleaning that up." Then they heard a muffled "we should make that a new rule," to Wesley.

"Okay, so no breaking anything. Jeez..." Elyse raked her hands through her hair. As the smallest member of their group, Viola was their last chance. She'd already tried and failed.

"Thirty-five minutes left!" Roger called.

Elyse froze. A memory stirred. Of sitting at the counter of the cafe and watching Roger slip his hands into the slim canisters. When an on-the-fritz grinder pelted the place with coffee beans, she saw Roger retrieve beans from vases and various hard-to-reach places.

"Yo Roger! Get your hands over here! We need your help."

Roger pointed a slender finger at the monitor. "We're less than half an hour in. We're screwed. Oh god, oh man, oh shit, oh man. Screwed!"

The four of them exchanged a look of exasperation.

With an impatient sigh, Aiden snatched the jug from Viola's gasp. "If he won't come to us, we'll bring the task to him. Come here..."

"No! What are you doing? I don't want to do this," Roger said, dodging Aiden's advance. "Don't you see? Time is running out!"

Aiden turned to Elyse for help.

"Roger!" Elyse said. "The sooner you cooperate, the sooner we can get out of here. Right now, you need to calm down."

"No!"

"Don't you dare 'no' me! I'm telling you for the last time—"

"Time!" Roger eyed the bolted doors, one panic attack away from running head first into them. "We're running out of time. We're going to lose. We've already lost."

"Enough of this!" Aiden hooked his arm around Roger's neck and drew him into a headlock. "Get his hands."

Elyse jumped at his order. With Aiden trying to hold him still and Roger trying to weasel his way free, getting the key was no easy task. At long last, the key popped from the jug. It was a bigger key than they expected, or perhaps it just looked bigger in Roger's tiny palm.

"Great job, buddy," Aiden said, swatting Roger on the back.

Roger's attention switched back to the clock. "It's over for us, guys. We should just give up now."

Aiden took a deep breath and walked away.

"We have the key, what do we do with it?" Elyse asked as Aiden joined them back at the bar.

"Wait," Aiden interrupted, his attention fixed on the mirror beside her. "Say that again."

"What are you talking about?"

"Breathe on the mirror," he ordered.

"What?"

"As if you're coming out of the shower. Do it."

"Twenty minutes," Roger announced. "Fifteen seconds."

"Lord, that boy is annoying," Coralee said.

Not one to knock Aiden's intuition, Elyse breathed on the mirror. "*Ha Ha Ha.*"

As if by magic, a message materialized in the condensation. Elyse squinted at the letters. "Play for the key," she read, then frowned. Beneath the message: C. D. E. A. C. D. E. A. "Well, this is helpful. We already have the key. Do you know what this means?"

"I'm stumped," Aiden said. "Is it a code?"

Viola tugged on the back of his shirt. "They're music notes," she said, pointing to the miniature piano at the opposite end of the hull. Sharing the same idea, they ran toward the instrument.

Viola tried to lift the cover. "It's locked."

"The key!" Seized by an *Eureka* moment, Elyse shook Aiden's arm. "Use the key."

Aiden fumbled with the key. The latch popped opened. The instrument began to self-play a haunting melody and then, the room fell silent save for Roger's repetitious countdown.

"What did that mean?" Coralee asked.

"The notes," Viola whispered. She sat on the bench, cracked her knuckles, and replayed the notes by memory. "C. D. E. A. C. D. E. A."

She repeated it. "C. D. E. A. C. D. E. A."

"Play for the key," Aiden said, tapping his chin. "That's the key. Those are codes."

Elyse scanned around the hull. "But where's the chest?" Nothing was ever easy.

"Fifteen minutes," Roger announced. "Five seconds."

Coralee slapped her hands together. "Crunch time. We need to dig deep, people. Move! Move! Move!"

What followed was a tornado of running around like decapitated chickens. They zigzagged from one end of the hull to the next, puzzle solving within an inch of their lives. They tied a sailor's knot and constructed a makeshift contraption of pulleys. Coralee proved surprisingly strong when she lifted a massive tome from the bookshelf to apply weight to flip a switch. The lid of an old sea chest popped open.

"Look!" Coralee peeked inside. "There's a trapdoor."

After a quick conversation, they all agreed that Viola was the only one who could fit inside the chest.

"What do you see?" Elyse hollered.

"I think I'm in the captain's abode," Viola said. "It's dark in here."

Aiden knelt beside her. "Do you see the chest?"

"I-I..." There came a crash followed by the thud of something hitting the floor. "I found it! I found it!" her muffled voice echoed through the floor.

"Good," Elyse eyed the remaining two members of her team.

Aiden slumped against the sea chest. Coralee praised the Lord. "Now enter the code."

"Ten," Roger said. "Nine. Eight. Seven..."

Viola sounded just as frantic. "I entered the code, but it's not working!"

"You're just nervous," Aiden shouted. "Try it again."

"Just concentrate, Vi," Elyse added.

Roger said, "Six. Five. Four."

"I can't think with Roger counting," came Viola's reply.

"Hey Roger," Elyse barked. "Shut up!" Across the chest, she met Coralee's eye. An unspoken understanding passed between them.

Coralee jumped to her feet. "I'll shut him up."

"Three..." Roger dug his fingers through his hair, his blood-shot eyes glued to the clock. He was too distracted to see Coralee running toward him like a linebacker. "Two. On-Oof!"

The buzzer signaled 'End Time' just as Coralee tackled Roger to the floor. Golden confetti showered the hull. The timer turned into graphics of toothless pirates dancing a merry jig on the deck of a ship. The double doors burst open. Olive and Wesley poked their heads in with big smirks plastered on their faces.

"You guys did it! You beat the escape room!" Olive said, coming into the room. She halted in front of Coralee, who was still sprawled on top of Roger, and frowned. Then she turned to Wesley. "Note to self, make participants sign a waiver in case of bodily injury."

"I'll talk to my lawyer," Wesley said, assessing the fallen pair. He offered Coralee a hand, nodding in approval at her pinning technique. "Figure four leg lock. Nice Ric Flair touch."

Roger did not look so amused.

"We are in no way liable if players harm each other," Olive added, stepping over Roger to congratulate the others.

Aiden stood. "We did it," he said, patting the dust from his jeans. He offered Elyse his hand. His fingers were warm and just a bit dusty. When he tugged her to her feet, the blood rushed to her head, dizzying her just enough to make her sway off balance. He steadied her with a firm grip to the shoulder. When she looked up, he was beaming from ear to ear. His happiness drew a smile from her.

"Do my eyes deceive me?" Elyse said. "Is doubtful Aiden actually enjoying trying new things?"

"That was the most fun I've had in years." His cheeks colored. He turned to Olive. "When can we come back again? Next time, we'll try to beat our time."

"I think you found a convert," Elyse said. Before she could say more, a hand clasped her ankle. "Oh no, we forgot about Viola!"

Viola's head poked out of the sea chest. "Did we win?"

13

"HELLO?" Aiden's voice echoed across the small studio space.

Poe poked his head up and dashed through the door. "Yip!"

"In here," Elyse called. "I'm setting up my gear."

Nestled between two silver umbrella-shaped reflectors, she could hear Aiden's dress shoes squeak on her distressed wood floor.

Aiden materialized in front of the white canvas backdrop, a navy blazer slung over his shoulder. Poe romped around him, filling the studio with machine gun fire barks until Aiden scratched him behind the ears.

"Hey," he said, eyeing the impressive collection of lenses on her equipment table. He was dressed to impress. Matching navy trousers. Freshly shined cognac-colored oxfords. A white dress shirt and red and white striped skinny tie.

Elyse wolf whistled. "Don't you look cute on your first day of prep school."

"I thought I had to dress up for the picture," Aiden said, loosening his tie. "Is it too much?"

"We're trying to sell barbecue sauce, not after school tutoring. I think you should lose the tie."

"Yip!" Huffing with excitement, Poe clawed Aiden's shin and tried to hump his leg.

"Bad dog!" Elyse dove for her pet. Scooping up the terrier, she carried him up to the loft. "Bad!"

"Sorry about that," she said, descending the stairs. "I've distracted him with Olive's Marvel Plush Tsum Tsum collection. He and the Avengers are becoming good friends."

Aiden's smile wavered on nervousness. "No worries. You'd be surprised how many times my leg has been violated."

"Nature of the job?" she asked.

"Occupational hazard." Clearing his throat, he gestured to the canvas backdrop. "So what do you want me to do?"

"Cooperate," she said. "And keep an open mind."

He arched a brow. "My mind is open. I'm giving you first crack at the label. Don't," he added with a hint of warning, "make me regret it."

"The only thing you'll regret is doubting me."

Aiden made a low-throated sound. Circling the set up, he rapped his knuckles on the wooden seat of a stool. "So where's your new assistant?"

"Viola? Church choir," Elyse said. "It *is* Sunday morning, after all. Sit down, you're making me nervous."

Aiden sat on the stool with his legs apart. Rubbing his sweaty palms on his thighs, his gaze traveled to the loft. "And Olive?"

"Over at One Enchanted Evening," Elyse said. "Making changes to her escape room, or so she says. Between you and me, I highly suspect her days involve sex in cosplay. One time I walked in on them—"

Aiden held up his hand, his ears swiftly turning red. "Sorry I asked."

Chewing on her inner cheek, Elyse propped her hand on her hip. "Let's get started. Today's the big day Mr. 'Face of the Company'."

"Hm." Aiden's shoulders lifted in a shrug.

"Don't look so excited."

"I think the label is just fine with Grandpa's face on it. If it ain't broke, don't fix it."

Elyse held up a finger. "Hold that thought." She dashed to the kitchen and returned with a bottle of Hines & Sons signature mesquite mop sauce.

Donning a bushy white mustache, walrus sideburns, and a raggedy old Stetson, Grandpa Hines resembled the lovechild of Mark Twain and Colonel Sanders.

"No offense, Aiden," she held the label to his face, "I'm pretty sure this is a direct rip off of KFC's IP and to be honest, Granddaddy Hines looks a little racist."

Aiden snatched the bottle from her. "He does not!"

"This face... this face says 'I fought on the wrong side of the Civil War.' But your face," she framed him with her hands, "handsome, wholesome, corn fed. You're a blank page. You're whoever the buyer wants you to be. You'll be loved from coast to coast."

"I may not be a marketing genius," he began, "but wouldn't Grandpa's face sell more sauce because it looks more authentic?"

"Don't fight me on this, Aiden." Elyse pinched her brow. "Can you just try... *try* to be cool?"

"So melodramatic," he muttered.

"I'm trying to hone my creative center and you're making me very unbalanced."

"I think you came unbalanced." Shaking his head, Aiden glanced over his shoulders, his body rigid with tension. "Where do you want me?"

"Perch yourself on that stool," Elyse said, picking up her camera.

Aiden tugged at the lapel of his blazer. "Should I wear this?"

"No," Elyse said, focusing in on his face. "Take it off."

"But don't you think it looks more professional?"

"Lose the blazer, Hines."

He stripped it off, folded it, and draped it neatly in his lap.

Setting her camera down, Elyse marched up to him and tossed the blazer to the floor.

"Hey! I just had that dry cleaned!"

"I'll pay to have it dry cleaned again. There, hold that pose," she said, running back for her camera, "perfect."

Snap. Snap. Snap.

"You shoot with film?" he asked.

"A true artist experiments with all the tools photography has to offer." *Snap. Snap.* "With digital, I have a million chances to get it right. There's too much distraction. You take a shot, you look at the picture. You fix it. There's more intimacy with film, more opportunity to interact with the subject. Plus, I like to challenge myself."

"Very hipster of you."

"You bet your ass."

That got the tiniest smile from Aiden. She tried to capture it, but something was not quite right. "Relax your shoulders. You're all rigid."

Despite following her instructions, Aiden still seemed visibly uncomfortable.

Frowning, Elyse prompted, "Try smiling again."

He flashed her a smile reserved for a forced family vacation photo. Her gaze followed the length of his rigid body. His hands clawed at his trouser legs. How could a man with a movie star face be so unphotogenic?

"Try relaxing your jaw." *Snap. Snap.* "No, don't clench it. You're clenching everything."

"Am not." He slumped a little, then it was back to the clench.

"I bet you're clenching your ass."

Grumbling, he shifted on the stool.

With a sigh, Elyse stomped over to him. His eyes shifted like a deer caught in the path of a barreling truck.

"What are you doing?" he asked, backing away.

Without preamble, she seized him by the collar and popped

the top two buttons of his dress shirt. The skin beneath his collar-bone was tanned and warm like honey. She was tempted to brush her thumb across his skin...

Elyse shook her head. What kind of thoughts were these?

"I know what we need," she said, grabbing the tail end of an idea before it zoomed by. "Music."

Aiden blinked. Was it just her or did he seem a little off-kilter too? "I could use some music."

Elyse yanked out her phone and synced it to bluetooth speakers. "Old people music, right?" she recalled that Aiden shared the same musical taste as her mom.

"Hey, The Bee Gees are a national treasure. Better than this E.P.N. nonsense you listen to."

"You sound exactly like my mother right now. It's E.D.M."

"That's what I said."

Elyse rolled her eyes. "Don't knock it 'till you try it."

"My mind is open." He folded his arms across his chest. "E.D.M. me."

"Okay, here," she said, pulling up 'Black Tie and Neon Lights.' "This is Eames Fawkes' most beloved mix." She hit play and watched Aiden's reaction. Loud, bouncing bass filled the studio.

His face changed from skepticism to disapproval to disgust. "You call this music?"

"Can't you feel the energy?"

Aiden jammed a finger in his ear. "Sounds like someone's banging a tin pot over my head. Where are the lyrics?"

"Sometimes he collaborates with vocalists," Elyse said. "Perhaps another track?" But one look at Aiden and she changed the playlist to The Bee Gees.

Aiden smiled as the sounds of the '70's filled the studio.

"You're a lost cause, Hines," Elyse said, shaking her head, though she had to admit, there was something soothing about those high-voiced brothers.

After a few more shots, it became clear that not even disco music could cure Aiden of his rigidity in front of the camera.

Frustrated, Elyse chewed on her thumbnail, studying her uncrackable puzzle of a subject. While he was stunning in real life, he was impossible to reach through the lens. It was as if he'd constructed a wall around himself, a wall barring her from getting the perfect picture.

"Let's try something different," Elyse said, ready to throw up her hand in surrender.

Aiden's shoulders deflated. "I'm up for anything."

"Really? You?"

He shrugged. "Anything to end this photo shoot."

"Hold that thought..." Darting into the storage room, Elyse pushed and dragged a battered steamer trunk into the studio.

"What's in there?" he asked.

Popping the latch, she pulled out a pair of silk stockings, a feather boa, a tricorn hat, and a Venetian plague doctor mask. "This is my prop box."

Frowning, Aiden shook his head. "I'm not—"

"'I'm not sure about this'," Elyse said, doing her best imitation.

"I don't sound like that," he said. "And I don't see how playing dress up is going to do anything for the Hines & Sons brand."

"I'm not going to photograph you with the costume on. I just need you to relax and since you can't chill naturally, I have to resort to props. Trust me on this. I do this for toddlers all the time." She shook a baby rattle in his face. "What does this do for you?"

"Funny."

She approached him with a Buffalo-check flannel shirt and a cowboy hat.

Aiden backed up. "What is that?"

"This is a barbecue sauce shoot after all," she said, holding out the costume to him. "Come on. Amuse me."

"Urgh, give me the hat."

Aiden unbuttoned his dress shirt. As he peeled his shirt from his body, Elyse turned away to offer him privacy.

Out of morbid curiosity, she snuck a peek, blushing at the way his undershirt molded to his hard torso.

"Take the undershirt off," she blurted out.

"Why?" he asked.

"It'll bulk up the costume."

When he hesitated further, Elyse cooed, "Come on, Hines. Don't be modest. It's not like I'm going to jump you and I'm pretty sure you'll wrestle me to the ground if I do."

Elyse could kicked herself for saying that. As if things weren't already awkward enough without bringing *that* image to the table. "You're stiffening up—" she cursed under her breath "—just do as you're told."

"This is highly irregular," he said, his mouth pressed into a thin line.

"Not that irregular. Most of my clients aren't prudes like you."

"Some of your clients are infants," he said.

"And none of them make such a big fuss about nudity."

"Because they can't speak."

"Hurry up now," Elyse said, losing patience. "It's not like I haven't seen your pecs before."

With great reluctance, Aiden tugged his undershirt over his head.

Elyse sucked in her breath.

Those abs again, six-packs of perfection, just asking to be photographed.

Snap. Snap.

She couldn't help herself.

Aiden froze, his arm half in-half out of the flannel shirt. "What are you doing?"

"Candids," she said.

He snapped the two ends of his shirt together and glared at her, looking thoroughly violated.

"Of your face!"

Reassured, Aiden resumed dressing without complaint, but when Elyse brought over her makeup case and rummaged around for her go-to foundation, Aiden's eyes widened.

"What's are you doing?" Aiden asked. His voice came out as a squeak.

Elyse squeezed a dollop of foundation on a sponge. "We don't exactly have the same complexion, but close enough," she said, advancing on him.

Aiden shielded his face. "No! No way. I'm drawing the line here. I'm not wearing makeup!"

"There's nothing wrong with make-up! Male celebrities do it, and male models like you certainly could use a touch up. If it makes you feel better," she said, reaching for her compact and a brush, "let me at least powder your nose. You're a little shiny."

With a scowl, Aiden slumped in his stool and folded his arms across his chest. Elyse flitted around him with the brush as he grimaced like a petulant child.

"You're tickling me," he grumbled.

"Small price to pay for beauty." Another dusting of powder. "There," Elyse said, standing back to admire her handiwork. "Bellisima!"

"What's that?" he asked nodding to the clear plastic box beside her costume trunk. "Your psychotic collection of human hair?"

"My mustache collection!" Elyse scooped the box from the floor and popped open the lid. Another brilliant idea struck her. She looked from the box to Aiden. "You wouldn't want to try one on, would you? Or are you too square for that too?"

There followed a long moment of silence. At last, Aiden sighed. "Why the hell not? I've already lost all my dignity. Lay it on me."

Elyse couldn't believe her ears. "You're serious?"

His lips pressed into a grim line. "Don't make me regret it."

"Yes!" Elyse leaped in the air. "Yes! Yes! Yes! Hold still, let me prepare the glue."

"Glue?!"

"How else do you expect the mustache to stay on? In for a penny, in for a pound."

"Yeah, yeah. Just get it over with," he said, bracing himself for the worst.

Elyse brushed the skin-safe glue on his upper lip. She worked quickly, afraid he'd change his mind. Holding her breath, she applied the bushy mustache with the utmost care, making sure the edges were on straight and smoothed out the gaps with her fingers. While she focused on the mustache, Aiden cast his eyes downward, fixed on a wayward point on the floor.

Once the mustache was attached to her satisfaction, Elyse stood back to admire her handiwork. She whipped out her phone and snapped a few shots.

"It's a good look on you," she said, showing him the results.

Aiden touched his upper lip. "Only if I want to get into porn."

"From what I witnessed a few nights ago, I'd say you have all the right assets."

"Um..."

Crickets.

Elyse cleared her throat. "Did I go too far?"

"When do you not?"

With an awkward glance over her shoulder, Elyse resumed the shoot. "So how are things with Liesel?"

Aiden's fake mustache twitched. "*Lisa* is doing very well."

"How did you patch that up?" she asked, and silently reprimanded herself for sounding over eager.

"I told her you were a troublemaker. That as an only child you were used to getting your way. You're an attention hog, a spoiled brat," he paused for a minute, "borderline sociopath."

Elyse grimaced. "Gee, thanks for coming to my defense. Anything else?"

"Oh, and you're selfish too," Aiden said.

"That comes with the sociopath territory. I can't believe you married me."

Aiden shook his head. "How you came up with *that* lie is beyond me."

"It just came to me in the heat of the moment," she said, then immediately clammed up. Her cheeks reddened as she recalled exactly how hot that particular moment had been. "So you and Libby are cool again?"

"*Lisa* and I have a lunch date next Wednesday," Aiden said. "*Don't* join us."

"I'd never dream of it." *Snap. Snap.* "Tilt your hat." *Snap.* "I'm very happy for ya'll. I'm sure you'll have a perfect life and make a brood of perfect babies together."

"We're not at marriage level yet," Aiden said, watching her. "You sound as if you're jealous?"

"Don't flatter yourself."

He shrugged. "Just making an observation."

Elyse set her camera aside. "Done."

He blinked. "Done already?"

"I've got everything I need."

A frown. "And you promise you won't use those shots for the label?"

"Don't worry," she tapped her temple, "I have a vision. All I need is your picture from the shoulder up."

"If you say so." He tugged on the edge of his mustache. "Ow."

"Don't do that. You're going to pull your skin right off." Elyse disappeared into the bathroom and returned with a hand towel and a basin of warm water. "Let me," she said, and began dabbing his upper lip.

Focused on the task at hand, she sensed a shift in the heavy cast of his gaze upon her. The air crackled with tension. His eyes tracked her every movement until she became self-conscious of her own breath.

Elyse froze, mulling over her task until she could figure out what to do. She felt like a spider caught in a web and every nerve of her body screamed 'Danger!' As long as she appeared blissfully ignorant, nothing would happen.

And then she looked up.

Time slowed. She became hyper aware of her surroundings. The hot studio lights. The raspy whisper of the AC unit on the fritz. Aiden's every inhale and exhale. The woody hazel of his eyes. The warmth of his skin beneath her fingertips. The sliver of a scar on his chin where she'd thrown a pebble (she was aiming for the brook) at his face when they were kids. She'd been seven and got quite the walloping from her mother because of it.

"Don't move," she whispered. "You're being so difficult."

"How am I being difficult?" he asked, his voice more raspy than usual. His eyes bore right into her, unraveling her in the most uncomfortable ways.

"Stop fidgeting."

He shifted, sitting with his legs planted wide apart. Aiden tipped his head back, studying her beneath the fringe of his eyelashes. "Better?"

A lump formed in her throat.

One step.

One step was all it took to close the distance between them.

And it was all up to her.

If she wanted to, she could step inside the circle of his arms, hook her arms around his neck, feel his hands sink into the small of her back, his fingers digging into her hips. The soft refrain of a '70's love song reverberated in her ears, desire coming to her on a summer breeze...

Her gaze fixated on his mouth. His bottom lip was fuller than the top and she wondered what it would feel like to nibble on...

Elyse shook herself like a dog out of water. What kind of sick thoughts were these? In one swift motion, she seized the edge of his mustache and ripped it off like a band-aid.

"Son of a—" Aiden doubled over. When he lifted his head, his upper lip was shiny and raw. He glared up at her, tears in his eyes. "What is *wrong* with you, Darrow?"

Elyse whirled around, her heart hammering in her ears. She couldn't turn to face him, couldn't let him see how something as innocent as removing a mustache had shaken her. Her legs wobbled as she walked the few feet to her laptop and shut off the music.

"That's a wrap," she said, feeling his eyes on her back. "You can go home now."

14

Cotton candy clouds rolled above a clear blue sky on the day of the Hincs & Sons anniversary barbecue. An egret cawed from the marsh; cattails swished in the wings of a crisp breeze.

Putting the last minute touches on her custom photo booth, Elyse sniffed the delicious air. Coal smoke streamed from the roasting box, an antique contraption of concrete and steel mesh. Her mouth watered; her stomach grumbled.

Since the crack of dawn, Aiden and three local barbecue joint owners had been tending to the pig, fanning the coals with cool water and slathering its crispy hide with Hines & Sons signature honey pepper mesquite. Elyse smiled. She couldn't help noticing Milo, the owner of The Pig Bar, amongst the pit masters. Aiden was making progress, expanding his horizons, widening his circle of friends.

At long last, the team popped the hatch of the roasting box. Elyse shut her eyes, inhaling the mouthwatering smoke. The men flipped the pig over for another round of marinating. Succulent fat dripped onto the coals. The pig's crispy skin sizzled with every brush of the mop.

"I can see you drooling from there," Aiden said, coming

toward her with a plastic plate full of pork shavings. "Just making sure you don't faint before the party," he said, offering her the plate along with a bottle of IPA from Indigo Bay's local micro-brewery.

"Oh thank God." Elyse snatched up the plate and devoured the shavings. She licked the fat from her fingers and guzzled the beer.

"That's not very ladylike," Aiden said, watching her down the bottle in one gulp.

Elyse stepped up to his ear and let out a massive belch. "That's not very ladylike either," she said, wiping her hand across her mouth.

Aiden shook his head. "Were you raised in a barn?"

Another belch greeted them. They both turned. One of the men tipped his beer at Elyse.

She turned to Aiden with a smug smile. "He approves."

"Hunter John also doesn't believe in regular bathing." Aiden stepped back to scrutinize the photo booth, a last minute add-on project that reeked of nepotism. Elyse wished Mama would stop meddling in her career, but with wedding shoots slowing down in October, she wasn't going to complain. She was told to create something 'tasteful.' Other than that, she had total creative control. So far, she thought she did an outstanding job.

Aiden circled the booth.

Elyse studied his reaction, her pride swelling with every beat of his silence.

"So?" she asked, practically bouncing on the balls of her feet. "What do you think?"

"It's..." Aiden tipped his head to the side. "It's... minimal."

Painted in matte black, her booth resembled a charcoal port-a-potty. "That's what I was going for. Understated."

"Uh huh."

Elyse whacked him on the arm. "If you hate my art so much, why do you keep commissioning my work? First the label shoot, now this. How much is my mother twisting your arm?"

"None at all. I make my own decisions." Scratching the back of his head, Aiden drank in the booth. "Guess I'm a sadist."

"Or," Elyse sidestepped him, trying to meet his eye, "you're a fan of my installations and you're afraid to admit it."

"I can assure you I'm *not* a fan."

"Tend to your pig," Elyse said, shoulder shoving him out of her way. "I've got work to do."

He lingered, hovering over her as she fiddled with the booth's electrical wiring. The unexpected end to last week's photo shoot was an elephant in the room, tiptoed around and best ignored for the time being.

"By the way, I talked to Viola the other day," he said.

Elyse glanced over her shoulder. "And?"

"She looks good," he said, rubbing the back of his neck.

"As in she seems *happier*, perhaps?"

Aiden shrugged. "Mm."

"Happier because she's no longer at her soul-crushing job?"

"I suppose," he said. "She didn't really say much."

She beamed. "So you're saying I'm right?"

He feigned an intense interest in his shoes. She thought she heard the barest whisper of a "yes." Knowing Aiden, it was probably a grumble.

"What?" she cupped a hand to her ear. "Am I hearing you correctly? Is Mr. Perfect admitting he was wrong? Are you saying I'm *not* meddlesome after all?"

"You're still meddlesome," he said, his lips twitching at the corners. "And a sore winner."

"Gracious winner."

"Gracious winners don't do silly jigs."

Elyse froze. She didn't realize she'd been River-dancing in triumph.

"That being said," he continued, "this Roger you're trying to set her up with..."

"What about Roger?" Elyse asked, alarmed.

"I don't like him."

She sighed. "Of course you don't. Is it because he lost it in the escape room? Some people can't handle the pressure. You can't really hold that against him."

Aiden held up his hand. "I think you should cool it with your matchmaking," he said, leveling her a warning look. "He's not right for Viola."

Baffled, Elyse asked, "Why? What's wrong with him?"

"He's smarmy and... grabby."

"With Viola?"

"With you. The guy has perv written all over him."

"That's ridiculous! He's—"

"Elyse!"

Turning at the sound of her name, Elyse spotted Lucie and Olive running toward her with Wesley in tow. Lucie wore a lemon patterned sundress with a flouncy skirt. Olive sported a T-shirt with The Three Little Pigs turning on a spit. Wesley came with his trademark mirror aviators; he looked exhausted.

They swarmed Elyse, sucking her into a squealing circle. Between the jumping and shouting and her friends talking on top of each other, she couldn't distinguish a word they were saying.

She turned to Aiden for help.

He wiggled his pinky in his ear. "This is my cue to leave. I have to um," he pointed to the roasting box, "tend to the pig."

Wesley glanced skittishly after Aiden.

"Fine," Olive said. "You can go play too."

He brightened up in an instant. "Thanks," he said, pecking her on the cheek. "Wait for me," he called, running after Aiden, grateful for an excuse to escape the company of screaming females.

"What's going on?" Elyse asked when they were alone.

Olive turned to her, wide eyed. "You mean you haven't checked your phone?"

"Kinda busy here." She gestured to the photo booth. "Immersive art isn't going to create itself."

Lucie dug into her wicker tote. "You have to look at Roger's latest Instagram post," Lucie said, holding out her phone.

The post in question was a decently framed (though heavily filtered) snapshot of his bedroom. Her eyes zoomed in on the picture hanging over his rumpled bed. In matte canvas: Viola in an angelic white gown, kneeling with a bouquet of yellow chrysanthemums. A light snowfall, added later in post, dusted the subject.

"That's my picture!" Elyse read Roger's concise comment: "Angel over my bed. Photo by @artistelyse."

Elyse broke into a big smile. Her heart flooded with warmth and a tiny bit of self-satisfaction. Being right never got old. "Did you see what he wrote about Viola?"

"She's going to freak when she sees this," Olive said.

Lucie frowned. "His bed is none too clean," she said, squinting at the picture. "That is one nasty pillow."

Olive enlarged the photo. "Whaaa! He takes his Funko Pops out of the box." She wrinkled her nose. "I can't say I approve of that."

"What's that contraption next to his bed?" Lucie asked. "It looks like the longest bong I've ever seen."

Olive shook her head. "Don't you know what a didgeridoo is?"

"Sounds like a nasty word," Lucie said.

"It's a musical instrument, dummy. Roger is Australian after all."

"Can we stay on track, girls?" Elyse snatched the phone away from Olive. "I thought Roger was taken with Viola during the shoot, but now I see that he's fallen head over heels in love with her." She glanced up, struck by a sudden epiphany. "Don't you see what this means?"

Two blank faces stared back at her.

Elyse took a screenshot of the picture. "It means I'm a better matchmaker than I thought!"

15

VIOLA RAN, huffing and puffing toward the group. A fine sheen of sweat coated her forehead. Her cheeks were flushed, her sundress wrinkled and grimy, her hair in disarray.

Elyse clasped a hand over her mouth. "My God, Viola," she said, and cast a quick glance at Roger, who had been boring her within an inch of her life with tales of his family's didgeridoo. Out of the corner of her eye, she caught Roger grimacing at the sight of Viola. It was the look you gave someone's dirty child.

In full-on damage control mode, Elyse seized Viola by the wrist and steered her toward the old-fashioned water pump behind the lake house.

"What happened to you?" she asked, working the pump as Viola held her hands under the stream of cool water. "How could you let Roger see you like this? Are you purposefully trying to undo all my hard work? You look like someone shoved you into a bush."

"Sorry I'm late." Viola apologized another three times. "I had a flat tire and got caught up changing the spare."

Elyse studied Viola, surprised. "You changed it yourself?"

"Yup."

"Why not call roadside assistance?"

"Why call for help when you can do it yourself? I've changed tires all my life, especially since Pa's always shooting them for rifle practice." Viola nodded toward Roger's turned back. "What were you talking about? You looked annoyed."

Elyse rubbed her temple. An hour of her life wasted hearing about the minutiae of taking care of one's didgeridoo. Polishing it. Cleaning the inside with a special brush. Storing it at a comfortable room temperature. Not being a proud didgeridoo owner herself, she couldn't relate.

But, *but*...

Just because she found Roger mind-numbingly dull didn't mean she had to ruin things for Viola. Different strokes for different folks. From what little conversation Elyse observed them having, Viola latched onto Roger's every word. As for Roger, he had many qualities to recommend him. He had a badass leg scar from a brush with a stingray while snorkeling in the Great Barrier Reef. He knew the subtle difference between the coffee beans of various countries and operated The Coffee Haus' elaborate contraptions of glass tubes and copper kettles with the deftness of a laboratory artisan. And the owning of a didgeridoo was definitely something to write home about, though in Roger's case, poor storyteller that he was, he might want to hire a ghostwriter.

"We were talking about you," Elyse said, not wanting to cloud Viola's opinion of Roger with her own. She whipped out her phone and pulled up Roger's Instagram feed. "Feast your eyes on this!"

In that moment, Viola resembled one of those characters in Olive's anime shows: huge eyes and a tiny little mouth, puckered into an O. "No!"

Elyse felt lighter already. She dearly loved delivering good news. "Yes!"

"No."

"Yes!" Elyse wagged her phone in Viola's face. "He has a picture of you in his room. The picture I took of you."

"What's he doing with a picture of me?" Viola asked, mind blown.

"To worship, of course." Elyse took a second gander at the photo. She could make out the tip of that blasted wind instrument. "Probably looks at it while polishing his didgeridoo."

Viola stumbled back a step. Her face flushed red. "Oooh."

Realizing her mistake, Elyse waved her arms. "No, not that kind of didgeridoo!"

AFTER ELYSE SORTED out the misunderstanding and reassured Viola that Roger wasn't a deviant, they returned to the picnic.

A crowd gathered around Aiden. He commanded his audience on the porch of the old lake house, beneath the sweep of red, white, and blue pennant banners. Three huge canvases covered in red velvet drapes formed a semicircle behind him.

"Thank you everyone for coming," Aiden began. He was a natural speaker, engaging and attentive to his audience. "Sixty years ago, my granddad settled in Indigo Bay after the war. He worked as a house painter, a sharecropper, a journeyman laborer, and finally, he got a job at Beau's Barbecue. He made 40 cents an hour, washed dishes by day, and perfected his signature smoky mesquite at night. Down by this very pit," he gestured to the roasting station where a savory plume of smoke spiraled into the evening sky, "he concocted Hines' famous honey pecan. At the age of twenty-five, he saved enough to buy the old cotton mill on 3rd and Grand. He had seven kids, a leg full of shrapnel, two dollars in his pocket after fixin' up that old mill. Now, on the 60th Anniversary of Hines & Sons we celebrate my granddad's American Dream with a good old-fashioned feast!"

He waited for the applause to settle before continuing, "But, this being the modern day and age, Hines & Sons desperately needs a facelift. To commemorate this new milestone, we've commissioned a new label design from Indigo Bay's own Elyse Darrow."

Elyse blinked, doing a double take at the unexpected windfall. "I got the commission?" *I thought I was applying for it.* A strange mixture of elation, confusion, and annoyance surged through her as the news sank in. "Mama," she said between clenched teeth.

Roger rubbed the small of her back in encouragement.

Viola shook a power-fist in the air.

Amid the applause, Elyse turned and gave the town of Indigo Bay a beauty queen wave. She caught her mother's eye in the crowd.

"Elyse, as you know," Aiden said, "is a multifaceted artist."

"Whooo!" Roger bumped her shoulder. "Yeah she is!"

Elyse cautioned one more glance at Mama. At the mention of 'multifaceted artist,' her mother took a pull of her Long Island Iced Tea.

"I haven't seen the photos yet," Aiden said, "but the board assures me they are a step towards a new direction for the future of Hines & Sons." Waiting for the applause to die down, he ripped off all three velvet drapes in one fell swoop.

A gasp swept through the crowd.

When she saw the center photo, Elyse stumbled backward, dizzied by her own incompetence. How could she be so careless?

"Well, there goes my career," she said, squeezing her eyes shut.

Frowning at the crowd's reaction, Aiden turned. He bent closer and studied the center photograph. A few minutes passed in heavy silence. He cocked his head to the side and studied it some more.

The other two photographs were standard commercial fare: Aiden's chiseled profile in black and white. The lighting, if Elyse could say so herself, was exquisite. Aiden was a movie star. Slap his handsome mug on a bottle of Hines & Sons hickory bourbon and watch the sales skyrocket.

The center photo was the mother of all screw ups. One word: Abs. The photo left enough of Aiden's face to know it was him, but the focus was on his abs. Naked. Toned. Six-pack. Okay, she might've tinkered around with it in Photoshop, adding dramatic lighting and extra definition to his torso, but those changes weren't meant to be seen by anyone—least of all the entire town of Indigo Bay.

"What the f—?" Aiden mouthed, glaring at her.

"Sorry," she mouthed back. To her friends, who were all staring at her for an answer, she whispered, "I must've mixed up the files by accident."

Seeing Aiden's ears turn pink, Elyse pushed herself through the crowd and climbed up on stage. "So a funny thing happened during post-production," she told the audience. She faced Aiden. "I wasn't trying to be provocative."

He opened his mouth to give her a public reprimanding when a collective sigh emanated from female members of the audience.

"I'd like to slather barbecue sauce all over *those* ribs," someone said.

"Hey Aiden," a woman called, "is this for your spicy sauce?"

Aiden turned to Elyse, wide-eyed with confusion. "I—I don't... know."

"You bet your tush," Mama climbed up on stage. She'd ditched her drink and was all business, protecting her twenty percent share in the company. "When I first saw this picture, I thought: 'That's my daughter for you, pushing the envelope again.' But then we realized that pushing the envelope was exactly what the founder of our label did. Adding Dr. Pepper to his recipe and jalapeños to his dry rubs sat none too well with the palate of the time and now they're beloved classics. So in the spirit of that rebellious old rascal Harlan Hines, meet the new face, or shall I say 'chest,' of our Sweet Heat line."

The crowd went wild. Amid the cheers, Elyse chewed on her bottom lip, watching the hushed exchange between Aiden and her mother.

"Why was I the last to know?" he asked.

"We all knew you would've thrown a hissy fit had you seen it before the unveiling. I've rounded up a majority of the votes."

Aiden glanced back at the photos, scowling. "Who says you have mine?"

"Aiden, honey. Do you hear the crowd? Voting 'No' now will only be shooting your granddad's company in the foot."

Aiden glowered at Elyse.

"Don't blame her," Mama said coming to her defense. "Elyse handed over three perfectly clean files and one 'eye-catching' one by mistake." She smiled at her daughter. "Once again darlin', I've saved you from being hoisted by your own petard."

The chime of a good old-fashioned steel triangle signaled the pig was ready. As the crowd dispersed, Mama patted Aiden on the shoulder. "Oh lighten up, silly boy," she said. "God gave you that body for a reason. Flaunt it while you can."

Aiden folded his arms across his chest. "Hmph."

"And don't pout. Think of all the money we're about to make."

Left alone, Aiden gave the photographs a thorough examination. He stroked his chin, frowned, got on his haunches and frowned some more.

"Aiden?" Elyse wrung her hands together. "Say something."

At long last, he glanced over his shoulder, his face solemn and grim. "Well, this wasn't what I was expecting," he began, "but I guess if my family is in the business of saucing meat."

"You're the choicest cut."

The barest hint of a smile flickered across his lips. He tipped his head to the buffet line. "Now that I've been exploited and objectified, there's only one thing to do." With great reluctance, he offered her his arm. "Let's eat."

16

THE BUFFET TABLE contained a veritable feast of ham, pulled pork, and ribs. A flight of Hines & Sons barbecue sauce was stationed three to a bench. A second table contained all the fixings for a Southern feast: red skinned potato salad, crawfish and shrimp seasoned with Hines' Cajun spices, cheesy grits and corn on the cob. Big glass dispensers of sweet tea and lemonade quenched the guests' thirst while the neighboring dessert table boasted peach cobblers, pecan pies, and fluffy rosemary-lemon meringue care of Confectionery Kisses.

With plates towering with food, Aiden led Elyse to a bench populated with the usual gang. She squeezed in next to Wesley, who was working his way through his tenth rib by evidence of the bones in his discard pile. Next to him, Olive's bone pile was no less impressive. They seemed to be having an eating contest.

"What I find interesting," Lucie said, cutting her smoked chicken with a fork and knife, "is *not* the fact that you mistakenly swapped the files, but you took the time to photoshop his abs."

Elyse gulped down her food. "I didn't do much photoshopping," she said, stuffing another biscuit in her mouth.

"I find it interesting, too." Aiden focused on the plate before him. He picked at his potato salad with a fork, singling out the celery bits. "My abs don't look like that in real life."

"So what are you suggesting?" Elyse asked, her mouth full. "That I spent hours ogling your bare chest?"

He gave her a smug smile. "All evidence points to 'yes.'"

"You are so full of yourself!"

As if on cue, a board member approached them. She tilted her head, studying the photographs on the porch. "I like it," she said to Elyse. "Don't know if your mother told you, but we've been getting a fair share of blame for promoting gluttony and unhealthy eating, but this," she gestured to the black-and-white abs, "anyone weaned on barbecue and still looks like this must be good for business."

"The board hid the pictures from me until the unveiling," Aiden muttered to Elyse. "I didn't know you won the commission till they handed me the cards."

"Why didn't you try to sneak a peek?"

"I trusted them."

"Knowing my mother's on the board?" Elyse *tsked*. "Why not leave the hen house unattended for the fox to have her day?"

He sank lower into his seat, his cheeks flushed beneath the patio lights. "This will never stop being humiliating."

"What's there to be ashamed of?" Elyse asked. "If I looked like that, I'd never wear a shirt. I'll just waltz around and flex my pecs."

Aiden drew his arms across his chest. "Treat me like a piece of meat, why don't ya?"

"You like it."

"I like to be objectified?"

Elyse returned to stuffing her face, but her attention drifted to Wesley and Olive's conversation.

"... so Eames has agreed to appear. With an astronomical performance fee, of course," Wesley said. "But the bride wants him to make changes to his set."

Olive shook her head. "That sounds like a homicide waiting to happen. How does she dare?"

"She's a senator's daughter. That's how she dared." Wesley grimaced. "I don't relish telling Eames that wedding deejaying is a lot different from performing a set in a club. Let's hope he doesn't kill the messenger."

Eames? DJ? Elyse choked on her sweet tea. "Wait," Elyse seized Wesley by the shoulder, her heart pounding with excitement, "did I hear you right? Eames? As in Eames Fawkes?"

"Yeah," Wesley nodded.

"*The* Eames Fawkes? You know him?"

"Uh, yeah."

"The Electric Ghost himself?"

"I don't call him that," Wesley said.

"They're best friends," Olive said, wiping a smudge of barbecue sauce from Wesley's chin with a napkin.

"We're just acquaintances," Wesley corrected. "I don't think Eames has any friends. I met him a few years back while I was still living in Vegas. He played a few gigs in my mother's chapel."

"I thought Eames doesn't work weddings," Elyse pointed out.

"He's just being humble." Olive leaned forward. "Didn't One Enchanted Evening, Vegas, host a couple of EDC events?"

"What's EDC?" Aiden asked.

Elyse blinked, horrified. "What's EDC? What's EDC? The Electric Daisy Carnival!"

Aiden took a swig of his iced tea. "That means nothing to me."

"You're hopeless! It's only the biggest EDM festival outside of Tomorrowland."

Aiden opened his mouth in question.

Elyse held up her hand to stop him. "No, don't ask me what Tomorrowland is. Just don't," she said, turning back to Wesley, star-struck with the possibility that Eames Fawkes, the creator whose music she listened to during her late-night photo editing sessions, was coming to Indigo Bay.

"When does he arrive?" she pressed.

"Next Saturday," Wesley said.

Her eyes widened. "Oh my god!" She leaned her elbows on the table. "Have you seen his face? What does he look like under the mask?"

"Wait," Aiden interrupted. He had this incredulous expression which told Elyse that he was on the brink of making another judgement. "He wears a *mask*?"

"Only in public," Elyse explained. "At first, it's because he was painfully shy and then it became his stage persona. His mask is made of carbon fiber and lights up in tune with the BPMs."

Aiden shook his head. "What a gimmick," he muttered.

"He's programmed it to sync with his mixes," Elyse continued, pretending she didn't hear him. She whirled on Wesley. "Is he hot? He is hot, isn't he? If he creates music like that, he has to be!"

Wesley shrugged. "I try not to check out my guy friends." He gave Aiden an uncomfortable glance. "He doesn't have your abs though."

"Thanks," Aiden said dryly.

Glancing over Wesley's shoulder, Elyse noticed Viola was sitting on the edge of the bench, attempting to listen in. "Vi, scoot in closer."

"Are you a fan of this masked DJ?" Aiden asked Viola. "It seems like he does nothing more than press the play button on his song list."

"A DJ does more than press play," Elyse snapped at him. "Eames composes all his mixes. In fact, he's not just a DJ, he's a producer."

"I agree with Elyse." Viola cleared her throat. The table hushed, leaning in to hear her soft-spoken words. "I'm a big fan of Eames."

"Really?" Aiden asked. "I thought you were more of a country music girl, myself."

"Vi listened to all the records in Whispering Vinyl," Elyse

piped in like a proud mother hen. "Unlike some, she has an open mind."

"I love all music genres," Viola said, braiding the ends of her hair. "And Eames' compositions are simply beautiful. When his music plays, it's like synesthesia."

"Even the ones without lyrics?" Aiden asked.

"Especially the ones without lyrics." Viola propped her hand against her cheek and uttered a dreamy sigh. "Eames Fawkes is classically trained. He plays the piano, violin, and has the most sonorous voice—that is, on the rare occasion that he sings."

"He never sings," Wesley said. "Not if he can help it."

"What's he like?" Elyse asked Wesley, her imagination running wild. Out of the corner of her eye, she noticed Aiden roll his eyes. "And where will he be staying?" She gasped. "Can I meet him?"

Before Wesley could answer all her questions, a body eclipsed him from view.

"There you are." Roger squeezed in between her and Wesley. "Make room there, mate," he said.

Elyse sighed.

"What's that you got there?" Wesley asked, nodding toward Roger's plate. It contained four biscuits slathered in a sticky brown substance. "Molasses?"

"Marmite." Roger stuffed a biscuit in his mouth. "Never leave home without it." He passed the plate around. "Want to try?"

Wesley held up his hand. "No thanks."

"Marmite, eh?" Aiden eyed the alien-looking condiment, then he whispered in Elyse's ear. "Marmite on Southern biscuits. I'm glad my granddad is dead or this will probably kill him."

"He's Australian," Elyse hissed. "They love this stuff. I've seen a documentary about it. You should try it."

"Yeah, mate," Roger said. "Give it a try."

Aiden folded his arms across his chest. "No."

"So much for keeping an open mind," Elyse muttered.

"Elyse?" Roger asked, pushing the plate toward her.

"Oh um... I shouldn't." She patted her stomach. "Ready to burst as it is."

"Viola?" Roger slid the plate over to her.

Viola shook her head frantically.

"Aw, come on. It'll put some hair on your chest."

Viola's eyes shifted to Elyse.

Elyse nodded. "Carpe Diem."

Viola plucked a biscuit from the plate. She took the tiniest bite and chewed. Her face turned green.

"What do you think?" Roger asked.

Giving him a thumbs up, Viola forced herself to swallow.

"That's what I call Aussie-Southern fusion." Roger stuffed another biscuit in his mouth. "So Elyse," he said, slinging an arm across her shoulder, "Have I told you about the many uses for my didgeridoo?"

"No," Elyse rubbed her temple, "but I know you're about to."

17

ELYSE'S finished photo booth stood between the inlet and the crepe myrtle grove. The booth was large and imposing, abstract and out of place amongst the fairy light-wrapped tree trunks and the patriotic decor.

"This reminds me of something," Olive said, stepping up to the entrance. She gazed up at the booth and tapped her chin. "What does it remind me of?"

Wesley snapped his fingers, then pointed at Elyse. "*2001: A Space Odyssey.*" He hummed the theme. "It's the monolith in the opening shot, the one that entrances the primates." He stroked his chin and studied the photo booth, his brows creased in thought. "Are *we* the primates? Is that what you're trying to tell us?"

Elyse folded her hands in front of her. "That's a good question."

"So what's the answer?" Aiden asked.

"I don't have the answer. The answer is within oneself."

"Oh, brother..."

"I wasn't thinking of Stanley Kubrick when I created this, but I like for my art to incite an intellectual discourse," Elyse said, glancing over Wesley's shoulder. "Aiden, you look like you have questions."

Aiden peered at the place card at the booth's entrance. "'*Man Stumbles Upon Starfield*': An Experimental Installation by E. Darrow," he read. Shaking his head, he muttered "okay" under his breath.

Elyse narrowed her eyes. She felt the skepticism radiating off of him in waves. Frankly, she was sick of it. Aiden was never impressed by anything she did. Sometimes she thought he was put on earth to question her every action and poke holes in all her accomplishments.

"I'm not being pretentious," she snapped.

Aiden held up his hands in self-defense. "I didn't say anything."

"I know what you're thinking," she said. "This isn't just your average photo booth. This is immersive art."

"I think we commissioned just an average photo booth, but—" He made the motion of zipping up his lip. "I'll try to keep an open mind."

Somewhat placated, Elyse gazed upon her small group of participants. "First: the ground rules. The photo booth holds two at a time. You can stay up to five minutes so feel free to go wild," she held up a cautionary finger, "but not *too* wild. Oh, and if anyone has a history of epilepsy, you probably shouldn't go inside." To Olive, she whispered, "Do you think I should have a waiver ready?"

"If you want to cover your ass," Olive said.

Aiden held up a finger, then clamped his mouth shut.

"Roger and Viola first," Elyse said, ushering the two forward.

Viola needed no further encouragement to partner up with Roger.

"Here's an idea," Roger halted at the entrance and hooked his arm through Elyse's. "As the creator, why don't you walk me through the booth?"

"Meh." Elyse slipped out of his grasp. "It's self-explanatory."

"But I'm new to immersive art installations," Roger stalled. "Maybe I need someone to hold my hand."

Elyse placed Viola's hand in his. "Your wish is granted." Before he could weasel his way out, she shoved them both inside and shut the door.

After a few seconds, she pressed her remote, and the booth lit up, outlined by a supernatural green halo. A frightened yelp echoed from within. In less than fifteen seconds, a photo strip slid from the front slot. Elyse gingerly picked up the photo and held it up to the moonlight. Roger and Viola stood inches apart for three out of five pictures. Immersed in a cosmos of green LEDs, they photographed as two bodies floating in space.

"Badass," Olive said. "How did you do that?"

"A trick with mirrors," Elyse said, frowning at the strip. The rest of the photos contained Roger snapping selfies while Viola gazed upon the camera like a deer in the headlights. "Well, this is underwhelming..."

"What did you expect?" Aiden asked, peering over her shoulder.

Sparks. Lust. Pictures you can't show your mother. She sighed. "A little more closeness than this."

Wesley and Olive were up next. They stayed way past their allotted time and when their strip developed, Elyse picked it up and showed Aiden.

He shielded his eyes. "Put it away!"

Elyse huffed in disappointment. She was hoping Roger and Viola's time inside the photo booth would look like this. She was starting to get the impression that Roger wasn't into Viola.

Could it be that I'm not as socially intelligent as I thought I was?

For a sliver of a second, Elyse was in turmoil. "Nah," she said, embarrassed for even doubting her matchmaking abilities. Knowing Viola, it was going to take a lot more than a dark photo booth to draw her out of her shell. As for Roger, well, she had to give praise where praise was due. No forward remarks. No aggressive advances. A complete 360 from her experience with him before. In fact, the more she thought on it, the more Elyse liked Roger. He was courting Viola like a 19th century gentleman in that he was courting her *slowly*. And there was nothing wrong with slow. Slow was romantic, the stuff of fairy tales.

She exhaled in relief. "I called it."

"You called what?" Aiden asked.

Elyse startled. She wasn't aware she spoke aloud. "Nothing," she said, a smile tugging at the corner of her mouth.

Aiden studied her closely. "Why are you looking so smug all of a sudden? You have a crazy glaze to your eyes." His brows furrowed. "What's going on in that brain of yours?"

She was in a good mood and was willing to overlook his acerbic remarks. Elyse glanced down at the two photo strips instead. "I just can't wait for Roger and Viola to get together. It's like watching a fairy tale unfold before my eyes. One day they are going to be as much in love as Olive and Wesley and they'll have me to thank for it."

Aiden pressed the back of his hand to her brow.

"What are you doing?" Elyse sputtered.

"Feeling for fever," he said, now touching his own forehead to compare temperatures. "One moment you saw zero chemistry between them and now you're planning their wedding. I need to make sure you're not sick."

She nudged his hand away. "I'm fine."

Out went Olive and Wesley.

"In you go, Lucie," Elyse said.

Lucie took one glance at Olive's rumpled hair and Wesley's mis-buttoned dress shirt. "Nope," she said, whirling on her heels.

"Lucie!" Elyse held her arms wide.

"I'm not going into that sperm trap."

"Party pooper!" Elyse's attention zeroed in on Aiden. "After you," she gestured to the entrance.

As she watched him tread inside, Elyse jumped on an impulse and slipped in after him. She intended for Aiden to experience the booth alone, but the opportunity to witness his reaction was too great to pass up. As much as she told herself that she didn't care about his opinion, a contrary part of her craved his approval.

Pitch blackness cloaked his face though she could feel his rational mind working overtime within the cramped booth. No matter which way she turned, her shoulders bumped against his.

"Are we supposed to do something?" he whispered in her ear. The sweet scent of peach cobbler still lingered on his breath.

"This is the first stage of my immersive experience," Elyse said. "A few moments of darkness to clear the gunk out of one's mind."

She felt his hand on the small of her back, steadying his balance until his eyes adjusted to the darkness. And then, just as suddenly, he snatched his hand away.

Elyse shifted to allow herself space. She tugged on her over-sized cami to no avail. The heat from his fingertips still left impressions on her balmy skin.

A steady *whoosh* played from a hidden stereo.

"Is that an air leak?" Aiden asked.

"It's my sound system. I'm trying to simulate flying through space."

"You've thought of everything, multifaceted artist." Another accidental bump of the shoulder. Aiden cleared his throat. "What's the second stage?"

"After darkness," she clicked her remote, "comes the light."

All at once, the LEDs she'd painstakingly installed lit up, shattering their cocoon of darkness. Greens. Reds. Blues. Yellows. Floor to ceiling. Wall to mirrored wall. Glowing and dimming into infinity.

"Imagine you're floating in deep space and stumble upon a star field. That's the immersive experience I was after."

Elyse studied Aiden's reaction. He did a complete 360 around the booth, shuffling as much as the cramped space allowed, his mouth ajar in awe.

"Well?" Elyse asked, after a few seconds of stunned silence. "What do you think?

"I think it's amazing." Aiden dragged a hand through his hair. His profile was bathed in pinpricks of lights. "Profound." Then he looked at her as if he'd never seen her before. "You're a very talented artist, Elyse."

"Oh, he's complimenting me now." She tried to sound sarcastic, but something went wrong with her voice. Usually she'd love nothing more than to rub how he'd underestimated her in his perfect face. Somehow, in this moment, the mood felt off. It wasn't a time for anything but sincerity. A hot flush swept over her cheeks. Elyse ducked her head, grateful for the distracting effect of the flashing LEDs.

"No really," Aiden said, a note of surprise in his voice. He studied her. "You're a pain in the ass, but you're beautiful," he tapped her gently between the brows, "you have a beautiful mind."

Another bout of silence followed. The time ticked. The lights flashed. On. Off. On. Off. Elyse's heart thumped in synchrony with the special effects. The interior was stuffy; only a sliver of breeze cooled her cheek.

"What's the third stage?" Aiden asked at last.

"Blatant party pictures," Elyse said. "We're in a photo booth after all." She invited him to sit on an inconspicuous, almost invisible bench.

The bench was big enough for one. Elyse had to make due by sitting on his knee. His arm wrapped around her midriff.

She exhaled a shaky breath. "Well, this isn't weird."

"Would you prefer I sit on your knee instead?" he asked, punctuating the awkwardness.

"I'd love nothing more." She rapped the back of his head. "Get ready," she nodded toward a cube-shaped cutout in the mirror, "Smile."

A bright flash illuminated the booth, complete with the retro sound effect of exploding light bulbs. They mugged for the camera, making a series of silly faces. Upon the fifth frame, Elyse threw her arms around his neck. She meant to peck him on the cheek, but in that exact moment, Aiden turned his head and her lips brushed against his. Her eyes widened in surprise yet she made no move to pull away. Nor did he. His arms tightened around her waist, lighting every nerve of her body on fire and turning her limbs to mush.

Flash.

The kiss ended before it began, prematurely cut off by a brilliant explosion of stardust. The booth was once again suffused in darkness, the sound of flashing bulbs giving way to a keen silence in which Elyse could hear her own heart drum a tattoo beat inside her chest.

She felt his hand slip off her waist and shut her eyes, dazzled by the unexpected turn of events. Slipping off his knee, she touched her lips with trembling fingers. She could still feel the feathery weight of his kiss.

"T-t-t-imes up," she said, stumbling out of the booth to save face. The cool breeze steamed her fevered cheeks.

Aiden followed her out. His body was rigid as if he were having trouble walking.

She made a beeline to the dispenser and snatched up the photo strip. "Do you want to keep it?" she asked, unable to meet his eye.

"I'll take half," Aiden said.

She sensed his eyes on her. A long silence descended upon them, the awkwardness meter tripling with every second that ticked by.

"Elyse!"

She glanced over her shoulder. Olive, along with the rest of the gang, huddled along the inlet's rickety dock. Fireflies danced in the tall marsh grass, flashing orbs of green light around the water's edge. A spectacular display of fireworks exploded in the night sky, casting sparks and Catherine wheels above the dark waters.

"Last chance for the boat rides!" Olive waved her over. "You coming?"

"Just a moment!" She glanced up at Aiden. "Are *you* coming?" she asked.

Aiden shook his head. "I'll pass. I've got investors to schmooze."

Elyse turned to go.

"Elyse?" he called her back. "The photo?"

"Oh, right." She tore the strip in half with clumsy fingers and shoved the other half in his hand. "Bye."

"Elyse!" Aiden called her back again.

She stopped in her tracks.

A frown furrowed between his brows. He glanced at the strip. "Keep on being... multifaceted."

Her mouth twitched into a smile, but as she jogged toward the dock, she studied the photo strip and brushed her thumb across the last picture. The two of them, locked in a kiss.

No one will ever see this.

Though on the off-chance someone were to see this picture, she'd tell them that stranger things were bound to happen... once upon a photo booth.

18

"ELYSE?" Olive waved a hand in front of her face. "Hello? Earth to Elyse."

Elyse snapped out of her daze. She was still clutching the photo strip.

"Are you still with us?" Olive peered at the strip. "Oh, I see..."

With a yelp, Elyse folded the strip and stuffed it inside her back pocket.

"What happened between you and Aiden in that booth?" Olive was wide-eyed with curiosity. "Did he kiss you? Did you kiss him? Did you kiss each other?"

Elyse regarded her, aghast. "*Nooo.*" Her laugh sounded too harsh, even to herself. "No." She shook her head. "Did we—of course we didn't. How ridiculous can you be?"

"Okay," Olive arched a brow at Lucie, "Just asking."

Lucie whispered into Olive's ear. "That's precisely why I didn't go into the booth. Talk about dirty."

"I heard that!" Elyse snapped.

"I didn't say anything," Lucie said.

Narrowing her eyes, Elyse scanned the small crowd waiting for the late night boat rides. Her attention zeroed in on Roger and

Viola. They stood a shoulder's length apart. Viola's face was still a touch green from the Marmite biscuits. Roger's eyes were glued to his phone.

Elyse shook her head. Their lack of chemistry had proven sorely disappointing tonight. In fact, it should have been Roger and Viola kissing in the photo strip instead of —

And now she probably couldn't face Aiden again. Her cheeks steamed, recalling the soft pressure of his lips. Who was to blame for this? Roger. She was going to make this match work or else tonight would be for nothing.

"Viola," Elyse said, as the paddleboat drifted toward them, "why don't you ride with Roger?"

Viola clutched her stomach. "I don't think—"

"Viola doesn't look like she's in any condition to get on a boat," Roger said, linking arms with Elyse and ushering her to the edge of the dock. "Why don't you ride with me?"

This hard-to-get dance again! Why did Roger persist in making her matchmaking endeavors so difficult? She got that he was going slow out of respect for Viola's delicacy but this snail-like pace was wearing on her patience.

"Actually," she spun on her heels and grabbed Viola's hand, "Viola was just telling me that she'd love to hear all about your didgeridoo."

Roger glanced at Viola, frowning. "That's nice, but I think it takes a special person to appreciate—"

Elyse held up her hand. "Stop right there. Viola is that special person and has three hours to kill, so..." and with a flutter of her hand, she shooed them toward the boat.

"Um," Viola's shoulders knocked into Rogers. "Elyse?"

"What? What is it now?"

"I think I'll sit this one out. I'm not feeling very well." A sheen of perspiration coated Viola's forehead. She furrowed her brows and gulped. "I think it's the marmite."

"My marmite?" Roger did a double take, sounding as affronted as if he were the inventor of marmite. "I've never heard of anyone getting sick over a little mar—"

As if to prove her point, Viola doubled over. A stream of savory-smelling, tar-colored vomit splattered the dock.

"Whoa!" Everyone jumped back.

"Easy there, little Sheila," Roger said, thumping Viola on the back. He turned to Elyse and held out his hand. "Come on, you're up."

"Nope. Not me," Elyse said, throwing her arm around Viola's shoulder. "I can't go on some pleasure cruise while Viola is sick."

"I'm all right, Elyse," Viola said, clutching her stomach. "I don't want to ruin everybody's fun."

"But Viola—" Elyse pleaded with her eyes, but Viola didn't get the hint.

"I'm pretty beat anyway," Viola said. "In fact I..." she gulped and slapped a hand over her mouth. Without another word, she raced off into the nerve center of the party.

Elyse chewed on her bottom lip as she watched Viola shove people out of her way in her race to the station of port-a-potties. She took a step away from the dock, but Roger's hand on her elbow spun her around.

He arched his brow in triumph. "Guess you're riding with me."

Elyse wrinkled her nose. She had a sour taste in her mouth too. "Lucky me."

———

"... an all natural wood oil is what I used to keep my didgeridoo extra shiny," Roger said, his biceps flexing as he paddled away from shore, "though I have experimented with a concoction of my own. What's the ingredient you ask?"

Huddled on the stern, Elyse rubbed her temples. "I didn't ask."

"Let me tell you."

"No," Elyse waved her hands, warding off the tedious soliloquy to come. "Please don't."

"Flaxseed oil..." Letting the boat drift, Roger leaned on the oars and counted on his fingertips. "... pine nut extract, a good cloth is essential for the care and maintenance, mind you."

"Kill me now," Elyse muttered. She slumped against the rim of the boat and tried to put her mind away.

Water lapped against the boat. Darkened cypresses bracketed the water, their overhanging branches dripping with Spanish Moss. The distant strings of lights glimmered on the shore where the guests congregated in chatty packs. To her satisfaction, she could see a line forming in front of her photo booth. Neighboring boats drifted by, a lazy flotilla under a canopy of exploding fireworks.

Nodding along with Roger's banal chatter, Elyse braced her cheek on her palm. She scanned the shore, plotting her escape, but the moment she spotted Aiden, she straightened. He was lost in avid conversation with a drop dead gorgeous blonde in a white picnic dress.

Elyse's nails dug into the boat's wooden rim.

Lisa.

"... so what do you think?" Roger asked.

"Think?" Her eyes tracked Aiden and Lisa. Aiden's mouth moved inaudibly, saying something that made Lisa laugh. "Think about what?" she asked absently.

Still laughing, Lisa leaned forward under the pretext of falling over, her hand pressed against Aiden's chest for support.

"Oh, come on," Elyse muttered. She'd known Aiden all her life and had never known him to crack a joke that funny. And here Lisa was practically rolling on the floor! Probably a ploy to get a ring on her finger.

"Elyse?" Roger tapped her on the shoulder.

The boat rocked. The oars, with no one to man them, banged against the sides of the boat. Roger rowed them to the far side of the inlet, within the tall screen of marsh grass. They were secluded from the other boats and far removed from the guests on the shore.

She gestured for him to be quiet.

"I've been doing a lot of heavy thinking," Roger began.

"About your didgeridoo polishing?"

Aiden and Lisa had left the crowd. Aiden took her hand and led her to the photo booth.

"Don't you dare take her inside *my* photo booth," Elyse whispered.

"I think there's something we need to discuss," Roger continued.

"Discuss?" she muttered absently, her heart rate spiking into overdrive. Yes. Aiden *was* taking Lisa inside her immersive art installation for five minutes of nooky. "Discuss what?"

"You and me."

"You and me?" Elyse frowned. What was he talking about? "What about you and me?"

Roger stood. The boat rocked some more. She heard the sound of a zipper. Elyse turned her head and something smooth and velvety, though not particularly imposing, poked her on the cheek.

Sputtering, Elyse backed away. At first, she thought she'd been hit by a flying fish but when her eyes zeroed in on Roger's crotch, she snatched up an oar.

"Put that thing away!"

"Hey!" Roger fumbled with his zipper. "Careful with that thing. I thought you wanted this. Talk about sending mixed signals."

"Wanted what? To get dick-smacked in the face?" She raised the oar, her body shaking with rage. "Mixed signals?"

"Parading around me with your skimpy clothes," Roger recounted while cowering at the opposite end of the boat. "Coming into the cafe in T-shirts without panties."

Elyse blinked. "You mean my shift dresses? They're a reaction against the feminine silhouettes imprisoning women in the hourglass figure."

"Whatever that means." Roger gestured to her current attire. "I mean, you've been flaunting your norks at me all night long. What am I supposed to think?"

Elyse glanced down at her black cami. She was barely an A-cup. She didn't need a bra. Why was that so hard to understand?

"Listen, *asshole.* I'll wear what I want when I want to wear it. I *choose* not to wear a bra because I'm freeing myself of the binding articles of my gender, not because I'm enticing you with my 'norks.' It doesn't mean I'm inviting you to assault me." The more she spoke, the angrier she became. "In fact, I can't believe we're having this conversation. How dare you call my breasts norks! I'm beyond offended."

Roger squared his shoulders. "I'm offended too."

Elyse grimaced. "What do you have to be offended about? I'm offended that you're offended."

"I thought you wanted to continue what we started."

Elyse laughed, unable to believe her ears. "Are you insane? That ship has *long* sailed."

She thought the feeling was mutual. Obviously, she was mistaken.

Roger didn't have the decency to pretend to be contrite. He actually seemed as angry as she was. "Then why do you keep inviting me to all these group events? The photo shoot, the escape room, this barbecue?"

"I was trying to set you up with Viola!"

"Viola?" Roger cursed under his breath. "That's the last person I'm interested in."

"What about her picture?" Elyse exploded. "You have it hanging over your bed!"

"I have the picture you took hanging over my bed."

"'Angel over my bed,'?" she said, air-quoting his words. "How do you explain that?"

"Everyone knows things you write on Instagram don't mean shit. Did you see that I went out of my way to tag you?" Roger pointed out. "I even invented all these clever hashtags to promote you."

Elyse threw up her hands in surrender. "Some heavy mental lifting for you I'm sure!"

"Listen," Roger advanced on her, "Viola's pretty and all, if you like that wilting lily type, but I'm not interested."

Elyse gasped, affronted. "Don't you dare insult my friend! Viola's worth more than ten of you."

Roger held up his hands. "No offense meant," he said, taking on the calming tone of a hostage negotiator. "Viola is a girl and I want a *woman*. Someone with experience. Someone who knows how to have fun."

Elyse clutched her temples. Her world was spinning. If she was wrong about this, what else was she wrong about? For the first time in her life, she began to doubt herself. Being wrong was not a pleasant feeling. Also, Roger just implied that she was a slut.

An intense bout of disgust washed over her. Disgust with Roger, disgust with herself for sleeping with Roger. Disgust with herself for foisting this creep upon Viola.

Viola! Oh shit. What was she going to tell Viola?

Her grip on the oar slackened. She looked up at Roger. "So you never had any feelings for Viola? None at all?"

"It was all for you," he said, brushing a hand across her cheek.

Elyse cursed under her breath. "I'm so stupid," she muttered. Viola's self-esteem was already low to start and after all that time and effort building it up, now it was all going to come crashing down. The news would inevitably crush Viola and any future efforts to build her confidence would be twice as hard if not impossible.

"I knew you'd come around," Roger said, ripping her out of her reverie.

"Come around? What the hell are you talking about?" Before she could correct him, Roger seized her by the neck and mashed his mouth against hers. His tongue rammed between her lips like he was trying to deep clean her tonsils. She tasted a sinister combination of Marmite and mesquite and thought she was going to gag.

"Get... Off of me!" Elyse's knee collided with his balls.

Roger's eyes bulged out of his head. He pitched forward, clutching his crotch.

Elyse leveled the flat of the oar against his temple. "You're lucky I don't smash your sex offender face in!"

"No." He shielded his face with his arms. "No, please!"

The sight of Roger squirming on the floor was enough to appease her. With a growl, Elyse pitched the oar over the side and kicked the spare into the water. "Have fun swimming back, asshole."

"Hey!" Roger said, when she mounted the prowl. "Where are you going?"

"Far away from you!"

"Cocktease."

She flipped him the finger and nose dived into the inlet, his insult still ringing in her ears. Freezing water hit her full force, momentarily stunning her, but rage and repulsion incited her to move. She frog swam to shore, emerging from the water to a stunned audience. The crowd parted for her.

"Elyse, darling," her mother shook her head, "can't we have a simple party without you trying to attract attention to yourself?"

Elyse drew her arms around her freezing body. Every inch of her exposed skin erupted in goosebumps. Her teeth chattered. "Not now, Mama," she snapped.

She plowed between Aiden and Lisa.

Aiden choked on his beer. He took in her dripping wet cami,

lingering for a moment on her braless chest. She was drawing the attention of more than one male guest. Beside him, Lisa rolled her eyes and said, loud enough for Elyse to hear, "So juvenile."

"What happened to you?" he asked, stripping off his jacket and draping it over her shaking shoulders.

"Men!" And without an explanation, Elyse broke into a run, fleeing the barbecue in a trail of tears.

19

FOR THE NEXT FEW DAYS, Elyse went into hiding. She avoided The Coffee Haus, steered clear of Aiden's pet clinic, and tried to say as little to Viola about Roger as possible. She harbored the hope that if she pretended Roger no longer existed, Viola would magically forget about him. But even Viola, usually so reserved, wouldn't shut up about that damned Australian.

"Why can't we go into the cafe, Elyse?" Viola asked, following her as they passed by The Coffee Haus. They were on the opposite side of the street and while Viola peered inside, Elyse kept her eyes fixed ahead.

"Move along, Vi," she said, more harshly than she intended. "We've got two newborn portraits scheduled for this afternoon."

"Sounds like you need your 3pm fix."

"I've given up coffee," Elyse said, though her head pounded from caffeine withdrawals. She hugged her chunky cardigan closer to her body. It was only mid-autumn, but Elyse was dressed for winter, no inch of skin exposed. She was even wearing a bra, and it was every bit as binding as she'd remembered.

Viola tugged on her sleeve. "I see him! He's making a macchiato. Oh, he's parted his hair a different way. Isn't he cute?"

Elyse adjusted her oversized sunglasses and picked up the pace. She touched her jaw, still feeling Roger upon her cheek like a penis-shaped brand. How was she going to explain *that* to Viola?

She ducked her head. "Hurry up! Those newborns aren't going to photograph themselves."

THE EVENING FOUND Elyse upon the doorstep of her childhood home.

Mama answered the door with her hair wrapped in a towel and her face slathered in a green clay mask. "Elyse! What are you doing here?" Her shrewd eyes narrowed in on her daughter's chest. "Heavens to Betsy! You're wearing a bra!"

"Not now, Mama," Elyse said, storming inside. "Are you busy? I need to talk."

Mama shut the door. "I was just about to settle in with my programs."

Even in the depths of despair, Elyse couldn't suppress an eye roll.

"You sound like nana. It's only six-thirty. You've got time." She flopped onto her favorite spot on the couch where the cushion conformed to her body. Kicking off her shoes, she snatched up a velvet throw pillow and curled into a pitiful ball.

The cushions shifted beside her. Mama switched on the television and the *Jeopardy* theme filled the family room.

"Oh, Mama..." With a cry, Elyse buried her face in her mother's lap. "I've made a big mistake."

Her mother patted her on the top of the head. "Tell me all about it, baby."

Elyse sobbed out the entire uncensored story. Her brief fling with Roger, her disastrous attempt to set Viola up with him. And last but not least, the cherry on top of her shit pie: "... and then he whipped it out."

"Well, that's not very gentlemanly." Mama sounded distracted and didn't seem at all shocked.

"I think he was trying to prop it on my shoulder," Elyse lolled her head against Mama's thigh, now soaked from her tears. "As if my shoulder is some kind of dick dormant. Oh Mama, I've never been so humiliated. What am I going to tell Viola? Thanks to me she thinks he's an Aussie coffee god." She groaned. "Why am I so influential? Now how do I break it to her without *breaking* her?" A minute lapsed without a response. Elyse figured her mother was trying to process the information—and there was a lot of information. "Do you have any advice? Any words of comfort?"

"What is Chernobyl?" Mama said.

"Huh?" Elyse cracked open an eye. She turned toward the TV. Alex Trebek unveiled the answer to '$500 for Nuclear Disasters.' "What is Chernobyl?"

"Ha Ha!" Her mother beamed. "I was right! Did you see that? I should be on that show."

"Mama! I'm pouring my heart out to you and you're watching Jeopardy? Were you even listening to anything I was saying?"

"I heard you admit you were wrong. I can't tell you how refreshing that sounds."

Elyse got up.

A hand on her elbow kept her in place.

"You need to tell her," Mama said, taking on a more serious note.

Elyse mulled this over for a spell and concluded this was not the answer she was seeking. "But it will crush her!"

"Quit your whining. It will crush her more the longer you wait. It's time you man up and be a good friend, as opposed to the horrible friend you are." Mama shook her head. "If I were Viola, I'd have kicked you to the curb long ago."

"Well, you're no help at all!" Elyse exploded.

"What do you want me to say?"

"Something helpful. Something that doesn't involve breaking Viola's heart."

"And maybe I should pull a rabbit out of a hat while I'm at it? I don't know what to tell you, baby. You've made your bed..." Then her eyes traveled over Elyse's head. "My word," she said, snatching an unruly tendril of her daughter's hair and rubbing the damaged strands between her fingertips. "How could you leave the house like this? You have a bird's nest growing on top of your head and your roots are showing."

"Mama, stay on track." Elyse whacked away her mother's meddlesome hands. She was beginning to regret coming here.

"How can I stay on track when my own daughter looks like she's been electrocuted? This lavender. Such a vulgar color!" Grabbing Elyse by the wrist, she said, "We're going to re-dye your hair."

"No!" Elyse dragged her heels. "Mama, no..."

An hour later, Elyse found herself bent over the kitchen sink as her mother rinsed the dye from her hair.

Just as she predicted, she accomplished nothing from this visit, though there was something comforting about her mother's gentle hands scratching calming circles onto her scalp. And while she never got the sage advice she was after, the world no longer seemed like a howling wilderness. She was even beginning to feel that everything was going to be okay.

Then the doorbell rang.

"Who is it?" Mama called.

"Just me, Mrs. Darrow," Aiden said.

Elyse's heart leapt to her throat. Memories of their accidental kiss in the photo booth swam to the surface. She stood up, spattering the countertop and her mother with brown dye.

"Door's open," Mama shouted, smacking Elyse on the arm.

"Sorry to come over unannounced," he said, shutting the door behind him. "I'm helping my sister bake pecan pies and we're all out of cornstarch." He halted on the kitchen's threshold. "Oh. Hello Elyse..."

Elyse dabbed at her temple with the corner of her towel. "Aiden."

"What are you doing?" he asked. A speck of flour dusted the hem of his heather gray T-shirt.

"Dying my hair."

"That's cool. What color?"

"Something of Mama's choosing. A poop brown."

Her mother shoved Elyse's head back under the stream of water. "Pantry. Third shelf," she said. "Help yourself."

"I'll just be a second," Aiden said, making a beeline toward the pantry.

Grateful for the interruption, Elyse shut her eyes and let the lukewarm water swirl over her head. She heard Aiden rummaging around and Mama ordering him to check behind the cake mix.

"So brittle and dry," Mama muttered, massaging in a color-protecting conditioner onto her scalp. "God knows what I was thinking allowing you to dye your hair at twelve."

Elyse couldn't help gloating. "Remember when I went from blonde to blue?"

"Then red to raven black. Pink to purple. You've had every color under the rainbow. I miss your original color."

"It was an unremarkable brown."

"Mahogany," Aiden interrupted.

They both turned. He got up from his crouch and shut the pantry.

"With auburn highlights," he added.

Elyse met her mother's eye.

"Great memory," Mama said, stunned.

Aiden cleared his throat and held up the cornstarch. "Found it. I've got to get back to... thanks." With a quick peck on Mama's cheek, he lit on out of there before either of them could comprehend what happened.

"What a nice boy," Mama said, dabbing Elyse's damp forehead. "Why can't you be more like him?"

———

ALL OF ELYSE'S friends worked the Reid-Blackstone wedding. As if ripped from the pages of a fairy tale, the bride arrived in a Cinderella carriage. Her gown glistened with sequins and her train was Princess Di-level long and required the help of all six of her bridesmaids. The groom was resplendent in a princely white tux. After the vows, ushers escorted the guests to a gigantic tent where a lavish banquet awaited.

Everyone was having a wonderful time.

Everyone except Elyse.

As the inebriated guests trickled onto the dance floor, Elyse pulled Viola aside.

"What is it?" Viola asked, sensing something was wrong.

Elyse took a deep breath. She'd rehearsed her speech throughout the ceremony, distilling her story into painless bullet points. Now, faced with the task, she seized up.

"So a funny thing happened out on that rowboat..."

"I'm so sorry, Vi," Elyse finished, watching Viola's eyes overflow with tears. "Please. Say something."

Cupping her hands across her mouth, Viola fled across the dance floor, knocking into a couple intertwined in the tango.

"Viola!"

Peeking her head out of the tent, she spotted Viola running across the damp lawn, strings of fairy lights providing a storybook backdrop to her heartbreak.

"Guess you told her," Olive said, coming up alongside her.

Lucie flanked Elyse's other side. "She reacted as I'd expected."

Elyse rubbed the spot between her eyes. "Telling the truth is the worst advice I've ever been given."

They watched Viola sprint back the way she came.

Olive frowned. "Where is she going?"

Lucie brought a hand to her mouth. "Poor thing, she's running amuck."

Squaring her shoulders, Elyse motioned for the others to follow. "Come on, we'd better go collect her before she flings herself in the pond."

Their rescue mission led them to the stables where they found Viola collapsed atop a bale of hay, sobbing her little heart out. In the stalls behind her, the horses whinnied, flicking their tails against a swarm of flies.

The trio approached her with caution. Olive, a self-proclaimed hater of hugs, threw her arms around Viola's back. Lucie massaged Viola's shoulder with her gloved hand.

Kneeling, Elyse smoothed Viola's disheveled hair. "This is all my fault," she whispered, unable to keep her own tears at bay. "I should've never tried to set you up with that low-life. I'm a terrible matchmaker and a horrible friend. You have every right to hate me."

Viola lifted her head and hiccuped. Her eyes were red-rimmed, her cheeks smeared with dirt and dried tears. "I don't hate you," she said, wiping her runny nose. "It's my fault."

"What?" Elyse blinked, saddened that Viola's first thought was to blame herself. "No, Vi..."

"Yes. I'm the stupid one for thinking Roger would like me over you. You're so stunning and accomplished while I'm... I'm small and plain. I'm a nobody," she said, descending into another violent bout of sobbing.

Elyse shared a helpless glance with Olive and Lucie. They'd come so far with Viola only to take a giant leap back.

"No, no, no," Elyse propped her chin on Viola's shoulder.

"Don't say that. Don't even think it. You're leagues above that sex offender—and a *way* better person than me."

With the cake cutting only minutes away, there was nothing they could do but fix Viola up and haul her back to the reception.

A dark cloud hung over Elyse as she snapped a picture of the bride smashing the cake across the groom's face. How could she be so wrong? She had never been wrong a day in her life. Maybe Aiden was right, and she knew nothing at all. Her meddling certainly caused more harm than good.

"One thing's for sure," she said to Olive as they watched the newlyweds' limo drive away, "I'll mind my business from now on."

Olive snorted. "We'll see about that."

20

VIOLA STAYED in bed for seven days.

Elyse brought her takeout from The Pig Bar and checked in on her regularly to make sure Viola didn't do herself in.

As evident by the pile of dirty dishes Elyse dutifully washed every night, Viola's appetite was fine. Viola had binged three series on their shared Netflix account. In light of these observations, Elyse had high hopes Viola was on the mend.

When the weekend came around and Viola still hadn't risen or showered, Elyse turned to Lucie and Olive in concern. "We need to get her out of this loft."

Olive brightened up, her auburn ponytail swinging with excitement. She pointed a finger in the air. "I have a spa Groupon!"

Thus commenced a day of primping and pampering. They indulged in full body massages, seaweed wraps, and dead sea salt scrubs. As part of the detox process, they spent one hour buried in a hot sand box and another hour freezing in the Arctic ice room.

"How do you feel?" Elyse asked Viola as they shivered upon a mound of snow.

Viola hugged her knees to her chest. Her limbs were turning blue and her eyes, abraded by the sand pit, began to water.

"Better," she said, her voice buckling beneath the weight of her sorrow.

Elyse sighed, a puff of icy air escaping her lips. What an absolute mess. She would give her right arm to mend Viola's heart but nothing seemed to be working.

Viola's teeth chattered from the cold. "Can we go home?"

The following day, Elyse suggested a mini work-related outing. She scooped Viola into her dented Honda Civic and high-tailed it down to One Enchanted Evening.

"I'm over Roger. Truly, I am," Viola said as they wandered the horse trails in search of the perfect photo spot for next week's wedding. Her tone was forced, not quite a skyrocket launch into emotional independence.

With a heavy heart, Elyse tucked a wayward strand of blonde hair behind Viola's ear. She motioned for Viola to stand next to the wooden fence post and lifted her camera to her eye. A mild breeze rustled the juniper bushes, carrying with it the sweet scent of grass and the pungent stench of the stables. The golden hour was upon them, the sunset cast a romantic haze over the stately Neo-Classical facade of One Enchanted Evening.

Viola looked lovelier than ever framed through the camera's viewfinder. Her pale lashes flickered against rosy cheeks and her hair fell in wispy tendrils against the swan-like arch of her neck.

Elyse snapped photo after photo, cursing Roger for being a fool, overlooking someone this lovely.

With an embarrassed smile, Viola tugged something from her pocket.

"What's that?" Elyse asked.

"The chrysanthemum Roger gave me." Viola cradled the shriveled yellow petals in her palm. "This may sound like the most pathetic thing in the world: I saved the bouquet and pressed it in my diary."

"Oh Vi..." Elyse didn't think it was possible to feel any more crummy than she did now.

"What's past is past." Viola opened her hand and let the petals slip through her fingers. "There is only the present, right?"

"Right." Elyse hesitated. "That was actually really beautiful. The sentiment, I mean. Hey, toss those petals again." She plucked a handful of dandelions from behind the fence post. "This would look great for my—I mean, *our*— portfolio."

"Sure. Um...what do you want me to do?"

Handing her the dandelions, Elyse said, "Strip off the petals like so and try to look morose. Let the petals drift from your fingers."

"I'm already morose."

"That's horrible and wonderful." Elyse raised her camera. *Snap. Snap. Snap.* "Yes, just like that..."

With each frame, both their moods lifted. This week started out in the dumps yet through the act of creation, Elyse was making lemons into lemonade. She caught a ghost of a smile on Viola's lips.

"What are you thinking about?" Elyse asked.

"Just trying to picture what Roger would say if I'm a famous musician."

"*When* you're a famous musician," Elyse corrected. "Success is the best revenge. One day, you'll perform in front of a captive audience and he'll—"

"Have a giant beer gut!" Viola clasped her hands over her mouth, shocked by her own spiteful words.

"Anger is good. It's healthy to vent."

"I hope he goes bald."

Elyse smiled. "If 'I hope he goes bald' is the closest you'll get to a 'fuck him,' I'll take it. Anger becomes you, Vi." She lifted her camera and snapped away. "Stay like that. Stay angry."

Upon her tenth frame, Elyse noticed movement in the background. She refocused her lens.

Behind the wooden fence railing, a horseback rider approached them at a steady pace. Elyse recognized the mare as part of the team that pulled the venue's Cinderella carriage.

He rode toward them in a bubble of absolute confidence, his long legs gripping the sides of his horse with the agility of a seasoned rider. His hair was midnight black, curling against the nap of his neck and topped off with a baseball cap.

He wore a pair of rugged jeans, ripped at the knees, perhaps more cosmopolitan than one would need for horseback riding, and a simple navy T-shirt. As he cantered closer, Elyse noticed that his forearms were covered with tattoos of musical notes and bars.

"Is this the way back to the stables?" he asked, skipping the 'hellos' altogether. His British accent caught them both by surprise. It was not the precise and posh accent of BBC newscasters, but the rough cadence of pub brawlers and prize fighters. Or so that was what Elyse imagined, fueled by a documentary about boxers in the East End.

"I'm new in town and bloody lost." His tone, while subdued, hinted at danger and invited recklessness.

"We figured," Elyse said, stepping forward to meet him. "The trails around here could be a maze if you're not careful. You'd want to follow the loop toward Ladybug Bridge and take a right."

He was even more handsome up close. Thick dark stubble covered a chiseled jaw. The whispering canopy of oaks made shadow spokes of his lashes and cast his face in a momentary mask of darkness.

Elyse's heart performed a series of erratic flip-flops. There was something familiar about this stranger. His devil-may-care slouch, the deftness in his arms as he gripped the reins, his swagger... All struck a chord of recognition, though she swore she'd never seen his face before in her life.

Elyse narrowed her eyes, studying the handsome stranger. "You on vacation?"

He tilted his head to the side. "Work," he said, his blue eyes smiling at her. His words were confident in a way that told her he said what he wanted and could give two shits what other people thought.

Elyse smiled back. He was her type of guy. She had a witty reply lined up when, out of the blue, Viola gasped and seized her arm.

"Oh my God," Viola said, so softly Elyse had to lean in to hear her. "Do you know who that is?"

Frowning, Elyse glanced up at the rider. "A gorgeous Brit atop a stallion?" she whispered back.

Viola shook her arm. "That's Eames Fawkes!"

"No way...How could you possibly know? No one has ever seen his face."

The mask was on the gimmicky side, but in an industry littered with strange personal quirks, The Electric Ghost's theatrics were not the strangest. The man watched their muffled back and forth with a bored expression. Maybe he was used to people talking about him as if he were not there. Elyse guessed it was part of the territory of being a 'ghost.'

"I subscribe to his podcast," Viola said, staring up at Eames with a mixture of terror and awe. "I'd know that voice anywhere."

There was only one way to find out. Elyse shielded her eyes. "Are you Eames Fawkes?"

"Yup," he said, aloof expression unchanged.

"No..."

"Yes."

"You're bullshitting us."

He shrugged. "Then I won't waste my breath."

He was brimming with *ennui* like an antihero from an artsy French film. Elyse found his listlessness and general discontent thrilling.

Viola tugged on Elyse's sleeve. "Look at his tattoos. Those are the notes to Neon Haunts," she said, referring to the single that skyrocketed Eames into the E.D.M. scene. Forgetting her shyness, Viola hummed the song beneath her breath.

The man who may or may not be *the* Eames Fawkes noticed Viola for the first time. A cynical smile flickered across his lips. "Almost, but not quite," he said, leaning forward in his saddle. "You missed the last bit. It goes like this..." he hummed the correct tune.

Turning scarlet, Viola clammed up and averted her eyes to the ground.

Elyse stared up at him. "So you really are... And your friend is Wesley. Oh my god, you're Eames Fawkes!"

"Yes, yes, I'm who I say I am. Imagine that," he said, sounding like he dreaded the prospect of yet another unstimulating conversation with two star-struck groupies. "Don't start wetting your knickers just yet, not before you guide me back to the stables. This horse is getting restless, as is her rider, who woke up this morning with a raging headache. So please, no sudden movements and for Christ's sake, don't squeal."

Elyse couldn't believe her ears. "You want *us* to take you back? Like escort you?" She turned to Viola and mouthed, "Eames Fawkes!"

Viola beamed, her heartache over Roger forgotten in the face of celebrity. "I know," she mouthed back.

Eames offered Elyse his hand. "Hop on."

Elyse hesitated. "What about Viola?"

"Saddle only fits one," Eames said.

"I can walk," Viola assured her.

Elyse would give her best camera to ride with Eames. Instead she pushed Viola forward, hoping that the experience will distract Viola's mind from Roger. "She'll ride with you. I'll walk."

Viola gave Elyse a terrified glance.

"Suit yourself," Eames said, taking hold of Viola's hand.

With Eames pulling her up and Elyse boosting her from

behind, Viola mounted the saddle like an ungraceful sack of potatoes.

"Wrap your arms around my waist," Eames said.

Viola turned white.

"Timid little mouse, aren't you?"

With great hesitation, Viola drew her arms around him.

"Come on, Viola," Elyse stepped in, "he won't bite."

"Unless you want me to," Eames added.

Viola blushed, caught off guard.

With a click of his tongue, Eames nudged his horse into a trot toward Ladybug Bridge.

"You look nothing like I'd imagined," Elyse said, falling into step beside his horse.

"What did you imagine?"

"Oh I don't know. Warts, perhaps? Big bug eyes and crooked teeth."

"You forgot disfiguring facial scars."

"You clearly don't have any of the above," she said.

"Not true." He gave her a wolfish smile, revealing sharp and slightly crooked canines. "My teeth are crooked. Blame the NHS. Are you disappointed?"

Elyse's heart skipped a beat. The way he looked at her made her feel like a tasty morsel he'd like to devour. She was Little Red Riding Hood, he was the Big Bad Wolf, and this flirtation could only lead to her being another notch on his bedpost.

Given what happened with Roger, Elyse knew she should proceed with caution. But it wasn't every day that an internationally celebrated producer made a pass at her. Caution be damned. She was an empowered woman. She could dance the dance and walk away unharmed. Notches worked both ways.

"I'm one hundred percent *not* disappointed," she said, winking at Viola. She hoped Viola was taking note: this is how you wrap a man around your finger. "If I had a face like that, I'd never hide it. Why wear a mask?"

Eames seemed charmed by her response. "When I started playing clubs, I was shy. The mask allowed me to perform in front of an audience. I played the role of The Electric Ghost and he took on a life of his own. I'm a package deal now: the music, the mask, the stage effects... one cannot exist without the other. Besides," he added with a twist of his lips, "I enjoy my privacy. I can do what I want when I want it without worrying about being hounded by the press."

Elyse met Viola's eye. "You can learn a lot from him."

Viola nodded.

Eames glanced over his shoulder. "So what's your story?" he asked Viola and got no response.

He turned to Elyse. "Does she talk?"

"My friend is a beautiful singer and talented violinist," Elyse supplied, causing Viola to flush from head to toe.

Eames gave an 'I'll believe it when I see it' shake of his head. "Aren't they all?"

"Would you like to hear her sing?"

Viola's eyes widened. "Elyse, no..." she said between clenched teeth.

"Maybe later," Eames said with a noncommittal shrug.

"Really?" Elyse pressed. "Do you mean it?" She slapped Viola on the shin. This was it. This was Viola's moment.

"Um, sure. Shoot me your SoundCloud demo," he said to Viola. "I'll listen when I have the time, but no promises—I have bloody little time."

"Oh." Viola's head drooped. "I don't have a demo."

"Make one," Eames said, sounding like he was losing patience. "Anyone who's serious about music has a demo. Maybe you aren't very serious."

"She's serious," Elyse answered.

Viola sputtered for a reply and tripped over her own words. "I-I-I guess I'll make one... um, right away?" She looked to Elyse for approval. "I mean, I'll make one right away!"

Elyse frowned. Viola hadn't stammered for weeks, but Eames' imposing, no-filter presence was making her relapse into her old ways.

"So you'll be my designated tour guide while I'm in town?" Eames asking, changing the topic. He'd forgotten about Viola again and had his full attention on Elyse.

She was amused. He was *definitely* flirting with her. "Are you staying awhile?"

"Deejaying for the senator's daughter," he said with a hint of distaste. "Keep in mind, I don't do weddings or private gigs anymore so *don't* recommend me to your friends. I'm too old for this shit."

"You mean too famous for this shit?" Elyse asked.

He laughed, then tapped Viola's shoulder. "Oy, listen up. Word of advice about the music biz: you say 'yes' to everything until you can say 'no' and then you say 'no' until you can say 'fuck off' and when you can say 'fuck off' then you'll know you've made it. Make sense, yes?"

Viola nodded vigorously. "Yes."

"Then why didn't you tell Senator Haywood to 'fuck off?'" Elyse asked.

Eames bared his teeth in an attempt at a smile. "That's for me to know, innit?"

"How much did he buy you for?"

"'Fuck off,' eh?" he said without real venom. "Anyway, when the gigs up—and it couldn't be over any bloody sooner—I'm taking a three week work-cation to compose my new album."

"What will your new album be about?" Elyse asked.

"Damned if I know. I haven't started on it. I'm having a bit of a block, but all will sort itself out." He didn't sound as convinced about the last part and Elyse wondered just how big of a block he had.

"Will you require absolute isolation?" she asked, imagining a high-tech creative cave packed with turntables and top-of-the-line mixers. She hoped he didn't intend to hideaway for the duration of his stay at Indigo Bay.

"I'll need to have fun from time to time," he said. "What's there to do around here?"

"We have a few cool cafes and stores."

"I've driven by," he said and his smile turned patronizing. "Quaint."

"I'm sure you've eaten at all the fancy Michelin star restaurants around the world." She colored, kicking herself for suggesting such dull entertainment.

He shrugged. "Most of them were shit."

"Oh." Elyse lowered her head. She was about to suggest they visit The Pig Bar, but if he was underwhelmed by the fanciest of international restaurants, he wouldn't think very much of their pedestrian menu. "Indigo Bay isn't the most exciting place," she said, feeling the need to apologize, "unless you plan to get married."

Eames laughed. "And why would anyone with any sense want to do a thing like that?"

"I know, right? Strange coming from a wedding photographer." She told him about her business and her dreams of opening a fine art photography studio in New York City, or any city for that matter. The more she talked, the more restless she felt. *Ennui* was contagious.

"You're in the wrong line of work, luv," he said. "How long have you been imprisoned here?"

"All my life." Elyse sighed. "I hate it here actually."

Viola, who had been silent this whole time, frowned at her. Elyse fixed her gaze on a distant point on the horizon. She felt Viola's gaze boring down on the top of her head.

"That's properly sad," Eames said. "And you can't find anything to do around here? Pretty girl in a pretty town?"

She glanced up at him. His eyes held the promise of change,

of adventure and rebellion. Elyse's lips twisted into a coy smile. Maybe Indigo Bay wasn't always so boring after all. "I'm sure we can think of something."

21

No one knew exactly why Eames Fawkes agreed to deejay a small town wedding. Rumor had it he owed his friend Wesley a huge favor. Some say he came to Indigo Bay to hide from scandal. Whatever the reason, Elyse was glad Eames was here to breathe life into what would otherwise be another stuffy money parade.

The guest list—an impressive gathering of politicians, businessmen, and C-list celebrities were here to celebrate the union of the senator's daughter with the son of a local shipping tycoon.

A majority of the guests didn't understand the music choice, but the twenty-two-year-old bride was a big Eames Fawkes fan and she was going to have her favorite DJ play her big day come hell or high water.

According to rumors, getting Eames to fly out to Indigo Bay put a hefty dent in her dad's wallet but the results were spectacular. For six very expensive hours, One Enchanted Evening thumped and boomed at a heart-pounding 128 beats per minute. A laser light show illuminated the night in brilliant hues of blues and purples. At the end of the night, Eames' traveling stage crew fired cannons of paint powder, showering the guests in a rainbow mushroom.

It was a spectacle, part of One Enchanted Evening's brand.

Elyse went into a picture taking frenzy, snapping the most exciting shots of her career.

The guests danced through the night and trickled drunkenly across the venue's Astroturfed lawn at the coming of dawn.

The next morning found Eames and Elyse slumped like derelicts on a bench outside Once Upon a Photo Booth. They each nursed a cup of black coffee, along with a massive hangover. Poe romped between them, clawing at Eames' chest and climbing to lick at his jaw.

With his head slumped against the bench, Eames seemed not to notice the terrier. Every so often, he'd scratch Poe's belly, earning a tongue-lolling yap of appreciation.

Poe liked him. Outside of Aiden and herself, Poe barked at everyone, including his own reflection. That was how Elyse knew Eames, despite his aloof exterior and caustic way with words, was one of the good guys. Case in point, a week had come and gone since she'd volunteered to be his Indigo Bay tour guide, and he hadn't tried to sleep with her.

"That was one of your greatest sets," Elyse said, massaging her temple. Even with a persistent hammer knocking away at her skull, she couldn't stop kissing his ass. "It was the set to end all sets, Eames. Truly inspired."

Eames rubbed his eyes behind his mirrored aviators. His baseball cap hung askew. He was three days short of a shave yet his scruffiness couldn't be more sexy.

"It was absolute shit," he said, yawning. "Hacked together on the plane ride over from songs the bride chose. All love songs, all the time."

"But it's a wedding," Elyse pointed out. "Love songs are kind of the norm."

"Trite, derivative drivel. There are songs about love, and then there are songs about *love*, you get me?"

"Yeah." Elyse nodded, though she had no idea what he was

talking about. Eames talked in riddles and he talked *fast*. Like 128 beats per minute fast. He was like a modern art installation on crack. Exhausting.

"When I cut other artists' tracks, I'm dead inside," he continued.

"But you do it so well!"

Eames threw up his hands in false modesty. "Off with you."

"You do," Elyse said. "Though I prefer your original compositions."

"Yeah, well that's dead too," Eames said, tugging the brim of his baseball cap over his aviators. "Between you and me, I haven't composed a decent album since Niccola left me and that's two bloody years ago. Know what that means? I'm officially done."

Niccola Costantini was Eames' featured vocalist and on-again, off-again lover. From Niccola's much publicized drug overdose to a late night arrest in London, their tempestuous and toxic relationship was perfect tabloid fodder. All fell apart when Niccola married the owner of a rival record label, leaving Eames without his muse.

"But you toured all last year," Elyse said.

"Playing the same songs. That's all anyone wants. The same damned beat, the same bloody drop." Leaning forward, Eames rubbed his palms together. He was jittery, itching to create something new yet tragically blocked.

Elyse frowned. She understood him completely. Even though they'd only known each other for a week, she felt a special kinship with him. Artist to artist. Creator to creator.

"You're being too hard on yourself," she said.

"No pity, I'll get it back." For a moment, he sounded more frightened than certain. "Who knows? Maybe I'll find my muse in this sad little hamlet," he said, looking at her in a way that made her stomach tighten.

She gave him her most winsome smile. "Am I your muse?"

He arched a brow. When he wasn't morose, he was actually quite charming. "Can you sing?"

"Not a note."

"Then no," he said in a blunt manner which others found offensive but she realized was his thorny way of cracking a joke. Then he gazed around the little section of downtown with its quaint storefronts and bowers of flowers at every window. His mouth twisted in disdain. "What a shithole."

"I wouldn't exactly call it a 'shithole,'" Elyse hesitated. "I mean, it's not the most exciting place, but it has its charms."

Eames lifted his aviators and stared at her with bloodshot eyes as if to ask, "Really?"

"I-I guess Indigo Bay's seen better days," Elyse backpedaled. "Urgh," she glanced around downtown in distaste. "What a dump."

"How can you stand to live here? Reminds me of where I grew up. The *coooountry,*" he said in a mock English countryside accent. "Everybody knew your name, every bloke knew your dirty laundry. If I were you, I'd have run long ago." He leaned back on his elbows and tipped his head to the sky. "But I suppose you like 'safe."

"Not me." She leaned back on her elbows too, mimicking his aloof posture. "I'm out of here as soon as I make enough money to move away."

He regarded her out of the corner of his eye. "What would you say if I asked you to run away with me? Right here, right now."

Elyse shook her head. "Be serious."

He nudged her knee with his. "I am serious. What do you say?"

"Woof!" Poe answered for her.

Elyse stood up more abruptly than she intended. "It's time for Poe's appointment."

"Just as I thought... safe." Standing up with her, he gave a mocking sweep of his hand. "After you, you so called-edgy artist."

"You're kind of a dick," she said.

"Not 'kind of.' I am. Completely unredeemable. The devil's own."

Elyse tipped her head to the side. "My, my... so much pride in being such a huge prick. Don't you ever want to be one of the good guys?"

"If I were, you'd probably lose interest, wouldn't you?"

She couldn't deny that she had a thing for bad boys and it wasn't every day she found someone just like her. He was a tool, true, albeit an amusing one, and despite his constant barrage of cynicism, she enjoyed his company.

Elyse felt his gaze boring into her back as she led him to Aiden's office. A chorus of barks greeted them as they entered the pet clinic. Expecting to see Viannie's grumpy face behind the reception counter, Elyse blinked twice.

"Viola!" Elyse set Poe on the counter. "What are you doing here?"

Viola peeked out from behind a tower of files and gave them a hesitant smile. "Viannie quit and Aiden offered me her job."

"That's nice of him, I guess," she said, eyeing the exam rooms beyond Viola's shoulder. "But you work for me. You're not quitting on me, are you Vi?"

"Of course not. I needed a second job."

"Don't I pay you enough?"

"No offense, Elyse," Viola said, blushing, "Being an artist is nice and all... I'm just not as persistent as you. And Pa's got all these bills he's yet to pay."

"It's not your problem."

"And my brothers are applying to colleges this year," Viola began.

"I understand you want to help your family, but Vi," Elyse said, shaking her head, "another soul crushing job?"

"It's not soul crushing. I find this job very rewarding. I'm learning a lot and I get to be around these cute animals. I get medical and dental, sick and vacation pay."

Absorbed by his phone during their entire conversation, Eames poked his head up at Viola's explanation. "A simple girl has simple needs," he said, taking Viola by surprise.

Her eyes watered. She lowered her head.

"Hey shut up," Elyse said, swatting Eames in the stomach. "He doesn't mean that. Tell her you don't mean that."

"I don't mean that," Eames parroted.

"Don't listen to him, Vi. He thinks everyone should dream big, which reminds me," she whirled on Eames, "have you listened to her demo? Or checked out her YouTube channel? Did you get the link in my text?"

Viola motioned for Elyse to stop.

"I'll get to it," he assured her, then added under his breath, "Along with the thousands of demos people send me. Yeah, I'll give it a go."

He sounded hassled. Elyse had a feeling Eames wasn't going to bite. She'd have to work harder to get him to notice Viola's talent.

She turned to Viola, who was busying herself with paperwork, her eyes downcast. It was hard dragging someone into the limelight. With one of the most famous EDM producers standing inches away from her and Viola doing absolutely nothing to advance her career, Elyse wondered if Viola wanted a music career as badly as Elyse thought she did.

As she contemplated Viola's ambition and Eames' abrasive comments, Aiden strolled out of one of exam rooms in the company of an elderly woman with a walker. He cradled her Siamese cat in his arms. The cat's tail was bandaged, its gray fur patchy and coarse. It narrowed its eyes and glared at everyone in the room with a surly expression.

"When will her fur grow back?" the old lady said.

"Give her time. The ointment will help. Make sure to apply it twice a day."

"But she is already ill-tempered enough as it is."

"That's all part and parcel with being a cat," Aiden said, dropping the Siamese inside the lady's wicker tote.

He spotted Elyse and smiled, but when his gaze traveled from her to Eames, a curtain of awkwardness descended upon the waiting room. Elyse glanced around. Eames was ruffing Poe's fur. The phone rang; Viola picked up the call. Did no one else notice the change in mood?

"Aiden," she said, after he'd ushered his patient to the door, "I don't think you've met Eames. This is Eames Fawkes." She bounced a little on her heels. "*The* Eames Fawkes. It's him. He's here." To Eames, she whispered, "Aiden appreciates um... music." She couldn't exactly say Aiden appreciated Eames' music, which, unfortunately, sounds nothing like the Bee Gees.

Eames held out his hand. "It's great to meet another fan," he said, with undisguised wariness as if he expected Aiden to fawn over him like everybody else.

Aiden made no move to take Eames' hand. He arched a brow at Elyse, and, after great reluctance, seized Eames' hand. Unlike Roger, Eames wasn't the first one to pull away. Aiden wouldn't budge either. Their hands turned red, then white.

"I've listened to some of your stuff," Aiden said, not taking his eyes off Eames. "It's not my thing. No offense."

"None taken, mate. Figured you're too old to be a fan, anyway."

"Yes, call me old fashioned, but I happen to enjoy *good* music," Aiden countered. "A nice melody now and then wouldn't hurt."

Eames shot him a tight smile. "That's the thing with critics. Every bloke thinks he is one."

Bones creaked. A sheen of perspiration coated both their brows. When they both were on the verge of keeling over in pain, Elyse scooped Poe up from the counter.

"Break it up, guys. Poe is getting antsy."

"I'll meet you outside, luv," Eames said, pecking her on the cheek. "Don't keep me waiting too long." With a quizzical arch of his brow at Aiden, he strolled out of the office as if he owned the place.

In the exam room, Aiden attended to Poe. Elyse leaned her elbows on the table and crossed her ankles. She tried to catch Aiden's eye. The silence was becoming overkill. She thought they left off on good terms. Now he seemed determined to treat her as if she were invisible.

"You don't like Eames, do you?"

Aiden pried open Poe's jaw. "No opinion."

"You look like the exact opposite of a man without an opinion."

"I try not to make snap judgements." Aiden kept his attention on the dog.

Elyse couldn't help smiling. "You're the most judgmental person I know. What do you really think of him?"

Aiden hesitated.

"Come on, first impressions," she pressed.

"You don't want to know," Aiden said, picking Poe up and shoving him in Elyse's arm.

"Believe me, I do."

He frowned. "Then you're more sadistic than I thought," he said. "Poe's fungal infection is improving, and he's gained weight."

Elyse nodded along with Aiden's assessment, suspecting he was trying to change the topic. As he escorted her out, she flipped around to taunt him. "I've never seen his face until now. Don't you think he looks like a fallen angel?"

One side of Aiden's lips quirked upward. "What kind of question is that?"

"Fair enough," she said, disappointed that she didn't get under his skin. "You never answered my original question: what do you really think of him?"

"Fine. Since you asked for it." Aiden took a deep breath. "I don't like him. Huge ego."

"You got that from a first impression?"

"Pretty much," he said. "I caught the tail end of his conversation, or lack of, with Viola. He wouldn't even give her demo the time of day."

"I don't know if you've noticed. He's kind of a busy guy."

"He didn't even try to be nice about it," Aiden continued. "Major superiority complex. Overall, a man of low character. An all around scumbag."

"Now you're not trying to be nice about it," she said.

"I don't approve."

"Okay." Elyse experienced a hint of annoyance. "You made your point, you don't have to go on and on."

He turned to her, brows furrowed. "First Roger, now this so-called 'DJ.'"

"He prefers to be called a music 'producer'."

"My point exactly. Only a very pretentious person would call himself that."

"A deejay cuts other artists' music, a producer composes his own," she pointed out.

Aiden shrugged. As if he gave a damn about EDM terminology. "I don't get women."

Elyse snorted. "No kidding."

"First Viannie, then you. I don't understand how you always fall for the guys that treat you like shit. Is it the accent or the asshole you're attracted to? Really, Elyse, you have the worst taste in men." Aiden gave her gray jumpsuit a quick once over and shook his head. "Amongst other things."

Elyse propped a hand on her hip. "Wow. Talk about an earful."

"You asked for it."

She was insulted and yet she had no room for complaints.

"You're the blindest person I know," he added.

"Yeah, well, you're the lamest person I know." Cringing at her own insult, Elyse clutched Poe to her chest like a protective shield and pivoted on her four-inch block heels.

She stormed out of the waiting room. "Bye, Vi!" she called over her shoulder. "You're too good to work here. Let me know if your boss gives you any trouble."

Viola waved back.

"I'll see Poe back in a month?" Aiden called after her. "Maybe when you've had some time to grow up."

Elyse flipped him her middle finger, but as she pushed the door open, she already knew she'd be back.

22

DESPITE HER CEASELESS complaining about boring Indigo Bay, even Elyse had to admit that there were perks to growing up in a wedding town.

There was always a party around every corner.

With One Enchanted Evening a permanent fixture in town, locals could count on lavish themed weddings, balls, and masquerades as part of the town's star attraction. There was no wedding planned for Halloween, but that wasn't going to stop Wesley and Olive from digging out the coffins and throwing a monster mash to remember.

Dressed as Sally from her favorite movie, Tim Burton's *The Nightmare Before Christmas,* Elyse arrived fashionably late, camera in hand.

She tugged the hem of her black baby doll dress over her thighs. Her arms, legs, and face were pale blue. Two hours in makeup, painting intricate black stitches across her mouth and eyes so she could resemble a demented rag doll.

"Come on, boy," she said, tugging on Poe's leash. His four Doc Martin covered paws scampered to catch up. His ghost hound outfit, complete with a full-body white cloak was the perfect accessory for her costume. Together, they were a ghoulish pair.

Joining a crowd of costumed guests, they strolled down the oak drive. Festive orange and green lights covered the sprawling branches. Cobwebs hung alongside dripping Spanish moss while gauzy paper maché ghosts haunted the oak canopies. Mini jack-o'-lanterns lined the spiraling walkway. Plaster coffins dotted the great lawns. The Cinderella carriage had been converted into a black coach drawn by stallions of death.

Just the sight of the ghoulish mansion smothered in cobwebs was enough for Elyse to forget her infuriating conversation with Aiden. Sure, she didn't have the best judgement with Roger, but blind? She wasn't blind. *He* was blind.

His words nipped at her all day and while she shoved them away to the back of her mind, they would pop up at the most inopportune moment and make her doubt herself. It never failed: Aiden's ability to get under her skin. He was as pervasive as Poe's fungal infection.

A bite of cool October air nipped at her bare arms, forcing Aiden and his unflattering opinion of her from her mind.

Elyse stopped in her tracks and shut her eyes, inhaling the delicious aroma of apple cider. Halloween. Her favorite holiday. She wasn't going to let Aiden ruin her fun.

One by one, the guests entered the mansion and stepped into the dimmed foyer. Cobwebs and spiders dripped from the banister of a sweeping staircase. A liquid nitrogen fog rolled around their legs.

Like an amusement park, the guests shuffled into the ballroom where they were treated to a delectable Halloween themed buffet, a veritable bacchanal worthy of Wesley's native Las Vegas. Caviar eyeballs, black widow cake pops, wooden buckets of Fuji apples covered in gold leaf, pumpkin gelato, and of course, no soiree at One Enchanted Evening was complete without a champagne fountain.

"Wow," Elyse said, joining Viola and Lucie at the gelato table. "When Wesley throws a party, he really throws a party."

Viola was dressed as a Celtic fairy, her lithe figure draped in a gauzy gown of ice blue accented with a pair of iridescent wings. Her blonde hair was tucked behind pointy prosthetic ears and piled into goddess braids.

Lucie had on a huge floral hat and a Victorian gown of ivory and black.

"What are you supposed to be?" Elyse asked Lucie.

"Rose Dewitt Bukater from *Titanic*." Holding her hat by its gigantic brim, Lucie struck a pose. "Don't I look like I belong in high society?"

"You already live in high society. The purpose of Halloween is to be someone else. Were I you, I'd come dressed as someone from steerage."

Lucie wrinkled her nose. "Well, that's not aesthetically pleasing."

"I'm the Lady of Avalon," Viola chimed in. "Except I added the wings. Wings are cool."

"They certainly are, Vi. You keep on keepin' on with your sexy fairy vixen self." Elyse scanned the ballroom for Wesley and Olive. "Where are the hosts?"

Viola pointed to the second floor landing. The host and hostess, dressed as Daenerys Targaryen and Khal Drogo from *Game of Thrones* were chatting with the guests. Catching Elyse's eye, Olive waved, then scratched her long white-blonde wig. A plastic baby dragon was perched upon her shoulder. Wesley was bare from the waist up. Medieval leather straps criss crossed over pecs no one knew he had.

"I didn't know Wesley had a six pack," Elyse said, impressed.

Lucie fiddled with the brim of her giant hat. "One hundred percent optical illusion. They're painted on."

"But he has abs! I've accompanied them to the spa. I've seen him get his chest waxed."

"Honey, no man has abs like those," Lucie said.

It was on the tip of Elyse's tongue to say Aiden did but she clamped her mouth shut. Aiden's abs didn't need her sponsorship.

"You think they dress like that when they," Lucie lowered her voice, "you know."

"Unfortunately I do know," Elyse said. "And the answer is... sometimes. Especially when she wants to ride his 'Great Stallion.'"

Viola cupped a hand over her mouth and giggled.

Still scanning the ballroom, Elyse spotted Aiden at the entrance.

"Figures," she muttered, giving his red coat with golden lanyards and brass buttons a critical once over. He had on sharply pressed black trousers with a golden strip down the legs and black dress shoes polished to a shine. His hair was slicked back and meticulously combed. Of course Aiden would come as a fairy-tale prince, an outfit without a hint of morbidity or imagination.

Elyse couldn't tear her eyes away from him. Maybe it was because he was so boring that he stood out from the decadent surroundings. Or maybe she'd become so attuned to his presence that it only became natural to pick him out of a crowd.

In the middle of a conversation, Aiden glanced up. As their eyes met, Elyse's heart skipped a beat. The ballroom and all its occupants began to blur until there was only one focal point: Aiden. Elyse opened and shut her hands.

Lucie said, "Aiden cleans up nicely, doesn't he? He's born to be Prince Charming."

"He came as himself," Elyse said dryly.

"He's gorgeous," Viola added with a sigh.

Elyse narrowed her eyes at the two. Hearing others swoon over him bothered her more than she'd care to admit. She didn't see what the big deal was. "Come on, he's just Aiden."

Aiden began to walk toward her.

Elyse smiled, all annoyance forgotten. That was the thing with Aiden: she could never stay angry at him for long. She squared her shoulders, readying herself for a playful sparring match with her favorite adversary when a man with his face painted in white stepped in front of her, blocking Aiden from view.

Recognition didn't click instantly, but when it did Elyse stared in opened mouth admiration at Eames' costume. Skinny black and white pinstripe tux. White face paint with hollowed out eyes and a stitched together mouth. A white bald cap covered his hair.

As a new track played, Eames extended a gloved hand. "Jack Skellington at your service."

She could still see Aiden out of the corner of her eye. He halted as soon as Eames entered the picture, retreating with a surly expression. On the opposite side of the ballroom, Elyse heard a familiar braying laugh. She turned just in time to see Coralee, dressed to the nines as Marie Antoinette, elbow her way through the dancers. Miniature sailing ships ornamented her white wig. Her pink gown took up the space of three people and made her look like a walking three-tiered wedding cake.

"Elyse!" Coralee called, flapping her fan.

Elyse's eyes widened. "Oh no. Here she comes."

Without a second thought, Elyse seized Eames' hand and pulled him out onto the dance floor. Ever the showman, Eames gave her a dramatic twirl, and she landed into his arms.

"Your dancing stamina is strong, I hope," Elyse asked, breathless from the suave maneuver.

Eames dipped her, then yanked her back up again in a way that made her body brush against his. "My stamina is strong in all things," he said, earning a blush from Elyse.

Eames was a superb dancer, light on his feet, anticipating her every move. The tracks changed, a remix of Eames' Neon Haunts.

Elyse raised an eyebrow. "I love this song."

"You might want to ease up," he said. "Your nose can't get any browner than it already is."

"I thought artists loved having their ego stroked."

Eames considered this, then his lips quirked into a mischievous smile. "No," he said, with a slight shake of his head. "I won't say it. It's too easy."

"A perv and a prick," Elyse said, batting her lashes. "Your mother must have done a number on you."

"My mother was a crack whore."

"What?" Elyse stopped dancing. "Are you serious?"

Eames stared at her solemnly. He nodded.

"I'm... um... sorry." Elyse nibbled on her bottom lip. She'd watched an indie movie about working class Brits who lived in a housing project. It was the kind of movie which required subtitles to understand. She recalled that the mother had to do tricks on account of her drug addiction and there was heavy swearing. "Did she use your dole money to buy her crack supply?"

Eames burst out laughing.

"What's so funny?" Elyse asked, peeved.

"Our 'dole money'?" He whipped the tears from his eyes.

"Isn't that what you call welfare in Britain?" She frowned. He was still laughing at her. "You mean your mother *wasn't* a crack whore?"

"My mother went to church every Sunday. Nicest woman that ever lived—too nice to know what's good for her," he said, taking her hand and resuming the dance. "The glass was always half-full. Everybody meant well, even when she was nursing a broken nose from dear old Da."

A dark squall crept over his face.

Elyse had loads of questions. Where was his mother now? Were they still in contact now that he was rich and famous? Did she listen to his music? But one look at his face and she knew he'd shut her down.

"Your friend reminds me of her," he volunteered.

"Which friend?"

He nudged his chin to a spot behind her. "The mouse."

Elyse glanced over her shoulder. Her mood plummeted as she spotted Viola sitting in a chair by the champagne fountain. "You mean Viola?"

"Another doormat," he said with a scowl.

Elyse stopped dancing.

"What's the matter?" Eames asked.

Elyse took another glance at Viola, who was staring at her phone, a blue glow illuminating her grim face. How could she have so much fun when Viola was so miserable?

"Excuse me." Breaking apart from Eames, she made a beeline toward Viola and took her by the wrist. "Vi! What are you doing here alone? Dance with us."

Viola shook her head. "No, I can't," she said, dragging her heels. "Three's a crowd."

"Eames won't mind."

"Eames doesn't like me," Viola said in a tone that made it obvious that the feeling was mutual. "I'd rather keep my distance from him."

Viola fell silent, her complexion turning an alarming shade of white.

"What's wrong?" Elyse asked, watching Viola's eyes fill with tears. She squinted through the crush of costumed dancers and whorls of dry ice fog. Roger and Viannie were twerking on the dance floor.

Elyse snorted, trying to make light of the situation for Viola's sake. "Since when is he with Viannie?"

"I don't blame him," Viola sniffled, her heartache evident in every morose pull of muscle, every teardrop. "She's so pretty. They're even going as Antony and Cleopatra. How perfect."

"Things didn't work out for Antony and Cleopatra you know." Elyse scowled. "Man, she sure knows how to get around."

"She's a confident woman," Viola said, coming to Viannie's defense, an act of selflessness that Elyse found both admirable and irritable. "Roger likes confident women."

"Who cares what Roger likes? I thought you were over him."

"I am," Viola said, blowing her nose into a napkin, "but I can't say watching this is making me feel any better. I think I'm going to go home."

"No! We just got here!"

At her wits end, Elyse spotted Aiden frequenting the cheese table. She patted Viola on the back. "Hold that thought and please, please stay."

She darted to the opposite end of the ballroom. "What are we going to do about your sister?" she asked, approaching him.

Aiden popped an hors d'oeuvre into his mouth. "There's nothing I can do about her. I'm her brother, not her father. Viannie is an adult, she's old enough to make her own choices."

"If I were you, I'd hose her off."

He gave a noncommittal shrug. "Threat has already been made, believe me."

Elyse sighed. "What if Roger tries to take advantage of her?"

He snorted. "It's more likely Viannie would take advantage of him."

"I don't care for your lackadaisical attitude."

Aiden turned to her, surprised. "And here you're always nagging me to relax... so this is me, relaxing. It feels good."

"Well stop it."

He gave her outfit a casual up and down. "You look nice. Did you plan to match with Eames?"

Elyse's cheeks burned. Aiden? Mocking her? Oh how the tables had turned. "What are you doing here, anyway? It's like you're trying not to have fun."

"I'm having plenty of fun."

"Standing here amongst the cheese?"

He popped a slice of brie into his mouth and chewed in spiteful relish. "I like cheese."

After some hesitation, Elyse stuck out her hand. "Do you want to dance?"

He looked at her hand for a long time. "With you?"

"Duh."

"No," he said matter-of-factly.

She gestured to the lonely fairy across the ballroom. "With Viola then?"

"I don't dance," he said with a note of finality. "Ever."

Elyse nodded to the abandoned baby grand piano at the corner of the ballroom. While Viola was primarily a violinist, she played a mean rendition of Beethoven's *Moonlight Sonata*. "Duets then? You could have your own private session."

He glared at her as if she'd lost her mind. "No."

"I know for a fact you've taken piano lessons," Elyse pressed. "Come on! It would draw Viola out of her shell."

"I haven't played since I was ten," Aiden said. "I don't relish embarrassing myself in front of half of Indigo Bay."

"No one's going to pay attention to—"

"No," he said with a note of finality.

Urgh. He was impossible.

"You suck."

"Mature, as always."

Tossing her hair back, she marched back onto the dance floor. She shoved herself between Roger and Viannie. "Has he shown you his didgeridoo yet?"

Viannie's black wig was askew, probably from all that grinding. "It's in the plans for tonight."

"Well I hate to disappoint, but it's nothing to write home about," Elyse said, heading straight back to Viola.

She didn't make it halfway across the dance floor before a hand seized her arm and spun her around. Strong arms wrapped around her waist.

"Eames," Elyse pushed at his chest, "I can't dance now. I have to comfort my heartbroken friend."

"She's fine," Eames said. "See for yourself."

Elyse checked over her shoulder. In the lull between tracks, Aiden had wandered over to where Viola was sitting and had struck up a conversation.

Viola's face lit up at the sight of him. Her smile was brilliant from sheer gratitude.

Aiden offered her his hand and led her to the piano. They sat side by side and, slowly, meeting Elyse's eye, he began to play a clunky rendition of *Thriller*. Several people around the piano turned and gave him a funny look.

Elyse's heart swelled at the sight.

"Christ," Eames said, plugging his ear. "What is that god awful noise?"

She bounced on her feet. "Aiden playing duets with Viola!"

"I can hear. I wish I were deaf."

"He was being so difficult and now look!"

"Somebody should stop him." Eames snorted. "No, seriously, somebody really needs to stop this butchery." He stepped forward. "Should I tackle him?"

"But don't you see? He's doing it so she wouldn't feel left out."

Aiden stopped playing and turned the keys over to a blushing Viola, who took over the rest of *Thriller* with steady, nimble fingers. Suddenly the scales sounded less like butchery and more like music.

"She's not bad," Eames said. "Though I played better when I was three."

Elyse swatted him on the shoulder. "All right, prodigy. Why don't you march up there and play with her then?"

Eames gave her a patronizing shake of his head. "I don't play with amateurs," he said, whirling her back around.

Elyse caught one more glance at the Celtic fairy and her prince before the lights darkened and loud dance music drowned out the brief piano interlude. Her mood brightened, her faith in the world restored—by Aiden of all people. Elyse couldn't stop herself from smiling. On that Halloween night, nothing seemed half as heroic as the ghastly piano playing of Indigo Bay's Prince Charming.

23

ELYSE BREEZED through the first week of November in a state of contentment. Her pumpkin spiced lattes tasted richer, the sun shone brighter, and maybe it was just her, but the clouds looked especially fluffy. She didn't know what had happened to her perpetual ennui. Or why every time the Halloween party crossed her mind, she'd catch herself smiling like a damned fool.

As Indigo Bay rushed into the thick of autumn, the air crackled with expectation. Autumn leaves littered the old cobblestones outside her studios, blanketing the sidewalk in reds, yellows, and oranges.

As she traveled through town, Elyse's mind swirled with visions of tailgate parties and cozy thermoses filled with hot cocoa, of wooly socks and flannel throws, of turkeys roasting in the oven and pumpkins pies slathered with mountains of whipped cream.

As the weekend approached, Elyse slipped on her favorite cognac leather booties, tucked a poncho-covered Poe under her arm, and drove to Mama's house.

Under normal circumstances, the prospect of spending an entire Saturday with her mother was as pleasurable as a root canal, but today, Elyse was high on pre-holiday buzz and filled with goodwill toward her fellow man. Besides, it wasn't every day Mama asked for her opinion, let alone her expertise on minimalism of all things.

An hour later, Elyse surveyed the monstrous task ahead of her, regretting her decision. Candles, teacups, crystal punch bowls, silverware, three sets of dish ware crowded the dining room table. The walls were bared, the paintings, along with all the furniture, tagged for sale. While the television was off limits, two decades worth of old electronics were piled on the floor. Word of the estate sale spread amongst Indigo Bay's senior community like wildfire, through Elyse couldn't fathom why anyone would want her mother's crystal punch bowl or collection of porcelain pigs.

"You do want to downsize, don't you?" Elyse asked her mother for the hundredth time today. "I mean, that's why you asked for my expertise and my expertise says, you don't need these."

Mama clutched the jade figurines. "I can't get rid of these. They were a gift from your great aunt Charlotte, who got them from an archeological dig in China."

Elyse pried the figurines from Mama's hands. "Aunt Lottie bought them at Pier One Imports."

"They're priceless! Worth at least—At least three thousand each. No, wait. Three fifty."

Elyse sighed. "Fifteen dollars with room to haggle."

"That's highway robbery!"

"They're made in China," Elyse said, turning the figurines over.

"Exactly! Unearthed from Mt. Jiuhua."

"More like unearthed from the clearance shelf of Pier One—"

Mama snatched the figurines back. "On second thought, it won't hurt to keep them around. They won't take up any room at all."

Elyse knew she had to act fast. If she let Mama rescue every item that held some sentimental memory they'd be here all day. "It's just an object," she asked, grabbing the figurine back.

"But I have so many fond memories," Mama said.

Elyse dodged her mother's reaching hands. "The memory is not in the thing. It's in your mind."

"What if I lose my mind?"

"Mama, you've already lost your mind."

"I'm keeping it."

"But does it 'spark joy'?" Elyse asked.

"Yes." Mama nodded. "I believe it does."

"That's bullshit, Mama. You hate dusting them. You've complained about it for years. Don't you want to go to Barbados? You're going to need extra cash for all those Mai Tais you're planning to put away."

Mama's mouth turned into a frown. "I suppose..." She set down the figurines and moved on to the next item: an old pipe and a rusty can of tobacco.

Mama threw up her hands in exasperation. "Well, I can't sell this."

"Really, Mama? Really?"

"That pipe was given to your great-great-great grandpa by Wild Bill Hickok."

The mention of 'Wild Bill Hickok' set Elyse off. She was ashamed to admit that she didn't know who he was... but that was not the point. He was an excuse to argue over this dirty pipe and waste another hour of her life. With a grunt of frustration, Elyse scooped up the pipe and tobacco tin and sprinted toward the trash compactor.

Between the grind of the compactor and battling off her mother, Elyse didn't hear the kitchen screen door open.

"So..." Aiden materialized in her peripheral vision. He stepped forward, ready to bolt in case things got hairy. "What's going on?"

"Helping Mama organize her estate sale," Elyse said in her

most dignified tone. It was hard looking dignified when your mother had you in a semi-headlock.

Aiden chewed on his inner cheek. "I can see that." He nodded toward the pipe and tin, which she held over the trash compactor. "What's that?"

He distracted Elyse just enough for her mother to pounce. Mama snatched the items from Elyse's hand.

"Leave me," Mama said, cradling the crusty pipe against her chest. "I'll take care of the kitchenware. Go to your room and clean up your own junk."

Elyse glanced at Aiden and her heart gave an unexpected start. Was it her or did Aiden look exceptionally delicious this morning? Maybe it was the way the morning sunlight showcased the subtle ripple of muscle under his navy T-shirt or highlighted the just-showered dampness of his hair. His aftershave smelled wonderful too, an alpine breeze cutting across the mustiness of her mother's antiques. Elyse fought the urge to lean forward and sniff his neck. Like that wouldn't freak him out.

"You want to help?" she muttered.

A ghost of a smile flickered across his lips. "That's why I'm here."

"Of course," she said, tearing her eyes away. Why did she feel flushed? She chalked it up to her heightened holiday senses, but as they climbed the stairs, she jumped when his arm brushed against hers.

"You're acting suspicious today," Aiden said, halting at the landing. He leaned over, peering into her face. "Like you killed someone."

"I was contemplating murdering Mama," Elyse said. "And my period starts tomorrow so you know..."

Aiden held up his hands and marched off toward her old bedroom. "Enough said. Sorry I asked."

Left alone, Elyse breathed a sigh of relief. Did she literally play the period card? What was wrong with her? Aiden's never made her this nervous. The change occurred after Halloween. A veil lifted over her eyes and she'd been on pins and needles ever since.

Aiden was standing in the middle of her bedroom, his arms crossed in contemplation. Elyse lingered by the doorway, admiring his powerful stance, the athletic flex of his back as he strolled to the window and yanked open the curtains. A stream of light stirred up the dust motes while highlighting the auburn in his hair. Sensing her eyes on him, Aiden gave her a curious smile over his shoulder.

Elyse's knees weakened.

"Your mother has turned your old room into a storage unit," he said, glancing around the eclectic collection of Ming vases, Christmas decorations, and boxes of craft supplies. Her four poster bed was somewhere underneath the storage boxes. Framed black and white photographs from her high school days still decorated her walls. The photo quality was out of focus and grainy, amateur hour compared to her current portfolio.

Rolling up her sleeves, Elyse began removing pictures from the wall. She came across an 'avant garde' photo of one single sneaker on the branch of a tree and scoffed.

"Looks like something you'd shoot now," Aiden said, peering over her shoulder.

Elyse whirled around, affronted. "That looks nothing like my current work."

"Really?" His forehead wrinkled in amusement. "Because I seem to recall a recent photo of a shoe atop of a fruit crate."

"That was a *bridal* stiletto shot for a rustic-country themed wedding. A still life of keepsakes are an industry standard," she said, removing the photo from the frame. She placed the frame on her dresser and crumpled up the photo.

Aiden took a step back. "You don't want to save that?"

"What for?"

He shrugged. "To remember how far you've come in your craft?"

"I have the digital files."

"For sentimental reasons then."

"I'm not a sentimental person."

"That's right," he said. "You're a stone cold minimalist."

Elyse studied a group photo of Olive, Lucie, Viola, and herself circa sophomore year. They were dolled up in prom dresses and grouped in front of a wall of silver streamers. "Let's get to work," she said, her fingers lingering on the backing. She glanced over her shoulder.

Aiden pulled a novel from her shelf. "*Twilight*. Keep or donate?"

"Donate them all. I have the ebook."

Aiden smothered a smile. "I'm learning a lot about you."

Elyse set the photo of her friends in the 'To Keep' pile. Maybe she was more sentimental that she thought.

Time passed in companionable silence. Elyse organized all her photos and was halfway through sorting out her closet when Aiden said, "What's this?"

She poked her head out of the closet. "What's what?"

He held up a fancy leather-bound book. "You kept a diary?"

Elyse didn't even blink an eye. "Several diaries. I'm a keen and clever observer of my generation."

"Of course you are. Regular essayist." Aiden flipped the book around, then glanced up at her with a sheepish look. "May I read it?"

"That's a weird thing to ask."

"Why? I thought you had nothing to hide."

True. She had an online portfolio of self-nudes. Elyse paused, raking her memory for embarrassing entries. She had no idea what kind of 'keen and clever' observations she made in her high school days, but whatever her musings were, they probably showed loads of insight. Leonardo da Vinci's journals were now public. As a fellow innovator, it wasn't a stretch to imagine that one day her journals would be consumed by adoring fans.

"Sure," she said, with a noncommittal shrug. "Ten minutes tops."

His eyes widened. "Really?" he asked as if he never expected her to say yes.

"Maybe you'll learn something," she said, ducking back into the closet to resume wardrobe sorting. "Be quick about it and box them up when you're done. I plan to digitize them later."

"You're sure?" he called to her.

"I'm an open book. No secrets, no shame."

"Okay..."

Elyse made it through her old winter coats when she heard Aiden chuckle.

"Oh hello," he said. "What's this?"

She froze, doubting her decision. With a measure of dread, she poked her head out of the closet. "What?"

Aiden, working efficiently, had skimmed through three journals and was holding an old school composition book. He leaned against her bookshelf, the corners of his eyes crinkling around the corners.

"March 23," he read, "Saw *Aiden* out my window with Mr. Gobbles tucked under his arm. Turkeys are gross with their waddles and their beady bird eyes but Aiden looked so good..."

Elyse dropped her coats and bolted out of the closet. Her heart rate spiked into overdrive. "Give me the journal."

"I'm flattered, Elyse," Aiden said, his cheeks tickled pink from amusement. "I never realized you thought I was so hot or that Mr. Gobbles was such a becoming accessory."

Was it possible to die of humiliation? Elyse made a flying leap for the journal.

Aiden dodged in a nimble sidestep, pivoting with a shoulder block. He flipped the page, holding the journal at arms length. She swatted him between the shoulder blades, pummeled his chest and biceps, but it was as if she were trying to fight a brick wall.

"What do you do? Live at the gym?"

He shrugged her away and continued to read, "'Aiden has the sexiest ass in Indigo Bay.'" He was in stitches, his eyes misting with unshed tears. "That's pretty powerful imagery for a—how old were you? Ten?"

She seized a handful of his T-shirt. "I swear to God, Aiden, if you don't drop that journal I will end you!"

Elyse pounced. She was going to tackle him to the ground if she had to. Aiden caught her around the waist and lifted her an inch above ground.

"Put me down!" Her legs kicked air. The back of her heel connected with his shin.

Aiden grunted. "You gave me permission."

"I take it back! I take it back!"

"Too late. Now I need to know." "'Between you and me, Diary',", he continued to read. "'Olive and I secretly call him the 'Gluteus with the Most-a-Mous...'"

"Ahhhh!"

"You were right," he said. "You are a fine essayist. Great descriptive passages for a ten-year-old. Do you still think I'm the 'Gluteus with the Most-a-Mous' now?"

"Oh fuck you Aiden. I will never forgive you for this shit!" Elyse amped up her squirming, her long legs wheeling in the air. She bent forward and backward, bending her body like a bowstring. She kicked her dresser and dimly heard her mother holler from downstairs, "What's going on up there?"

"Elyse and I are just reminiscing about the good ole days, Mrs. Darrow!" Aiden called, swinging her around to minimize damage.

The tip of her shoe smashed into a Ming vase. The vase nicked its neighbor. One by one, her mother's collection of pottery from Pier One Imports toppled and shattered in a horrific domino effect.

Aiden set Elyse down. They stared at the pile of blue and white shards in open-mouthed shock. They turned to each other. Aiden shut the journal and handed it back to her. Blinking, she took the journal dumbly.

He cleared his throat. "She didn't really care for those vases, did she?"

Mama's voice, full of fire and fury, bellowed from downstairs. "Elyse!"

24

"How many people can you fit in a hot-air balloon?" Aiden asked, climbing into the basket.

Wesley lent him a hand. "Enough. Why? Do you think we're over capacity?"

Aiden frowned at Elyse. "I don't know about this," he mouthed.

"Of course you don't," Elyse said, then snapped a picture of him brushing the wrinkles off his trousers.

According to Wesley, his hot-air balloon had a maximum capacity of seven people. Crammed in one corner: Elyse, Viola, Lucie, and Olive. Wesley manned the burner. Eames was perched on the rim, his ankles crossed as he barked orders to his music 'people' into his phone. Space in the basket was tight and they couldn't turn around without bumping into one another.

Ending his call, Eames poked Elyse in the ribs and nodded at Aiden, who was inspecting the rainbow-colored balloon for the slightest sign of wear and tear. Elyse stifled a giggle.

"I don't know why you persist in including him," Eames whispered in her ear. "He walks around like there's a permanent rain cloud over his head."

"Aiden is an old soul," she said. "Between you and me, I think he secretly enjoys these group outings. He just doesn't want to admit it."

Eames gestured to Aiden. "Does that look like a man who's enjoying himself?"

They watched Aiden circle Wesley as he was checking the blast valve. "Have you ever flown a hot-air balloon before?" he asked.

"Once or twice," Wesley said. "I just got my license, so it's still a steep learning curve."

Aiden glanced longingly at One Enchanted Evening's sprawling lawn.

"Why don't you come here, Aiden." Olive held up her picnic basket of gourmet cheeses, honey, figs, and champagne.

Since the merger between One Enchanted Evening and Cottage on the Green, Olive had transformed from reluctant wedding planner to gracious hostess, prepping their skittish guests for Wesley's' outlandish ideas.

"Hot air balloons are all the rage in the southwest," Eames said to Aiden. "Get with the program, man."

Aiden looked like he was about to murder Eames. Taking a deep breath, he turned to Elyse, who was busy syncing her drone controller to her phone.

"So what's the plan?" Aiden asked.

"Once we've made it to five-hundred feet, I let this bad boy loose," she said, showing him her drone. The Mavic Pro came with four propellers and a camera capable of shooting video in 4K. She'd practiced flying it over the course of the summer. Not content with traditional wedding photography, she wanted to get into videography and add aerial clips to her portfolio.

"I'll have shots of us ascending," Elyse said. "Once we're in flight, I'll do a 360 ohot of the group."

Elyse consulted the storyboard she'd hashed out with Wesley. The hot-air balloon ride was part of a joint promotional blitz between One Enchanted Evening, Inc. and Once Upon a Photo Booth. The final footage would be posted on both their respective websites and social media accounts. In order to succeed, one had to think big. That was what Elyse liked about Wesley: he was all about innovation.

The hot-air balloon campaign was a group project. Eames composed a short track to accompany the footage. Lucie took care of catering. Web design and various campaign GIFs care of Olive. Elyse had planned for Viola to play her violin several hundred feet in the air. As for Aiden, well, every promotional video needed a hunky face.

"Ready for take off?" Elyse called, untethering the balloon.

"Roger!" Wesley opened the blast valve, igniting a giant upsurge of flames. The basket wobbled. A second surge of fire... the balloon rose inches from the ground. "We have lift off."

At the last second, someone called from the lawn. "Wait!"

Elyse recognized that voice. Her blood turned cold.

Seven heads turned to the sight of Coralee sprinting toward them.

"Wait for me!" she called, holding the hem of her maxi dress over her knees. Chucking her wedges into the basket, she jump-hopped over the rim with the agility of an Olympic gymnast.

Aiden offered her his hand. She waved it off. "Sorry I'm late," Coralee said. "Time is not my friend. I even set my watch an hour early just so I wouldn't be late today, but then oops... ditzy me, I wore the wrong watch. This one matches my outfit, don't you think? Are the rhinestones too much? Speaking of which, what do you think of this dress? Will it look good on camera? Does coral make me look washed out?"

This set her off on an epic inventory of the items in her closet.

Elyse glared at Olive. "I can't believe you invited her," she said between clenched teeth.

Olive shrugged. "What was I supposed to do? She invited herself. She heard Wesley mention the hot-air balloon shoot and said she'd model for free." She gave Elyse a nervous smile. "The camera loves her, and she's always down for stunts. Who else do you know who could hop a balloon in mid-flight?"

Slipping her wedges back on, Coralee nodded to Elyse's drone controller. "What's that?" she asked.

Before Elyse could stop her, she snatched up the controller and began pushing buttons. The drone, hovering alongside the hot-air balloon, took a nosedive.

"Don't touch that!" Elyse wrestled the controller away from Coralee. The quadcopter narrowly missed slamming into a canopy of trees. She narrowed her eyes at Coralee. "Do you know how much this costs?"

Coralee was oblivious to her annoyance. "It's just a toy. If I break it, I'll buy you another one. Stop being so uptight."

Before Elyse could get a word in, Coralee turned around and asked Lucie about the cheese selection. This set her off on her favorite types of cheeses, most of which were simply 'cheese products.'.

Elyse turned her back on Coralee and gazed at the swiftly dwindling landscape. Horse trails and grand mansion rooftops lost in a sea of green. The low country beaches and inlets sprawled below them.

An hour trapped in a hot-air balloon with Coralee. How'll she survive it?

"What are the chances of survival if I jump?" she whispered to Eames.

Eames handed her a flute of champagne. "Bottoms up," he said with a cynical smile.

Elyse took the champagne and downed it in one gulp.

———

FLYING the drone while under the influence of alcohol was not one of Elyse's shining moments. At one point, everyone had to duck or risk getting sliced by the propellers.

"That's enough," Aiden said, wrestling the controls from her. "I'll take it from here."

Elyse tried to snatch the controller back, but her coordination was off. She slumped against Eames.

"You do know that piloting a drone under the influence is illegal right?" Aiden asked.

"What's the worst that could happen?" Eames came to her defense. "She gets a D.U.I. 'Droning Under the Influence'?"

"Actually," Aiden began, "According to the FAA..."

Eames rolled his eyes at Elyse.

"You don't know anything about flying a drone," Elyse said, then hiccuped. "I'm the only expert here."

"I'm a fast learner," Aiden said.

Like everything he did, Aiden learned quickly and within minutes, he was piloting the drone like a pro.

Elyse folded her arms across her chest and sulked. "If you delete my footage, it's your ass..."

He steered the Mavic Pro within grabbing distance and plucked it from the air. The spinning propellers came to a halt.

"Everything's in order," Aiden said, handing it back to her.

Elyse was even more petulant than ever. "Show off."

As Wesley prepared to descend, Coralee stood up and jabbed her finger in the air. "I have an idea!"

That wasn't something Elyse wanted to hear. She exchanged a long-suffering look with her conspirator, who seemed to share her dislike for Coralee.

"Oh no," Eames said to Elyse. "She hadn't spoken for a full minute. I thought we were in the clear."

Elyse cupped a hand over her mouth and whispered. "Where Coralee's concerned, no one is ever clear."

"I propose we play a game," Coralee continued.

"A game?" Eames asked, looking rather put off. "Why in God's name would anyone want to play a game? Who thinks of this?"

"I do." Coralee smiled, oblivious to Eames' slight. "Let's play 'truth or dare,'" she said to a speechless audience.

"Are we at a sleepover?" Eames whispered to Elyse, earning a snicker from her and another dirty look from Aiden.

"Who wants to go first?" Coralee turned to Aiden. "Are you game?"

Aiden hesitated.

"Truth or dare?" Coralee asked before he could give his answer.

He sighed. "Dare, I guess..."

"Aiden Hines, I dare you to..." Coralee cast her eyes around for victims. "Pick someone to kiss."

A gasp rippled through the girls. Everyone except Elyse.

"Anyone you like," Coralee said.

Looking like he'd rather be anywhere else, Aiden's scanned the basket's occupants, his gaze settling on Wesley.

Wesley held up his hands. "Whoa man, don't even think about it."

Olive was next. Wesley stepped in front of her. "Off limits."

He turned to Viola and Lucie. They sat up straighter, but when he passed over them, their shoulders slumped in disappointment.

Aiden's attention narrowed on Elyse. Not one to cower from the spotlight, she met his gaze with her usual bravado. Aiden came toward her. Elyse took a step forward to meet him halfway. She wanted to appear nonchalant. Her pulse was racing.

To her vast surprise, Aiden pivoted and turned toward Coralee.

It was meant to be a quick peck, but Coralee, sneaky opportunist that she was, hooked her arms around his neck and went in for a deeper kiss.

Eames leaned over and whispered in Elyse's ear, "Didn't her fiancé bang his sister?"

Elyse nodded, too stunned to eke out a 'yes.'

"Now Coralee and her ex have sampled some of Hines' goods, if you know what I mean," Eames said.

"Shut up," Elyse whispered, jabbing him with her elbow.

Her three friends giggled. Fuming, Elyse snatched a second bottle of champagne.

Eames grabbed her wrist. "Slow down."

"I think I want to vomit," she said between clenched teeth.

"I'd say you're on your merry way at the rate you're going."

Aiden pried himself from Coralee and wiped his lips.

Tipsy from the kiss, Coralee dabbed at her lipstick. "Gotta love truth or dare."

Elyse never wanted to punch someone as much as she wanted to punch Coralee. She turned to Eames. "I really don't like her."

"Why is everyone in this town so annoying?" he countered.

"Viola, you're up," Coralee said.

Viola's eyes widened.

Eames propped his elbows against the basket rim. "This ought to be good," he muttered.

Elyse shot him a dirty look. It didn't escape her notice that he had it out for Viola.

"Truth or dare?" Coralee asked.

"Um..." Freezing under the spotlight, Viola said, "Truth."

Coralee tapped her finger to her chin, pondering the most invasive question to ask. "How much does Aiden pay you?"

Elyse snorted. "That's the best you can come up with?"

"Well Viola doesn't look like she has any dark secrets," Coralee said with a shrug. "Truth Viola."

"Um..." Viola looked to Aiden for permission to disclose.

"Don't you think that's a bit personal?" Aiden asked.

"Hence the point of truth and dare," Coralee said. "Viola, you've picked your poison, now spill."

Viola stared at her shoes. "Seventy-five."

Elyse choked on her bottled water. "You mean seventy-five dollars an hour?"

"And eighty three cents," Viola added.

The group turned to Aiden, who cleared his throat, embarrassed by the attention.

"Damn, man," Wesley said. "How much barbecue sauce are you selling?"

Coralee's eyes widened. "Well, I declare, you're the most overpaid receptionist I've ever met. How much does Elyse pay you?"

"She only gets one turn," Elyse snapped. "And I sure as hell don't pay her $75.83 an hour. No offense, Vi. Holy shit. I'd go bankrupt." She locked eyes with Aiden. "I have half a mind to close my studio and work for you, too."

Aiden frowned. "You just described my worst nightmare."

Viola flushed. "You really don't need to pay me that much," she said to Aiden.

"Is she for real?" Eames asked Elyse.

"She deserves every penny," Aiden said. "End of story."

That put a stop to the conversation.

"Now it's your turn, Coralee," Elyse said, turning the tables. "Pick your poison."

Coralee squared her shoulders. "Dare."

"I don't think you can handle this dare."

"I can handle anything."

"It'll take you out of your comfort zone," Elyse said.

"Honey, I'm the queen of stepping out of one's comfort zone."

"Coralee," Elyse squared her shoulders, "I dare you to do something you've never done before. I dare you..."

Coralee stepped forward with a beauty pageant smile.

"... to be quiet and *stay* quiet for the remainder of the time we're in the air."

"Oh I see." Coralee surveyed the solemn faces around her. A

swift and uncomfortable silence descended upon everyone there. "Ya'll think I talk too much... I get it."

Elyse wasn't so drunk that she couldn't acknowledge she'd went too far. The one time her barbed comments didn't fly over Coralee's head and it had to be witnessed by one and all.

"I don't mean it like that," Elyse said.

"Of course she means it," Eames added.

She glared at him. Either Eames hadn't noticed her blunder, or he didn't care. He was either incredibly dense or more of a dick than she realized. Right now, he seemed hell bent on adding fuel to her dumpster fire.

"Oi Elyse, truth," Eames said. "Who would you like to toss out of this balloon?"

"Right now I'd like to toss you both out," Aiden muttered.

"He means me, right?" Coralee asked her.

Before Elyse could respond, Coralee's eyes filled with tears. "I didn't know you found me so annoying," she said, and fell into a hurt silence after that.

"No we don't," Olive said, stepping in to sit beside Coralee. Digging inside her pockets for a tissue, she shot Elyse a venomous look.

Sensing the tide turning against her, Elyse zipped her lip and glared at the encroaching lawn.

The landing was the longest ten seconds of Elyse's life. Her head spun and the cheese she ate sank to the pit of her stomach. She apologized every time one of her friends tried to console Coralee but it was as if her 'sorries' meant nothing. All she received were more dirty looks.

"What do I have to do?" she whispered to Eames. "Add an addendum to my apologies? 'I shit you not, this is a sincere sorry.'"

And, of course, Aiden *would* hear her say that. He glanced over his shoulder and shot her a look that made her hunch in her bench seat.

By the time the basket touched ground, Elyse couldn't wait to get out.

"I won't bother ya'll again," Coralee said, climbing out of the basket.

Olive grimaced at Elyse, then took off running. "Coralee! Wait."

Wesley followed Olive.

Lucie, who was never a fan of Coralee, glared at Elyse.

Even Viola didn't seem to want to be in Elyse's presence.

Eames offered her a hand. "Let's forget those losers," he said, helping her out of the basket. "Meet me by the pool."

"I didn't bring my swim suit," she said absently.

Eames smiled. "All the better."

She narrowed her eyes at him. "Sure. Whatever."

After Eames took his leave, Aiden cleared his throat. "Elyse, a word with you?"

Elyse swallowed as if she were about to be reprimanded by her teacher. His rigid posture told her he was displeased. She followed him a few paces away from the hot-air balloon until they were alone, shaded by the whispering canopy of the cypresses. His silence was oppressive, the atmosphere so cold that a crisp autumn freeze felt like an arctic blast.

Unable to handle the silent treatment, Elyse burst out, "Look, I know I shouldn't have gone there, but the truth is a bitch. If she couldn't handle it, she shouldn't have forced us to play 'Truth or Dare.'"

Aiden pinched the spot between his brow. "What is wrong with you?" He spoke calmly when she expected him to yell. Calm Aiden was scary Aiden.

"What's the big deal? Everyone thinks Coralee is insufferable but nobody has the guts to say it to her face. If left unchecked, she'd never shut up. Now thanks to me, she won't pester us anymore. Somebody has to be the social assassin."

"Oh you assassinated all right," he snapped. "And left a trail of carnage in your wake. Congratulations. Do you feel good now?"

"How was I supposed to know she'd take it so hard? She's usually so dense, everything flies over her head."

"Why would you say that to her in the first place? You know she's lonely! All her so-called friends left her after her break-up with Mason. You know Mason cheated on her and she had to cancel her dream wedding. You were there! You saw how hurt she was. Her pain is still fresh and here you are, throwing it right back in her face when she just wants a friend."

Elyse lowered her head. He did have a point. She hated it when he was right and it seemed he was often right nowadays. "Okay, fine. I'm wrong. I'm a bitch. Everything I do is wrong. I'm a poor excuse for a human being. What do you want me to do? Die?"

"You're not even sorry."

"I am sorry! I'll tell Coralee I'm sorry. I'll get down on my hands and knees and—"

"Shut up," he said softly.

Elyse frowned, taken aback. "What?"

"Look Elyse, I'm not going to argue with you anymore. You're a lost cause." With one last disgusted look at her, Aiden shook his head and began to walk away.

"What does that mean?" she called to his retreating back.

Silence. Something about the way he said that scared her. He sounded like he'd given up, like these parting words were his last words...

Alone in the shadow of the great balloon, Elyse called after him one last time. "I'm sorry."

25

Aiden came to Elyse's studio the next day, dispelling all notions that he was still angry at her.

"Hey!" Elyse couldn't help smiling. She found Aiden kneeling by the door, scratching Poe behind the ears.

"Yip!" Poe said, nuzzling against Aiden's hand.

Standing up, Aiden scooped Poe in his arms. One look at his face and Elyse's smile vanished. His gaze flickered over her for an instant before returning his attention to the needy terrier in his arms.

"I came by to check on Poe," he said in the professional, no-nonsense manner of doctor to patient, stranger to stranger.

"Poe has an appointment next week," Elyse said.

"I won't be in town next week."

Elyse frowned. "Really? Where are you going?"

"Nashville for business."

"For the sauce?" she pressed, trying to make conversation.

"Mm." He stared at a distant point beyond her shoulder.

"Well, that sounds fun." Elyse brightened up. "How long will you be gone?"

"Don't know yet."

"A few days? A week?"

"Depends on Lisa's schedule," he said.

"Lisa?" Gut punched, Elyse took Poe back from Aiden. She flashed him her most nonchalant smile. "Oh, so it's not just a business trip..."

"Lisa is the head copywriter of the ad agency we work with. New sauce label means new ad copy."

Elyse snorted. *Yeah, and I'm sure she'll want to study your abs for inspiration too.*

"Anyway," Aiden said in a tone that ended the conversation. "Poe's fungal infection is on the mend. A few more rounds of the ointment and he should be as good as new. I'll check out his joints when I come back."

Having said everything he needed to say, Aiden nodded and headed for the door. The overhead chimes tinkled. He was halfway outside before he turned around.

"I forgot something," he said, reaching into his pocket for an envelope and handing it to her. "Goodbye, Elyse."

"Good-"

The door slammed shut.

"-bye," Elyse finished, watching him walk away.

"Yip!" Poe pressed his paws against the window front and licked the glass.

Elyse ripped open the envelope. Aiden's half of their photo strip fell into her palm.

"Fine. Be a jerk." Her eyes watered as she stared at their smiling faces. In a fit of rage, she crumpled up the photo strip and tossed it in the trash.

"Yip!" Poe said, scurrying after her on his twiggy legs. His joint problem gave him a noticeable limp and made him list to the left.

"Quiet, you," Elyse said, picking him up. She took a few steps, but found herself lingering next to the trash can. Cursing under her breath, she dove in and scooped up the photo strip.

26

THE NEXT SUNDAY, Elyse met up with Viola at the farmers' market.

They passed stalls serving apple scones and steaming kettles of pumpkin chili, booths filled with kitschy handmade cornucopias, bouquets of Indian corn, and gourmet hot chocolate.

They strolled in silence, a norm for Viola, but an exercise in restraint for Elyse.

Stopping in front of a vegetable stall, Elyse pick up a tomato, absently squeezing it. She wore a clunky oversized sweater over tights and an ancient pair of cognac leather boots.

"I'm glad you want to hang with me," Elyse said, setting down the tomato and picking up its neighbor, squeezing for ripeness. "At least I have one friend. Olive and Lucie are giving me the cold shoulder. Even my mother is abandoning me for Thanksgiving for a cruise to the Bahamas."

"We're all still your friends," Viola said. Her blonde hair was piled on top of her head in a nest of braids. Her chin seemed to disappear inside the folds of her circle scarf. "But you must admit, what you said to Coralee was a little insensitive."

"I tried apologizing to her twice, and she ignored me."

"How did you apologize?"

Elyse lowered her eyes. "By text. And I know she read them."

"Have you tried calling her?" Viola asked.

"Calling? What are you? My mother? You know I hate the phone and imagine if I *did* get a hold of Coralee. I don't know about you but I don't have the patience for a three hour conversation."

Viola's shoulders lifted. "You might have more in common than you think if you'd just give her a chance."

Elyse brushed the suggestion away with a wave of her hand. "I saw there was an Escape Room 2.0 that I wasn't invited to," she said, changing the topic. "Interesting..."

Viola flushed. "It's basically the same escape room."

"But better?"

Without meeting Elyse's eye, Viola paid for the tomatoes. Elyse deduced from her silence that Escape Room 2.0 was a superior interactive experience. She drew her jacket closer, already feeling the chill.

"Olive and Lucie are just cooling their heels," Viola said.

"One drunken slip of the tongue and I've been blacklisted."

"Have you considered apologizing?"

"To whom?" Elyse asked. "As far as I see, the only person I offended is Coralee."

"Olive and Lucie are offended, too."

"What do they have to be offended about?"

"They're offended on *behalf* of Coralee," Viola pointed out.

"What about Wesley?" Elyse didn't need to ask about Aiden. He made his feelings clear enough. His crumpled half of their photo strip was tucked in the corner of her vanity mirror, right beside her half.

"Wesley's offended that you offended Olive, so that's two degrees removed. Otherwise, he's cool with you, but don't tell Olive that."

"Urgh!" Elyse stalked off, her head swimming. When did her friends get so touchy? "What about you? Did I offend you, too?"

Viola, bless her forgiving heart, smiled up at her. "You'll never offend me."

"Really?" Elyse frowned. "If anybody has the right to be mad at me, it's you. I'm single-handedly responsible for all your misery this year," she said, compelled to apologize. "That thing with Roger—I had no idea he would end up with Viannie. I didn't even know they knew each other."

Viola held up a hand. "No need to apologize."

"But—"

"Trust me, I'm over Roger."

Elyse eyed her in doubt. "If you say so."

They halted before a stall specializing in loose leaf tea. After making their purchase, they found a tiny table by the booth. Over a cup of Darjeeling with cardamon, Viola's big eyes sparkled with a dreamy light. "I'm over Roger because I'm in love with someone else."

"What?" Elyse leaned forward, intrigued. "Who?"

Viola cupped her tea. Wisps of steam rose from her mug, turning her cheeks apple red. She looked like a girl in love.

"He's far superior to Roger in every way imaginable," Viola said, leaning her hand on her cheek. "Oh Elyse, I can't believe I even liked Roger. Compared to him, Roger isn't fit to lick his boots. He's a gentleman in every way that Roger isn't."

Well, this was surprising. She'd been so self-involved with her own problems that she hadn't noticed the signs of a crush. "Is he cute?" Elyse asked.

"Gorgeous!" Viola wrapped her arms around herself. "Inside and out."

By now, Elyse buzzed with anticipation. It was cruel of Viola to leave her in such suspense. "Who is he?" She saw Viola hesitate and leaned forward, palms against the table. "Is it someone I know?"

Viola nodded. "Promise me you won't be mad..."

"Mad? Why would I possibly be mad?" The gears in her mind churned. She recalled all the times Viola displayed signs of infatuation, which, for Viola, involved blushing and full-fledged speechlessness.

Instances zipped through Elyse's memory: Viola's dumbstruck expression in Eames' presence, the two of them on horseback...Viola, so nervous she was practically shivering...

The answer struck Elyse like a thunderclap.

She nodded, pleased with herself for figuring everything out. "Vi, I know who he is!"

Viola blinked. "You do?"

"Of course," she said, tapping her temple. "Perceptive, remember?"

"You don't think it's insane? I mean, we're complete opposites and he's just so... intimidating."

"I think it's wonderful *because* you *are* opposites," Elyse said, placing her hand over her heart. "In my opinion, ya'll have more in common than you realize. Your passion for music for example."

"Music?" Viola frowned. "I guess we do. I'm surprised you're so enthusiastic. I thought that maybe you had feelings for him."

"Feelings?" The more time Elyse spent in his company, the more she'd concluded that they were more like friends. They'd kissed once and only once, a peck on the lips that started out passionate and fizzled into platonic. She liked the idea of Eames, his danger, his celebrity, his rebelliousness.

In the end, his dirty jokes, their double entendres were all talk, no action. They were so much alike and that was the problem. He didn't motivate or challenge her. He was a bad influence if her falling out with her friends had anything to say about it. Eames brought out the worst in her. Still, after getting to know Eames, she knew there was a good guy lurking underneath the arrogant jerk he presented to the world. He was even a bit lonely.

If anyone was in need of a compassionate person in his life, it was Eames. And Viola could benefit from someone who could teach her to be more assertive.

Why hadn't she seen it before? Eames and Viola. How right. How perfect.

"We're just friends," Elyse said at last. "You have my blessing."

"Do I really?" Viola's smile could light up the world and Elyse's heart filled with joy. At last, Viola was a radiant, confident, and multifaceted woman.

"I'm just happy to see you happy." Elyse took a sip of her tea. "Now tell me when this whole thing began."

Viola's face flamed. "It's wildly inappropriate considering."

"Considering what?"

"That I work for him."

Elyse choked on her tea and sprayed the table.

"Oh wow," Viola jumped up with a handful of napkins, "are you all right?"

Elyse wiped her mouth on the back of her hand. Her levity vanished, replaced by a heavy lump of dread. "Wait, who are we talking about?"

Viola frowned. "Aiden. Who did you think we were talking about?"

"Eames!"

"Eames?" Viola looked at her as if she'd lost her mind. "Why would I like Eames? I hate Eames. He's gone out of his way to be mean to me."

"He's mean to everyone. That's just the way he is," Elyse paused, realizing that this wasn't exactly a glowing recommendation of Eames.

"He isn't mean to me. He's pleasant when we're alone."

Viola grimaced. "I can't imagine."

"He's not so bad once you get to know him."

Viola shook her head, putting the kibosh on that idea. "I never want to get to know him."

"But you never hate anyone."

"I wholeheartedly dislike him then," Viola said. "I've had it up to here with assholes."

"Whoa, whoa." To say Elyse was blown away by Viola's sassy new attitude was an understatement. She'd never heard Viola speak so much in her life, much less use such forceful declarative sentences. "You sound just like me..."

"You empowered me."

Elyse frowned, not sure how she felt about the news. "So Aiden, huh?" she repeated, trying to get used to this idea and feeling her body grow numb. "You like *Aiden*?"

"I love him."

"Those are strong words, Vi," Elyse said, while she herself was at a loss for words—something that had never happened to her in her life. "H-h-how did you arrive at that conclusion? And are you sure your feelings are reciprocated?"

"Definitely," Viola said.

Elyse rubbed her abdomen, feeling the beginnings of a stomach ache. What was happening here? Her world had flipped on its head: she was stammering while Viola had morphed into an overconfident—and arrogant—version of herself.

"How can you tell?" Elyse asked.

"It's the little things," Viola said. "How he went out of his way to hire me. He didn't have to do that. And remember when he played duets with me during Halloween when no one would?" She uttered a deep, heartfelt sigh. "He's the best man I've ever known."

A dark cloud lingered over Elyse's head, threatening never-ending rain. "He certainly is," she whispered, recalling all the times Aiden swooped in to save her from her self-inflicted troubles.

"Maybe he doesn't love me the way I love him," Viola continued, "But 'like' could turn to love, couldn't it?"

"But don't you think... love is..." Elyse paused, searching for the best way to put it. "Aiden would do that for anyone."

Viola sat up. A frown wrinkled her brow. "What do you mean?"

"I've known Aiden all my life. There isn't anybody or anything he wouldn't rescue. Remember when he charged into that frat house to save Mr. Gobbles? He's got a massive hero complex and you're a damsel in distress. It's only natural he'd come to your aid."

Her response was met with a long, uncomfortable silence.

"So you're saying I mean no more to him than a turkey? That I'm not special?" Viola asked.

"No, no," Elyse backtracked. "I didn't mean that."

"What did you mean then?"

"I don't want you to read too much into things. We misread Roger's actions and look how great that turned out. I just don't want you to get hurt," she said, taking Viola by the hand.

Viola snatched her hand away. "Meaning he couldn't possibly be interested in me?"

"That's not it at all!" Why couldn't she stop putting her foot in her mouth? "Listen, Vi—"

"No, *you* listen. I hoped you'd be happy for me."

"I am," Elyse said, her words sounding like a lie even to her own ears.

"Then why do you look like I told you someone died?"

"Vi... don't be like this."

Viola stood up, her chair legs scraping the sidewalk. "You encouraged me to make my own decisions and now you're trying to discourage my choices." Her eyes filled with tears. "I'm beginning to wonder if you care about me at all."

"Of course I care about you," Elyse said, her own eyes flooding with tears. "How can you doubt that?"

Shaking her head, Viola snatched her bag from the chair and ran off, her parting words stabbing Elyse like a storm of arrows.

Left by herself, Elyse slammed her fist on the table. The teacups bounced and rattled against their saucers. The couple in the next table over glared at her. Passersby gave her funny stares as she broke into ugly sobbing.

"What are you looking at?" she barked at a man in a peacoat. "You've never seen a girl in a bad mood before?"

The man scurried past her.

Blowing her nose on a soggy napkin, Elyse picked up her empty teacup and stared at the leaves. She didn't need to be a fortune teller to read the forecast of her future: cloudy, with a chance of offense. She'd already offended her last remaining friend—all in a day's work.

27

"OLIVE?" Switching on her studio lights, Elyse glanced up at the loft. "I'm home and you wouldn't believe what happened."

Silence.

"Olive?"

"Woof!" Poe said.

"Guess she's spending the night at Wesley's again," Elyse said, her mouth tucking into a disappointed frown. She was expecting a cathartic late-night therapy session with Olive. Now she'd have to settle with the dog. "Well, it's just you and me Poe."

In reply, Poe squirmed and clawed at her forearms. Getting the hint, Elyse set him down.

"I need alone time anyway," she said, ascending the spiral staircase to her loft. Each step was a journey as she replayed her argument with Viola.

By the time she reached the top, she had analyzed every word, every gesture, every facial tick until she was sure she'd gone mad. What an absolute train wreck of a day. Elyse couldn't fathom why she reacted so badly to Viola's crush on Aiden. She agreed with Viola completely: Aiden was smart, loyal, honest, handsome, chivalrous. He was good for Viola. He'd treat her like a queen.

Wasn't that everything she wanted for Viola? Together they made a handsome couple. They were both her friends and two of the most kind-hearted people she knew. No logical person could object to pairing Aiden with Viola.

Except her. Indigo Bay's self-appointed matchmaker. More like backstabbing bitch in training.

She had not only objected, but she had flew off the handle and tried to sabotage Viola's crack at happiness. And for what? Sometimes she didn't understand herself.

As she stripped off her clothes and slipped into her heather grey Ansley Mills kimono, Elyse massaged the knots from the back of her neck. There was a lot of tension in her shoulders and every time she thought about Aiden and Viola, she felt like hurling.

Perhaps the best way to pass a lonely night was to minimize her negative thoughts, much like she minimized her stuff.

For the next hour, she put on some soothing post-rock music and lit her soy-based stress relief candles. She slapped on a clay face mask and rubbed Argan oil into her scalp. She brewed a batch of oolong tea, loosened the ties of her kimono, and descended the stairs to the sounds of rainfall in a bamboo forest.

Poe greeted her at the bottom step with a volley of high-pitched barks. He scampered toward the door with his tongue lolling out of his mouth and pressed his snout against the glass.

Elyse peered outside. Main Street was a ghost town in the purple dusk. She spotted pigeons loitering on the sidewalk outside her studio.

Poe barked at the pigeons, then turned around and stared at her with big pleading brown eyes.

"No! I've already walked you," Elyse said. "You can chase the pigeons tomorrow."

"Yip!" he said, displeased.

She propped a hand on her hip. "Well, we can't always have our way can we?"

Poe bared his bottom teeth.

"Do you see the face mask and the kimono? I'm staying in."

"Yip!"

"Don't back-sass me." She snatched up Taytos the Monkey, Poe's favorite squeaky toy. The monkey was still damp with saliva. One of his legs was a tug away from falling off.

"Here," she said, squeezing the nasty stuffed monkey. *Squeak. Squeak.* "Gnaw on this."

"Yip!" Poe seized the monkey and trotted off to the corner. *Squeak. Squeak.*

Satisfied, Elyse took her tea and headed into her 2001: A Space Odyssey photo booth. The interior was dark and cool. She sat on the bench and sipped her tea, trying to cleanse herself of negativity, but the sound of Poe growling was making it hard for her to concentrate.

Elyse pushed the curtain aside. "What are you doing?" she asked, glancing from the discarded monkey to Poe's stunted tail.

"Yip! Yip! Yip!" Poe was back to scratching at the door.

"I'm trying to mediate!"

In reply, Poe lifted one hind leg.

"Don't you dare!"

A stream of pee splattered her immaculate hardwood floor.

"Fine!" Storming out of the booth, Elyse scooped him up from the floor and opened the door. "You want to go out? Wish granted."

"Yip!" Poe barked in her ear.

"Out you go!" She dumped him on the sidewalk. "Don't wander far."

"Yip! Yip! Yip!" *Snarl.*

"Well 'yip you' too." Elyse slammed the door.

Alone at last, Elyse peered over her shoulder. Poe had all but forgotten their argument and was in doggie heaven chasing the pigeons. That should satiate him for five minutes, which was all she needed to sort out her troubled mind.

Heading back to the photo booth, Elyse shut the curtains and activated the LEDs with her remote. The interior flashed in reds and blues, greens and yellows.

In the distance, Elyse could hear Poe yipping with glee.

"Spoiled, entitled mutt," she muttered.

The lights changed again, soothing her with the illusion that she was floating in a star field. She hitched up her legs, shut her eyes, and tried to drown out the outside noise.

Red. Blue. Green. Yellow.

"Om..."

A memory of herself perched on Aiden's knee came to mind. His arm around her waist. Of mugging for the camera and the unexpected kiss, a contradictory sensation of the familiar and the foreign, safe yet thrilling. She had liked it. Quite a lot.

"Om."

Her thoughts took a darker turn: she imagined Aiden and Viola kissing and cuddling on a lazy Sunday afternoon. She saw them slow dancing at their wedding, his arms wrapped around her tiny waist, his lips, the same lips that kissed her in the photo booth, nuzzling Viola's neck.

It was wrong. *They* were wrong on so many levels. But for the life of her, she couldn't put her finger on why. The thought made her ill and her mind drifted toward a different direction. The same image replayed. Aiden was still slow dancing with someone, his arms wrapped around her waist, his lips nuzzling her neck—but it wasn't Viola, it was her.

Elyse sat upright, returning to reality with an intense jolt of clarity. She began to shake. She gazed around her as if seeing the world for the first time. The lights of the photo booth turned into living pinpoints of color.

Aiden had been such a permanent fixture in her life that she'd taken him for granted. She'd never really looked at him or thought about him as anything other than Mr. Perfect. And now, awakening from a deep slumber, she realized that he was indeed perfect.

Perfect for her.

It wasn't that she begrudged Viola's happiness, but when it came to Aiden, she couldn't see anyone with him that wasn't herself.

"Could it be that..." she spoke aloud.

The soothing music ended, followed by silence. The lights dimmed, submerging her in darkness and then, with a simulated light bulb pop, the hidden camera flashed, taking her by surprise. "I—"

Flash.

"Love."

Flash.

"Aiden."

———

ELYSE STUMBLED out of the booth on shaky legs and retrieved the photo strip. She stared at her photo's dazed face, certain her 'Ah Ha!' moment mirrored Thomas Edison's expression when he invented the light bulb.

Like a zombie, she headed for the door. She stood on the sidewalk in a dumbstruck state, trying to process the new revelation. That she might—No, she *had* feelings for Aiden all along.

Was it too late? Did she completely wreck things between them? Last she saw of him, he'd been disgusted with her conduct, so much so he couldn't even bare the sight of her. When she angered him in the past, she expected him to forgive her. But she couldn't expect that now? Even Aiden had his limits.

At long last, Elyse shook her head and snapped back to reality.

"Poe," she called, wrapping her kimono closer to her body. "Your five minutes are up."

The pigeons were roosting on a bench, but her dog was nowhere in sight. At first, she wasn't alarmed. She'd let Poe out before and he'd never strayed farther than a few feet from her doorstep. Poe had a touch of separation anxiety and he was not a curious dog. As the seconds ticked by, Elyse's own anxiety flared.

"Poe?" she took a step into the deserted street and scanned the halo of golden light beneath the nearest streetlamp, the stone fountain, and under every shadowy store awning. Her feet moved on their own accord until she was running like a bat out of hell with her kimono flapping behind her and her face covered in green clay. "Poe!"

28

Running down Main Street in her fluffy unicorn slippers and kimono, Elyse was aware she appeared insane. Her eyes were red from crying, her voice hoarse from calling Poe's name.

"It'll be okay, Elyse." Olive assured her over the phone. "He has bad hips. He couldn't have gone far."

Elyse pressed her phone to her cheek, mindless of the damage to her Matcha clay face mask. "I was so mean to him. I kicked him out without his shoes. I've never walked him without shoes before. His paws are tender and—" she gasped, recalling his fungal infection. "Oh god, Olive, what if someone dog-naps him? What if he trots his way in front of a car? Or he gets into a tussle with a fox? He thinks he's bigger than he is. He'll 'yip' himself into a fight I'm sure!"

"Don't jump to conclusions," Olive ordered. "Wesley and I are scouting the south side. Lucie and Viola are covering the west side and Coralee's plastering Indigo Bay with reward posters."

A pang of surprise and gratitude tugged at her heart. She broke down into a fresh batch of tears. "Viola and Coralee are helping me find Poe?" she asked. She was also impressed that

Olive could churn out posters so fast. Her friends were efficient little machines.

"Of course," Olive said. "Even Aiden's in on it, though there's not much he could do from Nashville. He's taken care of the reward money though. Hold on a sec."

Elyse's phone dinged. Wiping her eyes, she enlarged a thumbnail of a cobbled together "Lost Dog" poster. She almost dropped her phone when she saw the reward amount beneath a picture of Poe's derpy face.

"I'd say 5K is asking too much for that ugly, deranged mug," Olive said, voicing her thoughts. "Aiden's way too generous."

"He's the best man I know," Elyse said softly.

"What was that?"

"Nothing." Elyse shook her head before she became too overwhelmed with emotion to be of use to the search party. "Listen, I'm going to keep searching."

"You should really call it a night," Olive said, sounding concerned. "It's cold as hell out here and you've been at it for hours."

"Just a few more minutes and I'll come back home. I promise."

Before Olive could protest, Elyse ended the call. One thing was certain: she wasn't going anywhere until she recovered her dog.

"Poe!" she called into the night. "Poe! Where are you?"

Elyse wandered the coast highway, hugging her thin kimono around her shivering body. The cotton felt clammy to her fingertips and the bracing November air was creating fissures in her clay mask.

She warmed herself by imagining how she planned to pamper Poe once she found him. A full body massage. A pigeon chew toy. She'd make it rain kibbles if it meant he'd return to her safe and sound.

In fact, Elyse had an endless parade of apologies for everyone.

Viola. Aiden. Coralee. She bowed her head. She'd been busy these last few weeks.

A gust of wind shaved the top layers off the sand dunes. Patches of sawgrass and cattails swayed while whitecaps broke along the shore.

Sensing a storm coming, Elyse picked up the pace. Halfway down the street, an engine roared behind her.

Startled out of her reverie, Elyse glanced over her shoulder. A motorcyclist on a sleek black Ducati zoomed through the street. He pulled up beside her and revved his engine. He acted as if he knew her, but she had no clue who he was.

Elyse squinted, trying to ID him through his black helmet. "Do I know you?"

The rider tugged off his helmet, blue eyes sparkling with mischief.

She squinted in the darkness. "Eames?" The Ducati, the leather jacket, the devil-may-care attitude—it was a good look for him. Under normal circumstances she'd be impressed. Right now, he was distracting her from her mission. The more time they wasted, the more likely something might happen to Poe. He was an indoor dog, ill-equipped for survival in the wilds of Indigo Bay.

"I thought that was you." He paused, his gaze traveling from her green face to her fluffy unicorn slippers, now ruined from her trek. "I'm going to be honest with you, Elyse. This is not a good look for you."

"Don't I know it," she said, anxious to set off.

"Aren't you going to ask about my new bike?"

"Nice bike," she said absently. "Look, I've got to go."

He noticed her wringing her hands. "What's wrong?"

"I was meditating and Poe ran away."

"Poe?"

"My dog? We took him to the vet?" She frowned. "Tell me you remember Poe!"

"Ah yes," he nodded. "The rat dog."

"He can't help that he looks like a rat! Anyway, he's lost. He could be hurt or dog-napped. His former abusive owner might've scooped him up."

"To do what?"

"Beat him again!"

His mouth curled at the corners. "I seriously doubt that."

"I don't care for your attitude," she snapped. "Poe loved you!"

"He loved my leg."

"While I'm wasting my time talking to you, Poe's probably already dead."

"If he's already dead, what does your time-wasting matter?"

"Flattened like a pancake," she continued. "Mauled by raccoons."

"Melodramatic," he said under his breath.

She whacked him on the arm. "Are you going to help me or not?"

He propped his helmet back on and fastened the straps. "Actually, I'm late to a prior engagement."

Elyse shook her head. "I don't know why I bother."

"It's a meeting with the head of my label."

"Don't—" she held up a hand. "You don't have to explain. You have something more important to do. Do it. Go, just go." She stomped away, then on impulse whirled around and marched up to him. "You know something, *Eames?*" she said, jabbing a finger into his chest. "I defended you when all my friends called you a prick. Now I agree with them. I have seen the prick upon your soul."

Eames raised his eyebrows, unfazed. "I don't know what that means, but okay."

"And you know what else?"

"There's more?"

"Your last album *sucked.* You had one decent track, everything after that sounded exactly the same."

"Funny, I could say the same about your photo booth. Last I checked, someone already invented the infinity room." He flipped his visor and hunched over his bike. "Hope you find your rat, Elyse. Have a nice life." And with a deafening roar of his engine, he was gone before she could get the last word.

"Yeah, well, your name is stupid!" she shouted after him.

Embittered by their conversation, Elyse watched him ride until his taillight became a speck of red on the horizon. She hunched her shoulders against the cold, prepared to continue this rescue mission alone. Her legs moved sluggishly through the chilly night air.

I really am a terrible judge of people.

"Poe! Poe!" she called, scanning the darkening beach walk and wondering if she should've had a better plan to find her tiny dog. Survey the sand for paw marks, perhaps. Search for signs of poo.

Seconds later, the sound of an approaching motorcycle startled her out of her reverie. She shielded her eyes from the headlights' glare, surprised to see Eames riding back toward her.

He slowed his speed, did an expert turnaround, and came to a sliding halt beside her.

"Come back to run me over?" she asked.

He tossed her a spare helmet. "Hop on."

———

"Poe!" Elyse scanned the swampy embankment for a patch of black fur. "Where are you? Poe! Come home..."

Acres of marshland and miles of Atlantic Ocean passed in a blur. The salty sea gale whipped her hair up behind her helmet and a light mist sprayed her face shield. Her bedroom kimono flapped against her skin.

"Elyse!" Eames called over his shoulder. "I can't breathe."

"Oh, sorry." She didn't realize she had his waist in a death grip.

To the darkness, she shouted "Poe!" for the thousandth time that night.

"Not to be a naysayer in your time of need," Eames said, "but the mutt knows his name is 'Poe' right? He *does* answer to his own name?"

"Well, he—" Elyse fell into a contemplative silence, recalling the many times Poe refused to heed her commands. "He's a very bullheaded dog."

"Maybe he goes by another name? Rex or Spot or Boo?"

"Nonsense. Those are stupid names."

"Why are they stupid?" Eames said. "They are all common dog names."

"His name is Poe, all right," Elyse snapped, refusing to believe she wasted her time. "I've had him for months. He can't be that dense."

"Hate to break it to you, luv," Eames said, "but he looks pretty bloody dense."

Elyse grimaced. She was liking Eames less and less though she did appreciate the ride. "Poe!"

"Boo!" he echoed.

"Shut up! You'll confuse him!" She heard him chuckle over the howl of the wind and fought the urge to slug him. "And slow down, we'll drive right past him. He isn't exactly fast. Maybe we should get out and forage."

"Forage?" Eames snorted. "He's a dog, not a mushroom. Listen, Elyse, I doubt we'll find him tonight. I say resume in the morning."

"And leave him outside overnight? I'm shocked by your heartlessness. *Shocked.*"

Eames glanced over his shoulder. "I don't see how driving around aimlessly without a game plan is going to help us find him."

"I don't see how being an asshole is going to—"

The headlights illuminated something small and furry scurrying across the road. She squinted, assuming the critter was a possum or a black cat. Then her eyes widened in recognition.

Poe stopped right smack in the middle of the road.

"It's him! Stop, I see him! Let's scoop him up!" she shouted.

Elyse tightened her grip around Eames' waist. He wasn't slowing down, nor was Poe showing signs of moving as their motorcycle barreled toward him. "Do you see him?"

"See what?" Eames called over his shoulder.

Her heart leap into her throat. He wasn't stopping. Soon it would be too late. "Eames! Watch out!"

"Yip!" Poe said.

Eames whipped his head around. *"Shit!"* He swerved a hard right, and the motorcycle tipped over, skidding across the asphalt.

29

ELYSE WOKE up in a hospital bed with an IV drip in her arm and her head groggy from painkillers.

Olive's freckles swirled into focus. "Whaaa!"

"Where am I?" Elyse's voice was raspy and, as far as she was concerned, she was still sprawled face first in the muddy embankment, a sullied unicorn slipper lying beside her head.

Olive brought a paper cup to her cracked lips. A gentle hand caressed her matted hair. "Drink."

Elyse gulped, choking on the tepid water.

"Easy, easy," Olive said, dabbing a napkin to her chin. She waited until Elyse drained the entire cup.

With her throat feeling less parched, Elyse gazed around the sterile white room. A hospital room.

"Do you remember anything from yesterday?" Olive leaned forward, bombarding her with questions. "Do you remember your name? How many fingers am I holding up? How do you feel?"

Elyse rubbed the spot between her eyes. Scraped knuckles. A bandage upon her temple. "Eames crashed his motorcycle. My name is Elyse. You're holding up two—now three fingers. I feel surprisingly fine. How long was I out?"

"Those are the drugs talking."

"Give it to me straight," Elyse whispered. "How long was I out?"

"Two hours."

"I was in a coma for two hours?!"

"You were never in a coma," Olive said. "You were asleep. The nurses laughed about how much you snored."

Olive's phone dinged. "It's from your mom," she said, showing her the text, "her plane just landed. She'll be here in a few hours. If it makes you feel any better, she bought you a conch shell from this famous souvenir palapa in Barbados."

Elyse sighed. "I'm a minimalist. What am I supposed to do with a conch shell?"

Olive nodded in approval. "The fact that you can remember you're a minimalist is a good sign. It shows you're on the mend."

Elyse tried to sit up and found, to her terror, that her neck was in a brace. "I can't move. Oh my god! I'm paralyzed!"

"You have a mild case of whiplash," Olive said, adding an extra pillow to her pile.

From her vantage point, Elyse could see her left leg was in a cast all the way to the thigh. She wiggled her toes and didn't feel any pain. Not yet. The color of the cast displeased her.

"My cast is pink," she said. "Not just pink. Hello Kitty Pink."

"They had some fun plaster from the children's ward," Olive said, "so I Face Timed your mom and she gave the thumbs up. She thought a splash of color would cheer you up."

Grumbling, Elyse folded her arms across her chest. They were bruised, but she thanked her lucky stars that she could move them. "Okay. I'm ready," she said, bracing herself. "What's the damage?"

"You have some hairline shin fractures and a sprained ankle.

Your leg will have to be in a cast for a few months. And the whiplash, of course."

"Internal injuries?"

"Nope."

Elyse groaned. "Broken ribs?"

"Your ribs are fine."

Elyse glared down the tip of her nose at her cast. "Will I be able to walk again?"

"Of course."

"But I'll need physical therapy," Elyse said.

"Not really. Your doctor said you'll be able to walk as soon as the cast comes off. Three months tops."

Frowning, Elyse held up her finger. "I have a cut."

Olive handed her a Band-Aid. "There you go."

Once she was reassured the cut on her finger wouldn't result in a life-threatening infection, Elyse asked, "Are you my only visitor?"

"Lucie and Viola are in the waiting room," Olive said. "We would've come in all together, but the hospital only allows one visitor at a time."

Elyse laid back against her fluffy pillows. "And A—" She stopped herself before she said too much.

"He booked the first flight home as soon as I called," Olive said, reading her mind.

"Well where is he now?"

"The only flight he could book has a three-hour layover on account of the storm."

Elyse closed her eyes. Tears dribbled down her cheek. Bright, painful flashbacks of the marshland and their head-on collision with Poe. She recalled skidding across the black tar and scraping the entire left side of her body. Eames took the brunt of the fall, cushioning her impact with his body.

Dizziness swarmed her the moment she tried to sit up. "Poe..."

"Safe and sound," Olive said. "Just a bit of shock at nearly being turned into roadkill."

Her heart seized up with worry. "Poe doesn't do well with shock. He can't handle the stimuli. He needs a stable environment and Taytos his squeeze toy."

"He's just fine."

"Where is he?" she asked, grabbing Olive's hand.

"Back at your place. Coralee is dog-sitting. She gave him a bath and wrapped him up in an electric blanket. He's as cozy as can be considering he caused the crash."

Elyse sank back against the pillow, somewhat relieved to know Poe wasn't traumatized one bit. "And Eames?" she asked. "How is he? Does he have whiplash too?" She figured if she and Poe came out of this ordeal unscathed, Eames was probably fine. "Don't tell me he got away without a cut."

Olive's cheerful demeanor vanished at the mention of Eames.

Elyse bolted upright, her veins filling with icy dread. "What is it?" she asked, sorry for making light of a serious situation. "How is he?"

"He's alive," Olive began.

"But..." Elyse fished. "Just tell me already!"

Sitting on the edge of her bed, Olive took her by the hand. "He's in the burn ICU."

"Oh my god." Elyse clasped a hand over her mouth, then paused for a beat. "He was burned?"

Olive nodded solemnly.

"But how? I don't even remember there being a fire..."

"That's because you were unconscious," Olive said. "If that trucker hadn't stopped to pull him out of the wreckage, he could've been a lot worse. He could've been dead."

Elyse shut her eyes, imagining all the horrible possibilities that might have befallen them. She shuddered. "What's the damage then?"

"Do you want the good or the bad?" Olive asked.

"The good. Always start with the good."

Olive hesitated. "On the bright side: no internal injuries."

"If you can call that a bright side," Elyse said dryly. "What's the bad?"

Olive grimaced. "He's incurred several burns. Over his body, the entire left side of his face is... I don't know the details, but I'm told it's pretty bad."

It was a while before Elyse could find her voice. "How bad is bad?" she managed to croak.

"He'll live, but he won't be pretty."

30

Upon her insistence, Wesley wheeled Elyse into the burn ward, stopping just outside Eames' room.

"I'll check if he's awake," Wesley said, patting her on the shoulder.

He opened the door a crack.

Elyse peered inside, briefly glimpsing Eames surrounded by a network of tubes and bleeping monitors. Bandages covered his arms, shoulders, and the entire left side of his face. Save for a deep scrape along his cheek, the right side of his profile was remarkably intact. His unbandaged eye stared up at the ceiling. Sensing their presence, his eye flicked toward her. He registered recognition but no emotion.

"Hello. Look at you," she said, rolling herself inside his room. "You look good." The moment the words left her mouth, Elyse wanted to slap herself upside the head.

Eames lifted two fingers, prompting her to halt at the doorway. His eye flickered toward Wesley and he crooked his finger, motioning Wesley forward.

Wesley glanced at her apologetically. "I think he wants to see me alone. Wait outside a moment."

The door shut behind him, leaving Elyse alone in the hallway. Her pink cast was obnoxiously cheerful against her sterile surroundings. An orderly wheeled an empty gurney past her. Elyse rolled herself out of the way, bumping her foot against the wall.

"Mmm!" She stifled her moan by biting into her knuckles.

The door opened. She glanced up hopefully at Wesley and her heart sank at his grim expression. She peered around him. The door shut in her face.

"He doesn't want to see me?" she asked as Wesley wheeled her back the way they came.

"He doesn't want to see anyone."

"But won't his family come visit soon?"

"He has no family," he said. "Not much in the way of friends."

"But you're his friend."

Wesley was silent for a moment. "We're not really close, but I suppose I'm the only friend he's got."

Elyse swallowed the lump in her throat. "That's so sad."

"Yeah," Wesley said softly. "Yeah it is."

———

THE NEXT DAY, Elyse was released from the hospital. Her friends and travel-weary mother fawned and fussed over her, each one vying to make her comfortable. Even Poe was considerate, sitting docilely on her lap, licking her ever so sweetly on the wrist.

Her heart filled with gratitude at all the love and attention, but the thought of Eames, injured and alone in his hospital bed, dampened her spirits and riddled her with guilt. That morning, she had tried to see him one more time and had been turned away by his nurse. Eames wanted no visitors. The encounter made an otherwise joyful release day bittersweet.

As the others helped arrange her mother's Cadillac to accommodate her wheelchair, Viola sidled up to her and gave her a big hug, crushing Poe between them.

"Yip!" Poe said, displeased by the impact.

"This is all my fault," Viola broke into tears.

"Vi! Stop this nonsense." Baffled by the unexpected flood of emotion, Elyse patted Viola on the back. It wasn't long before Viola's tears dampened her shoulders. With a whimper, Poe wiggled his way out and sprang from Elyse's lap.

"You had nothing to do with this," Elyse said. "You didn't force me to get on the back of that motorcycle. Or make Poe run away."

"Yes, I did!" Wiping her eyes, Viola hiccuped. "If I hadn't riled you up, you wouldn't have needed to meditate and Poe wouldn't have run away. It's a simple cause and effect in which I'm the cause and this," she gestured to Elyse's cast, "is the effect."

Elyse's brows furrowed. Viola's explanation didn't sound simple.

"You've done so much for me," Viola continued, "and how do I treat you in return? Try to muscle my way into your territory."

Elyse frowned. "What territory?"

"It wasn't until I heard about your accident that it hit me. I'd mistaken my crush on Aiden for something more."

Elyse's eyes widened. "You mean to say you don't 'love' Aiden anymore?"

"I do 'love' him but only as a friend," Viola said, blushing. "I-I suppose I was so caught up in being like you that I might've inadvertently single-white-femaled you. Is that creepy?"

"Just a little." Elyse held back a smile.

"Everybody knows you and Aiden have a thing," Viola went on.

Elyse let out a hollow laugh. "What thing? We don't have a thing," she said, wishing the exact opposite. It only took a lost dog, and a broken leg to make her realize a 'thing' with Aiden was what she wanted all along. A heavy dread settled over her heart. Was it too late? She covered Viola's hand with hers. "No need to apologize, this was nobody's fault. Well, it's kind of Poe's fault, but it's not like I could hold it against him."

"I suppose..." Viola sniffled. "So am I forgiven?"

"Only if you forgive me first."

"Me forgive you?"

"Yes." Elyse chewed on her inner cheek, contemplating the best way to phrase what she had to say. "I had a lot of time to think and it's been brought to my attention by someone," she said, recalling her argument with Aiden, "that I was being selfish. I realize now that I've probably steered you too forcefully toward quitting your job and dressing like me. Do you even like your minimalist wardrobe?"

Viola hesitated.

"It's all right. You can say it."

Viola breathed a sigh of relief. "I like color," she said at last. "And ruffles."

"Then I encourage you to go forth and wear ruffles," Elyse said.

Viola smiled, her eyes flickering over Elyse's head. "I think there's someone who wants to see how you're doing."

"Aiden?" Elyse tried to turn her head and grimaced. The neck brace made movement difficult.

"Sorry I'm late," Coralee said, stepping up to her with a bouquet of succulents.

"They're beautiful."

Coralee gave her a shy smile. "Anyway, I just wanted to give you these and see that you're okay. I won't stay long." She turned to go.

Elyse glanced at the succulents, a frown wrinkling her brow. Her cheeks burned with shame.

"Wait!" she called, prompting Coralee to turn around. "There's been talk about an Escape Room 3.0. You're in, right?"

"You're inviting me?" Coralee asked, taken aback.

"We'll text you the date when it's all set up."

Coralee was trying hard to suppress a squeal. "And maybe we can all have dinner afterward?"

Out of the corner of her eye, Elyse caught Olive eavesdropping on their conversation. Olive gave her an encouraging nod. "Where?" she asked.

"At the new molecular gastronomy restaurant that opened downtown. *Quintess—*"

"*Quintessence?!*" Elyse's eyes widened. Now they were talking. "I heard they have 23 courses, including a deconstructionist take on pecan pie, edible balloons, scallops baked in gold leaf, and a somber four-note soundtrack to accompany your meal."

"And all the servers dress in grey dystopian robes," Coralee continued. "They never smile at you or answer your questions. Heck, they don't even tell you what you're eating. I'm told they're trained to ignore you so you can contemplate the meaning of your own existence. Hence, 'What is the—'"

"Quintessence of dust!" they said in unison.

Elyse heard that the famous dish at Quintessence involved three raviolis, arranged in order of diminishing size upon an artful drizzle of pesto sauce. The dish was called 'The State of Hope.' It was avant-garde and soul-crushing in its deepness.

"We have to invite Aiden too," Elyse said. "He'll hate every minute of it."

"I'll make the reservations," Coralee said.

Elyse gave her a thumbs up, feeling the burden of the past few days lift from her shoulders. The accident had been eye opening, attuning her to what really mattered in life. From this point forward, she was going to put friends and family over her own grandiosity. She was going to try to be nicer and make amends to those she'd offended.

"Ready?" Mama asked, taking charge of her wheelchair.

Elyse scanned the hospital turnaround, her heart sinking with disappointment. There was one face that was noticeably missing from her 'Welcome Home' send off.

"I guess so," she said, jumping a little as Poe hopped back on her lap.

Mama and her friends were in the middle of hoisting her out of her wheelchair when the muddy grill of a rental sedan pulled up to the curb. The door swung open and Aiden hopped out looking like he'd been through a war. His suit was rumpled, the leg of his trousers muddied around the hem, and his jaw sported an impressive five o'clock shadow. His bloodshot eyes scanned the turnaround, zeroing in on Elyse. An array of emotions flickered across his face as he took in her neck brace and hot pink leg cast.

Caught in the crossfire of his intense stare, Elyse sat up as straight as her neck brace would allow, her fingernails digging into the arm rests of her wheelchair. For a moment, everyone else blurred into the background. Only the two of them existed, the only thing separating them were words left unsaid, words she didn't know how to say.

Realizing she had feelings for him was the best and the worst thing that could ever happen to her. She used to burp in his presence—and sometimes in his face—without batting an eye. Now she wondered if her hair was behaving or if the yellow dress her mother picked out for her made her skin look sallow.

She was grateful when Olive tapped her shoulder.

"Um, Elyse?" Olive said. "I'm suddenly famished. In fact, we all are."

"We're going to check out the cafeteria food," her mother said. "We'll just leave ya'll to..."

"Catch up," Lucie finished. She eyed Viola, who gave Elyse a thumbs up.

Scooping up Poe, Mama pecked Elyse on the cheek and shooed everyone toward the cafeteria. Her friends scattered in seconds, leaving her alone with Aiden.

Taking a deep breath, Elyse dared to meet his eyes. "Where the hell were you?"

"My connecting flight was cancelled due to the storm," he said. "There were no other flights out, so I rented a car and drove all the way back. When I heard you were in an accident, I thought about the last thing I said to you and I—" He broke off, his voice ragged with emotion.

"You never thought you'd see me in a collar of shame?"

Aiden laughed and swiped a hand over his eyes. "It's a good look on you," he said, kneeling beside her.

Up close, she could see the dark circles under his eyes and the dark grain around his jaw. Aiden frowned, his attention resting on her cast. "How are you really?" he asked. "Are you in a lot of pain?"

"Not right now," Elyse said. "They've given me something for the pain and believe me, I've never been so inspired to create conceptual art in my life."

The corner of his lips lifted. "You look... colorful."

Elyse smiled, relieved that they were once again on bantering mode. She gave a half-hearted eye roll. "Mama took charge of bringing my clothes. Hence this monstrosity," she said, plucking at her lacy skirt. "I look like I'm about to go on an Easter egg hunt. Don't laugh."

Aiden bit his bottom lip. "I wouldn't dream of it."

"Help me up, will you?"

Taking her gently by the wrist, Aiden helped her out of the chair. His hand came around her waist, anchoring her against his body as he lifted her into the backseat. There ensued a lot of awkward maneuvering on account of her cast. At last, they determined the best way for her to fit was to flatten the passenger seat.

"I take it you were worried about me," Elyse said, watching him buckle her in.

He met her eye. "You've given me white hairs all my life, what's a few more."

She searched his expression for something more than what he was giving her. He cared about her, but in what capacity? As far as she was concerned, he still regarded her as a friend and nothing in his actions suggested otherwise. His tone hinted that there was more under the surface, his nearness implied chemistry. But did it really? In the past, she relied on her intuition, on her uncanny ability to read people. But through a series of embarrassing events, she came to the sad conclusion that she had no ability to read people whatsoever.

"What's the matter?" Aiden said, noticing her frown.

"It's just that..." So many words rested on the tip of her tongue and she couldn't express them. The realization of her love, the wealth of her emotions, all buzzed around her. She didn't want to be the first one to pull the trigger. Suppose he didn't feel the same way? Suppose he rejected her? Overwhelmed by the multitude of embarrassing possibilities, Elyse glanced at her lap and tried to shake her head. "My neck hurts."

"When I'm around you, my neck always hurts," he said.

His joke only underscored her assumption: if she were to admit her feelings for him, he would just assume she was kidding. He'd never take her seriously and why should he? She had never been a very serious person.

"Please close the door," she said, watching his smile fade at her unexpected coldness. "And please tell my mother I want to go home."

31

Elyse spent the first few days of her recovery mired in a swamp of self-loathing. She had ample time to reflect and what she found was a person she didn't like. Everyone had forgiven her, but what did she really do to earn their forgiveness besides breaking her leg? In fact, it was more of a pity forgiveness.

Her thoughts took a dark turn the more she contemplated her actions. She'd been nothing but mean to Coralee, who proved to be a better person than Elyse had ever been. And while she genuinely wanted to help Viola, in hindsight, she had to admit that the mentorship was feeding her own sense of grandiosity. Guess Aiden was right yet again. She was vain, selfish, and a closeted egomaniac—why did they put up with her? She didn't deserve any of their friendship and she was, sadly, unworthy of Aiden.

The accident was a wake up call that left her temporarily crippled and permanently humbled. All this time she thought she had the world figured out. She thought she was killing it at adulting when in actuality she was just doing the same old narcissistic shit she did in high school. She knew she needed to change.

But how?

For days Elyse spiraled down the existential rabbit hole in the comfort of her mother's freshly decluttered living room. They had decided that she'd move back home until she got back on her feet—no pun intended. A brilliant idea dawned on her while she was on the couch. She had her pink cast propped up on a pillow and was absently watching *Jeopardy* with Mama when Poe stood up on his stumpy hind legs and pawed her knee.

Elyse picked him up and held his squirmy body against her. She wrinkled her nose at his rank breath. Almost losing him made her appreciate him more. He was like her elderly dog baby. Rescuing him was the only purely selfless deed she'd done all year, she thought as she stroked Poe's soft fur. If only there was some way she could do something like that again...

The epiphany landed like a sparkling package wrapped in a silver bow. Elyse sat up with a gasp.

"What's wrong?" Mama asked, her brows wrinkled in concern. Final Jeopardy had just concluded. "Is your leg hurting you again?"

"Can you hand me my phone, Mama?" she asked, reaching over the coffee table. "Poe just gave me the most brilliant idea."

Her mother darted a suspicious glance at Poe, who was fast asleep with his tongue lolling out of his mouth. She handed Elyse her phone.

Elyse called Aiden.

He picked up on the second ring. "Is something wrong?" he asked.

"Why do you automatically think something's wrong?"

"You're calling. You never call. Are you in pain? Do you need me to drive you back to the hospital?"

"No, Aiden," she said, "but I need you to take me to the pound."

"I think you're being too hard on yourself," he said, chuckling at his own joke. "Why do you need to go to the pound?"

"Puppies, Aiden." She was so excited she couldn't form a rational train of thought. "And the cats too. I'm not a cat person but I've gotta have all of them. And snakes. I'll take them too."

Radio silence on the other end.

Mama reached over and felt her forehead. "I'm okay, Mama," she said, shrugging her head away. "Did you hear me, Aiden?"

He cleared his throat. "Let me get this straight. You want to adopt all the animals in the pound?"

"It's going to be brilliant, Aiden. The best... We'll dress the dogs in bow ties and little tutus and the cats will have tiny little hats. I can see it now."

"Oh boy," Mama muttered.

Now she could hear Aiden taking a big gulp. "I know I shouldn't ask, but *why*?"

———

THE TURN OUT for Indigo Bay's First Annual Pet Adoption Festival was the highest anyone had ever seen. Certainly the highest Elyse expected on such a time crunch.

As Olive wheeled her around the lake house veranda, Elyse had the satisfaction of seeing her idea come to life. Festive booths lined the grassy banks serving kettle corn, hot chocolate, and mulled wine. Guests roasted chestnuts around a fire pit while cheery Christmas music filled the air. As this was first and foremost a Hines sponsored event, the roasting box was in full use, churning out delicious plates of ribs and pulled pork slathered in one of their mouthwatering sauces.

The stars of the show were the rescue animals. Greyhounds and terrier mixes, alley cats, hamsters and iguanas, and even a litter of teacup pigs. Each animal had been washed and groomed, fed and cared for by Elyse and her team.

She spotted Aiden at the far end of the bank. He was crouched on his haunches, his brows furrowed in concentration as he examined a goat. A line of people cradling cats and holding dogs on leashes waited patiently behind him. Viola stood behind a booth, checking in newly adopted animals.

"Nice of Aiden," Olive said. "Volunteering free vet services."

A smile ghosted Elyse's lips. It was in her nature to utter a boasting comeback like 'he owes me a favor' when Aiden never owed her anything. "I owe him," she said instead. "For more than you know."

They both stared at Aiden. Deep in conversation with the goat's new owner, he gave the goat a tap on the back. The goat uttered a contented bleat and began nibbling on the hem of Viola's skirt.

As if he had a sixth sense that he was being watched, Aiden glanced their way. Elyse's heart skipped a beat the moment their eyes met. She felt like she could leap out of her wheelchair and run a marathon and like she wanted to throw up all at once. She returned his smile with a limp-wristed wave that would've gone on forever if Olive hadn't stepped in and wheeled her around.

"We've got work to do. Pet portraits, remember?" Olive said, handing Elyse her camera. "You guys can undress each other with your eyes on your own time."

"We're not—" Elyse sputtered. "Do you think he was undressing me with his eyes?"

"No, but you were giving him a sultry stare." Olive shook her head, her auburn ponytail bouncing from side to side. "Elyse, not in front of the goat."

They arrived at a simple photo booth consisting of several chairs and a faux marble background. There was just one light box and a steamer trunk loaded with props. A booth displayed artistically somber black and white photos of the pound animals: an existential close up of a pug, a cat draped sluggishly atop a shoe box, and a bunny staring morosely at a carrot.

"Quite the turn out," Olive commented, checking out the line amassing beneath the Soulful Pet Portraits banner. "Who would've ever guessed so many people wanted somber pictures of their pets? When it comes to trends, you've got your finger on the pulse of the ultimate weird."

"It looks like we're cleaning out the shelter." She beamed with pride at what she and her friends had accomplished.

"Right on time!" Coralee ran up to join Elyse. "This crowds' getting restless and there are ten corgi pups driving me bananas. I have them posed and looking as depressed as possible, but they have resting 'happy face' and are being so uncooperative. You better take their pictures before Lucie bails on us."

They turned to Lucie, who looked hassled with a boa constrictor around her neck and a hamster perched atop her head. "Hurry," Lucie said between clenched teeth. "Something tells me we'll be a subject short if you don't get started soon."

"Yeah, what's the hold up?" Roger called. He was third in line and cradling a hairless Sphynx cat. "We're waiting. Aren't we, Sheila?"

The cat, who held an uncanny resemblance to a plucked chicken, gave them an indifferent stare.

"That one has natural ennui," Elyse whispered to Olive. "I think I found my inspiration, but first the corgis." She wheeled herself into position and readied her camera. "Coralee, if you'd please stop that one from chasing his own tail..."

———

ELYSE SPENT the better part of the day catering to her pet photo booth. She took more pictures than she could count and had an interesting time wrangling a veritable menagerie of subjects to stay still. By the time she snapped the last portrait, she was sparkling with an overwhelming sense of satisfaction. Despite a few fumbles, she still considered herself a natural matchmaker, except this time she was matchmaking animals with new homes.

As late afternoon dwindled into dusk and the triangle bell

signaled guests to the barbecue feast, Elyse perched her camera on a tripod and gathered everyone for one last picture.

What followed was a chaotic game of musical chairs. Over a long session of elbowing and bickering, it was decided that:

a) Coralee could have her teacup pig in her lap.

b) Viola would not stand next to the goat who seemed to have a fetish for her skirt.

c) Lucie didn't mind posing with a cockatoo on her shoulder as the cockatoo was a fastidious groomer and far more desirable to stand next to than Olive and Wesley, who, being parted for the day have finally been reunited.

"Not in front of the goat," Elyse said, wheeling herself between the couple. "Were you two born in a barn?"

"Are we ready yet?" Lucie said. "This bird is clawing me in the neck."

"Just about." Elyse scanned the lakeside. "Yo Aiden! Get your ass in here."

Aiden hustled toward them with Poe tucked under his arm. Elyse shooed Olive and Wesley aside to make a spot for him beside her wheelchair. With a mumbled apology, Aiden dropped Poe in her lap, and, in one swift move, swooped in and pecked her on the cheek.

Elyse blinked, blindsided. She turned to him and caught him smiling, his eyes crinkling at the corners. Aimed the surrounding chatter, Elyse touched her cheek. A goofy grin broke across her lips.

"Elyse?" Viola poked her in the arm, breaking the spell. "Will you please take this picture? This goat is worrying me."

Poe squirmed in her lap. "Yip! Yip!" he said, hurrying her along.

Elyse shook her head. She held up her remote, thumb on the trigger. "Hey everyone!" she hollered in what Aiden once called her 'cafeteria lady' voice. "Shut up and pose. On the count of three..."

"Cheeeeese!"

"Meeehhhh," said the goat.

And Poe, not to be outdone, said, "Yip!"

32

WITHOUT THE USE of her leg, Elyse had been forced to depend upon her mother to keep her photography business afloat. Mama surprised her by being a regular spitfire, hauling ass from wedding to wedding in addition to working through the indoor portrait sessions and on-site engagement photos.

"Not bad," Elyse had said, scrolling through the proofs. Given her mother's dated portfolio, she expected a lot worse. The photos, while ordinary by Elyse's standards, were elegant and tasteful.

"What do you mean 'not bad'?" Mama stuffed an extra pillow behind her back. "I may come out of retirement yet."

Elyse raised her eyebrow and fought the urge to say anything.

Another pillow joined the first.

"Did you take your painkillers?" her mother asked.

"Took them fifteen minutes ago."

"Good, good." Her mother wrung her hands together. "Are you thirsty?"

"No, Mama."

"Should you really be sitting at this angle?"

Elyse stifled a groan. While she was grateful for all the fuss and attention, a month of living at home had been a test of her patience.

Taking a deep breath, she wheeled around. "Mama, I want to move back to my loft."

Her mother frowned. "But the loft is not wheelchair accessible."

"I think I can manage."

"Can you?" Mama said with a skeptical tilt of her head. "Can you really?"

"Mama! We've been over this..."

After a storm of squabbling, Elyse moved back to her loft on the condition that Mama was given a spare key and the go-ahead to check in on her. It was not the ideal situation for an independent woman such as Elyse, though Mama's tupperwares of chicken noodle casserole were always appreciated, her constant nagging... not so much.

Much to Elyse's chagrin, her loft was the absolute worst place for a wheelchair. The wrought-iron spiral staircase, while aesthetically pleasing, was a bitch to climb. Most days, she meandered around the bottom floor. Come evening, as if by clockwork, Aiden dropped by after work, lifted her into his strong arms, and carried her up the stairs.

On the rare occasion that Aiden couldn't come over, Olive, Viola, and Lucie would find a way to maneuver her upstairs. Moving her from place to place became a team effort for Elyse who, while slight of body, was surprisingly heavy and inept at moving herself about with her cane. Coralee, who was surprisingly strong thanks to her regular yoga regime, would often offer to haul her up the stairs. Elyse's friends treated the offer like a godsend. Once confined to her bedroom, Elyse tackled her greatest adversary: boredom. Under normal circumstances, she slept very little; now she was forced to sleep more than she wanted. She itched to be out and about. She longed to return to the hustle and flow of her busy life as a full time wedding photographer.

In the midst of her boredom, her mind wandered to Eames, and she'd experience a pang of regret. He was still hospitalized, still ignoring her. Elyse doubted he'd want to speak to her again after the accident. In fact, she imagined that he was probably kicking himself for sticking his neck out for her rat dog. The one time he did a completely selfless deed and *Bam!* A month in the burn ICU.

In the evenings, her trusty camera was her sole source of entertainment. Wheeling herself to her window, she'd play with the telephoto lens, capturing stills of the lavender dusk and the pink streaks of sunset over downtown Indigo Bay. Mostly she spied on her neighbors as they closed up shop for the night. She zoomed in on Sam from Old Hollywood Cinema as he propped up his ladder and changed the letters on the marquee from *Gone with the Wind* to *Rear Window*.

She could see a cloud of liquid nitrogen whisking from underneath Icy Cauldron's red door. She snapped stills of the shopkeeper from Bowler Alley changing the window display. And then there was Aiden, locking up his office, the collar of his raincoat tugged up. He glanced from side to side, appearing shifty as he crossed the street.

"What's he up to?" Elyse muttered to herself, tracking him with her lens. He disappeared inside The Pig Bar, leaving moments later with a bag of takeout. Stunned by the revelation, Elyse pried her eyes away from her camera. She blinked several times and then her lips twisted into a smile. "Caught you!"

The next evening, it was Aiden who caught her.

She had him in frame and was waiting for him to lock up his practice when he suddenly whirled around. Tilting his head up to her window, he raised his hand.

Elyse gasped. The back of her wheelchair bumped against her iron bed frame. Her heart leapt to her throat. Taking a shaky breath, she raised her camera, focused her telephoto lens. Aiden had disappeared.

Her buzzer went off. At the same time, her phone dinged. She snatched up her phone and read Aiden's text: *I have a key. Can I come up?*

Her thumbs went to work. "Okay..."

No sooner had she hit Send did she hear the door open and his footsteps climb the spiral staircase. From his doggie bed, Poe lifted his head at the sound.

"Yip! Yip!" he said, darting down the stairs. Soon the first floor studio exploded with Poe's excited barks.

"Down boy!" came Aiden's muffled voice. "Good boy!"

Left alone, Elyse wheeled herself to a mirror and tried to do what she could with her messy bun. It was while she was tugging at an especially stubborn knot that she realized she was only clothed in a see-through bralette and granny panties (she'd taken to wearing these around the house as they were big enough to stand in for pants). In a fit of panic, she snatched a kimono from her dressing screen and draped it around her shoulders just as Aiden appeared on the top step.

"Are you decent?" he asked, his head lowered.

"Enter," Elyse croaked. Then she realized she was still holding her camera. With a soundless gasp, she tossed the incriminating device on her bed, and lounged back in her wheelchair as if she didn't have a care in the world.

With Poe dancing around his legs, Aiden stepped into her tiny loft with a puzzled expression on his face. His attention rested on her camera and his lips lifted into a knowing grin.

"So what are you doing?" he asked, the question designed to tease.

"Relaxing," she said, gesturing to her lounge wear. The kimono was grey, threaded with black and silver lotus blossoms —another recovery gift from her mom. For a triumphant second, she was the picture of nonchalance. Until her broken leg began to itch. Elyse sat up. With a grimace, she hiked up her kimono and scratched her thigh above the cast.

Aiden cleared his throat, his eyes crinkling with amusement. "Do you need help?"

Desperate now, Elyse pointed to the top of the dresser. "Can you hand me my Chinese back scratcher?"

He handed her the back scratcher. Folding his arms across his chest, he watched her work on her leg. The tips of Elyse's ears reddened. So much for dignity.

"This is a nice conch shell," he said, picking the object up from the scattered array of knick knacks atop her dresser. "Do you ever use it?"

"Mama brought it back from her cruise. And yeah, I use it to summon Olive and Viola when I need something from downstairs. Very *Lord of the Flies* and better than any bell. I suspect I'll find it smashed to pieces soon."

Aiden set the conch shell back. He was staring at her in a funny way.

"What?" Elyse said, feeling self-conscious.

"It's come to my attention that I'm being spied upon."

They both eyed her camera and telephoto lens. Sensing he'd been pushed to the background, Poe leapt on the bed and nestled beside the gear.

"I've been hearing complaints from my patients," Aiden said. "Some voyeur from across the street has been snapping photos of my customers."

"By customers you meant the animals."

"I've sworn an oath of doctor-animal confidentiality."

Elyse held up her hands. "You caught me. I got multiple snapshots of an elderly St. Bernard, an obese iguana, and a shedding cockatoo."

Aiden crossed his ankles and draped an arm casually against her dresser. "Sick."

She hung her head. "I have a problem."

"What do you plan to do with these pictures?"

"They are for private use," Elyse said, peeking up at him through her lashes. "I also caught something that would be of particular interest to you."

Aiden raised a brow.

Keeping her eyes on him, she reached for her camera and received a lick on the wrist from Poe. The terrier let out a whine and flopped on his back, exposing his belly for scratches.

"Maybe you'll want to oblige him," Elyse said, searching through her camera's files. Aiden knelt beside her and tended to Poe. Out of the corner of her eye, she could see Poe's tongue lolling out of the side of his mouth. He was in doggie heaven.

"Ah, here..." Leaning toward him, she showed him the incriminating slideshow of Aiden leaving The Pig Bar.

Aiden inclined his head toward her, his face expressionless. His eyes flickered over the photos without interest, then settled on her profile.

Elyse's hands began to tremble. A swift flush crept from her collarbone to the tips of her ears. Her mouth suddenly felt as dry as a desert.

Clearing her throat, she steadied her camera. "How do you explain yourself?" she asked, trying to sound unaffected, though she was certain her words escaped as a squeak.

"It was the cilantro sake ponzu sauce," he said. "I couldn't get it out of my mind. Then I gave the pig's ear and quail salad a second shot." He lowered his head sheepishly. "I've been ordering take out from The Pig Bar every night this week. I even tried the hoof..."

"Do my ears deceive me?" She turned to face him. He was very close. If she leaned forward another inch, they were in danger of bumping noses. "Are you saying The Pig Bar is better than Applebee's?"

"I wouldn't go that far."

"Well," she said, "it's good to see I've affected your life in some small way."

And then he did something unexpected: he reached out and touched her face, his fingers gently grazing the slope of her cheek. He took her chin in his hands, demanding her to look at him. To *really* look at him. The lines of his shoulders were tense and there was a noticeable wrinkle between his brows. The hand that held her chin shook. At this close distance, with only an inch separating them, she knew he was as nervous as she was.

"In a small way?" Aiden repeated, his lips twitching into a sardonic smile. "Elyse, you've been a constant source of chaos in my life ever since you were born. You're a tornado on my sunny day, the rain on my parade."

Elyse blinked. Well, *that* wasn't the confession of undying love she was expecting. "You're quite the poet, Hines."

"What I meant to say is that you make me uncomfortable."

"Is that a good thing?"

He took a long time to answer. "Sometimes it's good to be kept on one's toes."

"Indeed." A shared silence befell them as Elyse contemplated all the ways Aiden had changed and all the ways he'd managed to change her. He was a little less closed-minded, and she was a little less oblivious. "Speaking of which, did you happen to notice the new photo booth I'm building downstairs?"

"Even while ailing?" he nodded, impressed.

"Would you like to be the first victim?"

Aiden turned to her dresser mirror where a carefully taped together photo strip of the two of them was tucked in the corner. Their eyes met in the mirror.

"Amuse me," she said, turning away to hide the rapid flush of her cheeks. "I'm climbing the walls with boredom."

With a smile, he scooped her up. Maneuvering her cast out the door and down the stairs was no easy feat and there was a turn which required all of Aiden's concentration. Elyse linked her arms behind his neck, trusting in his balance and quick footwork. Sparks of heat zipped through her good leg as his fingers dug into her thigh. In the tussle, the ties of her kimono loosened, revealing her bralette and a scandalous swath of midriff. She glanced up at Aiden. Except for a slight tightening of his jaw, he gave no indication that he noticed, but when he set her down, the front of her body skimmed against his.

In the dim studio, Aiden gazed upon her new photo booth. While the exterior was unpainted, preliminary stenciling on the side suggested a carnival themed interior. A red velvet curtain covered the entrance.

"What's the mind-blowing concept behind this?" Aiden asked.

"Sorry to disappoint. It's just a normal photo booth. Even multifaceted, groundbreaking artists sell out. Sometimes the most mind blowing thing I can think of is just being normal." She scrutinized his face. Did her eyes deceive her? In place of his trademark skepticism, did she spot a... *spark of curiosity?*

"Shall we?" Elyse asked.

Offering her his shoulder for support, they entered the photo booth. The bench was almost big enough for two but the bulkiness of her cast forced her to half-sit on his lap. In the heavy silence that followed, Elyse could hear Aiden's heart galloping at the same frenetic pace as her own.

"Elyse, I..." he broke off, shaking his head. She could hear his mind churning. At last, he managed to choke out the words that were on both their lips. "Are you as nervous as I am?"

She swallowed the lump in her throat. "Terrified."

Her answer gave him the courage to take her hand. His palms were sweaty. Their fingers intertwined. "Of me?"

"Of what comes after."

"Between us?"

'Us.' The most beautiful word in the English language. "Before my accident, I had an epiphany," she began, casting her eyes to her lap. Mushy love confessions didn't come easily to her. She took a deep breath. "About you," she said at last. "And the fact that there had always been an 'Us.' I just didn't see it until now. It may come as a surprise, but I can be short-sighted."

"You?" He gave her a sidelong look. *"No."*

She felt the close-shaven bristles of his jaw against her temple. His lips were inches away from her ear. "Where do we go from here?" he whispered.

There was only one road from here. Elyse twisted toward him, her kimono slinking off her shoulder. His hand tightened around her waist, the pads of his fingers sending singular points of heat against her bare skin. He planted a kiss on her shoulder, and another, on her neck, on her chin. Suddenly he brought his head back, his lips hovering over hers. He gazed down at her in question, waiting for her to give the okay.

Leaning forward, Elyse let her kimono pool around her waist, "Shame on you."

His brows lifted. "Shame on me?"

"I'm a poor, defenseless one-legged girl. How dare you try to go down on me..."

Even in the darkness, she could see Aiden's cheeks redden. "Is that a request?"

She pressed her lips against his and gave him his answer.

"What will our friends say when they find out about us?" Aiden asked, kissing her collarbone, the swells of her breasts, her bare stomach, her inner thigh. He tugged on her granny panties and she helped him out with a wiggle of her hips.

"I'll tell them it happened... *we* happened..." Elyse dug her fingers into the bench, bracing herself for dear life. Aiden was perfect at everything and he was a pro when it came to this. "Once upon a photo booth."

———

OLIVE CAME HOME to a dark and empty studio. She trounced up the stairs to the loft. "Elyse, are you up there? A bunch of us are going to the Christmas tree farm."

The small bedroom she shared with Elyse was empty.

"Hellooo? You didn't have an old lady accident did you?"

Poe answered her from below. She followed the sound of his bark back downstairs, hoping she wouldn't find her roommate sprawled in a corner somewhere. Poe greeted her on the last step, his stumpy tail wagging.

"What is it, boy? Where's Elyse?"

"Yip!" Tongue lolling, Poe pawed her ankles and scurried toward the unfinished photo booth. "Yip!"

Olive's attention traveled to the clothes on the floor. A discarded kimono. A man's oxford. A pair of granny panties which she knew Elyse had taken to wearing as shorts. Poe sniffed the panties and sank on his haunches.

"Yip!"

"Yes, boy," Olive frowned. "There's certainly something fishy afoot."

As if on cue, a strip of film slid from the slot. Olive hesitated. She really shouldn't tempt fate, but she found herself picking up the strip anyway.

"Whaaa! My eyes!" The strip fluttered to the floor. She wasn't the most socially savvy person, but even she knew that when your roommate's photo booth is a-rockin', don't come a-knockin'.

Scooping Poe into her arms, Olive tiptoed toward the exit and locked the door behind her.

EPILOGUE

"Visitor for you, Mr. Fawkes," the night nurse said.

"Visitor?" Eames winced as he tried to sit up. His side was in agony, but broken ribs were the least of his problems. Half his face was covered in bandages and though he had not yet seen the extent of the damage, he knew it was bad. As he swam in and out of lucidity, he picked up on a few disheartening terms from the endless parade of doctors and nurses.

Third-degree burns.

Disfigured for life.

Will need extensive plastic surgery.

Eames was in no mood for visitors. And speaking of which: who in God's name would want to visit him? Wesley was his only friend—if a business partner could be considered a friend. The only way that lot of jackals he called family would fly to the States would be to rejoice over his funeral rather than visit him in the hospital.

Someone knocked on his door.

"Enter," he croaked, more out of curiosity than anything else.

The door creaked open and in stepped Elyse's friend. He tried to recall her name and drew a blank. The mute one. Elyse's

270

shadow. She huddled at the entrance, her hands clasped hopefully in front of her. Her hair was pulled back in a loose ponytail, the blonde flyaway strands framing an elfin face.

Even with one good eye and painkillers coursing through his bloodstream, Eames sensed she was nervous. As he watched her knobby knees knock together, he recalled how her reticence irritated him before his accident. That feeling hadn't changed.

"What do you want?" he barked.

No reply. No sound. No hint of leaving him alone.

"I'm not in the mood for autographs."

"I-I don't want your autograph," came her quiet reply.

Eames leaned back against a nest of pillows. "Then get out." She was no longer in his field of vision, but he sensed that she hadn't moved. "Let me make myself clear," he said, staring up at the sterile white ceiling. "Get the fuck out."

Over the beeping of his monitors, he could hear her take a deep breath. Instead of obeying his command, she stepped closer. A chill whispered through the room. Eames shifted in bed, his body suddenly tense in her silent presence. Her footsteps, much like her very being, glided across the linoleum floor. She reminded him of a ghost—and, like a ghost, she persisted in haunting him.

Coming to his bedside, she gazed down upon him. Her eyes were big and blue and doe-like; they were the most innocent eyes he'd ever seen, and the most determined. The glaring overhead light framed her from behind, transforming her from a mousy shadow to an angelic specter. Wisps of white blonde hair escaped from her band and drifted across her freckled cheek. She was pretty. Beautiful even. It occurred to him that he'd never really looked at her before.

"What do you want, mouse girl?" he repeated, his voice more unsteady than before. Without realizing it, Eames clutched his sheets.

"I-I want..." She took a deep breath and stammered again.

Every word was a struggle. If he let her go on like this, it would be an eternity before he got any rest.

"Out with it," he snapped. "I don't have time for this. Start by telling me your name." In the recess of his memory, he recalled that Elyse had introduced them before. He had written her off as too insignificant to remember. Now, her name piqued his curiosity, though he would never show it.

"Viola."

"And what, Viola, do you want from me?"

She opened her mouth.

"Don't you dare stammer. One word at a time. I don't suffer imbeciles."

Viola squared her shoulders and blurted out, "I want a music career."

"Good for you," he said. "And what the hell do you expect me to do about it?"

"Make it happen."

Eames considered her request, and then, as quickly as his bandaged arm allowed, he hit the call button. "Nurse... Nurse. Get security."

———

THANK you so much for reading my quirky little book. I hope it provided you with an escape and a few chuckles. If you had as much fun reading it as I had writing it, **please leave a review** on Amazon or your preferred book retailer.

Reviews help readers discover my books, motivating me to write *more* books. I read and learn from every review. Not only do your words help me improve, but I save screenshots from some of them to refer back to when I'm in my creative low. So you see, Dear Reader, your thoughts mean more than you know. Please leave a review:)

Cybersecurity consultant Elliot Cole lives and dies by efficiency.

He's never late for a meeting and has *never* missed a flight.

Until *she* walked into his life.

Coralee Davis was trouble...

Trouble in athleisure and a daisy scrunchie.

Coralee, his cousin's beautiful and *extremely chatty* ex-fiancée.

They're on the same flight.

Stuck in the same storm.

Strangers turned travel buddies crashing in a never-ending string of airports and forced to share a bed in a fleabag motel.

All the while, Coralee names off all the fish in the sea and forces him to watch *Beaches*.

Elliot left Iceland refreshed. Now he finally understands why his cousin calls her 'Hurricane Coralee.'

She destroys everything in her path with her non-stop chit chat.

She's also the sunniest person a grump like him has ever met.

Will Elliot make it back to Indigo Bay without losing his mind —and his heart—to Hurricane Coralee?

———

KEEP READING for a sneak peek of SYMPHONY IN THE SNOW! (COMING OCTOBER 2021)

VIOLA FLEXED HER FINGERS, ready at the drop of a pin to bolt for dear life. Fleeing, however, would pose a problem. She couldn't move a muscle. Her legs felt like cement blocks, her tongue felt as heavy as lead. She knew she appeared like a deer in the headlights, but with flight out of the equation, her only alternative was to stand her ground and fight.

Viola counted her lucky stars that she hadn't peed her pants. She spent her life in constant fear of many things:

1. Public speaking.

2. Disappointing her friends.

3. Dealing with angry people and ugly situations.

4. Her father's drinking, for example, which usually led to angrier and uglier situations.

5. Eames Fawkes.

Eames Fawkes terrified her most of all.

It wasn't because Eames was an internationally famous EDM producer. Nor was it because at an impressionable age in her life, she'd listened to his debut electronic dance album *Electric Haunts* every night for weeks on end and memorized every note, beat, and drop.

It was because Eames hated her.

Not just hated her.

He simply detested her.

From the moment they met, he either ignored her existence or went out of his way to be mean to her. Viola was used to people ignoring her. Trying not to offend was her goal in life. For twenty-four years, she'd become the living, breathing equivalent of the color beige.

It baffled her that as much as she tried to stay under his radar, Eames had not only noticed her, but went out of his way to pick on her. Calling her simple. Nicknaming her 'church mouse.' Viola wondered if her more worldly friend Elyse Darrow noticed Eames' behavior, though it seemed Elyse was too enamored by his celebrity and British accent to notice.

Whatever the reason for Eames' dislike of her, Viola equally disliked him. He was a bully trying to pick a fight. Under normal circumstances, she avoided him like the plague.

Today she was desperate.

"What do you want, mouse girl?" He asked in a rasp whisper, every word dripping with thinly veiled contempt.

Viola flexed her fingers again, wiping her sweating palms on the leg of her jeans. The rusty creak of a gurney's wheels passed through the hallway. The beep of his heart monitor amplified her spiking anxiety.

She took a deep breath. She had an eloquent speech prepared in her mind, but one look at Eames' impatient scowl and she couldn't remember a word. He had a knack for making her feel dumb and incompetent.

"I-I want..."

"Out with it," Eames barked. His speech rate was ten times the pace of normal American speech. One hundred times the pace of the lazy Southern drawls of Indigo Bay. A 128 beat per minute rate of talking which left Viola dizzy. His British accent was so thick that whatever he was trying to say sounded like babble, punctuated every few beats by an F-word or two or twenty. Viola strained just to understand. She didn't dare ask him to clarify. If only he came with subtitles.

"I don't have time for this," he said. "Tell me your name—if you can manage."

Viola frowned. She'd been on a horse with him, his arm wrapped around her waist. They'd been confined to a hot-air balloon together, their shoulders inches apart. They'd been introduced and reintroduced. Yet even now... he still couldn't remember her name?

Was she that forgettable?

Was she that much of a loser?

It was one thing to think you were nobody. It was another thing for someone to confirm your insecurities.

She considered the injured man before her. There was nothing physically intimidating about him. Bandages covered the left side of his face. The right side was still handsome, his jaw shadowed by whiskers, his cheekbones hallowed by pain. His unbandaged eye, an otherworldly shade of blue, picked up on her nervous ticks and told her she was wasting his time.

A motorcycle accident landed him in the hospital. There had been a mysterious fire. Eames bore the brunt of the injuries; Elyse escaped with a broken leg.

Apparently, Eames was helping Elyse search for her runaway dog, so there must be some redeemability to the man before her. There must be, or he wouldn't have bothered to help Elyse.

"Viola," she said, finding her voice. *My name is Viola, you asshole.* She drove her thumbnail into the web between her fingers.

"And what, *Viola*," he sneered, "do you want from me?"

"I-I—."

"Don't you dare stammer. One word at a time. I don't suffer imbeciles."

Viola squared her shoulders, dragged in a fortifying breath, and blurted out, "I want a music career."

Eames was as surprised as someone with a bandaged face could get. After a beat, he said, "How the fuck do you expect me to help you with that?"

"You can make it happen."

Silence. Judgement. Eames' IV drip morphed into a mighty splash.

After the longest pause of her life, Viola watched in horror as Eames' bandaged arm reached for the call button.

Viola panicked. "What are you doing?"

Wincing, he picked up the remote. "Nurse... Nurse. Get security."

"Oh no, don't do that!" She checked over her shoulder, half expecting a pair of burly orderlies to appear and drag her out of his room.

No one came.

His thumb lingered over the call button, but he'd never pressed it.

A *whoosh* of relief threatened to topple Viola over. Her knees wobbled like wet spaghetti.

He'd played a mean trick on her. Even in his indisposed state, he still had time to bully and coerce.

She didn't want to believe anyone could be so horrible. She'd known plenty of mean people in her life, yet found good in everyone. But Eames Fawkes made her lose faith in mankind. Maybe he was just an irredeemable asshole?

"Jumpy little thing, aren't you?" he said, tossing aside the remote, "I'm not going to throw you out. *Yet*. I'll give you five."

"Five?"

"Five seconds to state your case. Go ahead, entertain me."

A tear dribbled down her cheek.

"Cry and I'll not only have you thrown out, I'll press charges. You have four minutes." His voice echoed through the sterile corners of the room.

Viola wiped her eyes on her sleeve.

Eames stared her down like an insect. Maybe he was testing her. Maybe he was just amusing himself again at her expense.

"Fine," he snapped. "Seems like I have to do all the heavy lifting even through I'm obviously not in the mood seeing as I don't have a fucking face." He dragged in a lengthy breath, coughed. "So. A music career, eh?" he said, his cold blue eye tracking her up and down. "Doing what? Let me guess: you want to be a singer like all the other girls."

He sounded so sure of her ambitions.

Viola's indignation flared. Who was he to judge her? He didn't know her history and the obstacles she had to overcome to get to this point. He knew nothing about her.

"I can sing, yes."

"I suppose you want to be a star?"

"No," she said. "I'd rather not be famous if I can help it."

He snorted. "That's the first I ever heard. Why the hell not?"

"You're famous and you're the most miserable man I know."

She held her breath, waiting for his reaction.

He half-smiled, half-winced in pain. "So what is it you want to be if not famous?"

"I want to be a composer like you."

"A *composer*?" He laughed. "Do you hear yourself? Are you living in bloody 1791? Do I have a fucking powdered wig? I'm not a composer. No one ever calls me that. No one *sane* anyway."

"But you *are* classically trained," she said, recalling an ancient

YouTube video of a five-year-old Eames Fawkes playing the piano. As a prologue to an unconventional life, he toured with the London Philharmonic in his teens, working on private musical projects on the side. When he was nineteen, he uploaded a sample into the comment section of a famous EDM blog and caught the eye of a music exec. "You appreciate all genres of music. You—" she stopped herself before she could give away how much she admired him. Used to admire him, anyway.

"I don't know where you've formed such a high opinion about me. I'm a sell-out. I don't appreciate shit."

"That's not true…"

"Let's get to the point," he said. "How do you think I can help you? I haven't put out an album in two years. Have you read what they say about me? I'm finished."

Viola squared her shoulders. Here was her opportunity. "It's more like what I can do for you."

His eye widened. She'd spoken out of turn. Once the words were out, there were no take backs. "*Phantoms* was derivative of *Electric Haunts.* You took what made the first album great and altered the notes, changed two chords, sped up the middle, and added some vocals. Like this…" She hummed the similarities.

Viola's reticence disappeared when she spoke of music, and a more articulate power possessed her. "Anyone who knows music knows it was a rehash. Your lyrics were lazy. It's almost…"

She halted, afraid to continue.

"What is it?" he barked. "Don't stop now."

"It's almost as if you lost respect for your listeners just to make a quick buck."

"Listen," he said. "I don't know who you think you are. The day you command six figs for a set is the day you can give me advice. I don't have to listen to this. What the fuck do you want?"

"To collaborate."

His eyes widened. "Collaborate?! Ha! Get out. I've heard

enough." When she hesitated, his finger smashed the call button. "Nurse. Nurse. Get security."

A woman's static voice crackled from the other end of the line. Viola stepped backward. "Please, h-h-hear me out."

"I can't hear a fucking thing," he said with a tone of finality.

"Okay." Viola reached into her pocket and set down a transparent cassette tape on his night table.

Without meeting his eyes, she fled the room.

———

WITH THE PEST GONE, Eames Fawkes, alone and in pain, picked up the cassette tape. His brows furrowed in annoyance— a running theme since he arrived in Indigo Bay. The town was packed with eccentric people and that was saying something coming from a D.J. who donned a carbon fiber mask during performances.

He studied the cassette. "Strange girl," he muttered, popping open the rose-gold case. The cassette was transparent, housing a spool of neon pink tape. It was the overpriced, prefabricated retro junk you'd buy at a hipster record store. He doubted that a wilting flower like Viola could come up with a stunt like this herself. This had Elyse's influence all over it.

Big, brash, grabs-life-by-the-balls, Elyse. Bohemian love child, lavender-haired Elyse.

Elyse Darrow was the reason he was in the hospital. After weeks of trying—and failing—to bang her, he'd gone out of his way to help her search for her runty dog. The next thing he knew he was in the burn ICU with a catheter jammed up his knob, bandages all over his face, and the stench of burning petrol forever seared in his memory. Except for a broken leg, Elyse escaped the accident with minor injuries. As for her dog? The *reason* his motorbike crashed... that dog didn't have a scratch on him.

Eames hadn't seen his injuries. He was sure he looked like Two-Face. Quite the price to pay for a piece of ass. And the ironic part? Wait for it... he'd never even slept with her.

He was done with Elyse. Fuck Elyse. Fuck her dog. And fuck her bumbling Disney Princess friend and her goddamn stupid demo.

"Who the fuck uses a cassette?" he said to his empty hospital room. Only the beep of his heart monitor answered him.

He mentally replayed Viola's critique of his second album. Derivative? Lazy? What did she know? *Phantoms*, creatively shitty as it was, made a mint. All his concerts sold out within minutes. He made boatloads of money. She didn't know what the fuck she was talking about. That he was even giving her opinion a second thought catapulted him into a boiling rage.

With a grunt, Eames tossed the cassette in the trash. The tape hit the can with a ping and clattered to the floor.

―――――

VIOLA RACED through the hospital corridor and burst into the parking lot. The sky crawled with gray clouds. A bracing November wind chilled her from head to toe.

Without stopping for breath, she dove inside her rusty Ford pickup and slammed the door. Blood rushed inside her ears. She clutched the steering wheel to stop herself from shaking. White puffs of breath clouded her car window. She was close to fainting.

I did it. I can't believe I just did it, but I did it.

Speaking to Eames Fawkes was frightening enough. Leaving behind her demo was perhaps the most terrifying and coura-geous thing she'd ever done.

It took weeks to work herself up to this point.

She almost chickened out more times than she could count.

If someone were to tell her three months ago that she'd make a daring business proposition to The Electric Ghost himself, she would never have believed it.

It was surreal.

Like something that would happen to someone else in the movies.

Today it was happening to her.

All because she'd made it happen.

And she had Elyse to thank for it.

Elyse had intended to make Viola over, transforming her into a confident woman, but all Elyse changed was Viola's wardrobe. Viola knew she would never wear crop tops, shredded jeans, and messy high buns as well as Elyse. Rather than embrace Elyse's 'don't give a fuck' chic, Viola felt like she was playing dress-up. After a week of not washing her hair and wearing nothing but shredded denim and shapeless sack dresses, she smelled like a hobo. While she never transformed on the scale that Elyse had hoped for, something inside Viola had changed.

She'd been content with her small, quiet life...

Living in the shadows of her twin brothers.

Existing as a shadow in her own right. She'd worked at Whispering Vinyl when she was seventeen and never thought about moving some place else. The job paid the bills and filled her days with music. She can boast that she listened to every record in every genre from '40's big band to '80's synth pop.

Then along came Elyse, who pushed and cajoled and bullied. Because of Elyse, Viola saw she could *be* more.

She never had trouble keeping a tune, but she never realize she made a damn good vocalist until Elyse pushed her to sing at a wedding, secretly filmed her, and uploaded the video on YouTube.

Once the mortification of watching herself on YouTube wore off, Viola saw her subscriber base grow. Playing first fiddle in her family string band was a side hustle, but it wasn't until she saw that strangers actually loved her performance that she began to wonder...

What if?

Could she make a career out of her hobby?

She became hungry...

What was the point of merely existing?

What did she have to lose?

The worst thing Eames could do was laugh in her face. He already laughed at her anyway. Was it not better to try and fail than to have never tried at all?

Eames reacted exactly as she'd expected.

She knew the odds going in. The chances he'd listen to her demo were slim to none. Propositioning Eames would bring her no closer to a music career than singing in the shower.

But she had done it. She had done *something*. She'd marshaled up her courage and marched up to the one man who terrified her, and she'd stood her ground.

Viola jammed her keys in the ignition. Her car sputtered to a start. With a shaky sigh, Viola hooked up her phone and hit play. *Cloudburst*, Track 8 of *Electric Haunts*, filled her car. The tempos were slower than his normal mixes, the composition deeper and richer, a synthesized symphony on a cold winter's morning. The song was uplifting and hopeful, even idealistic. The first time she heard it, she imagined a young and optimistic musician with the world at his fingertips.

Was she wrong!

Viola shut her eyes as a sudden pang of sadness struck her. She almost wished she never met Eames. She liked him better when all he was to her were crisp, melodious notes and an albums' worth of long, haunting beats. Funny how he seemed more human in music than in person.

She leaned forward, her hand tapping her tattered leather dashboard. A fine dusting of snow coated her windshield, reminding her that if she didn't leave now, she'd be late for job as a receptionist at Aiden Hines' veterinary practice. If she remembered correctly, Aiden had a pug and a cockatoo scheduled in the morning.

One courageous thing was all she could muster. Except for today's crack in the stone wall, life went on as normal.

———

"YOU BRING IT TO HIM," a female voice whispered from outside Eames' door. "I brought *him* breakfast, lunch, and dinner all week."

A male voice responded, "I did dinner duty yesterday and got soup tossed in my face."

"He's *your* friend."

"He likes you better," he said.

"He's been mean to me all week."

"Olive, please..."

"No, Wesley. No! Get your ass in there!"

"Please..."

"Fine," Olive sighed. "We'll both go."

Several tense minutes passed. They were probably taking deep breaths and doing positive visualization exercises.

Eames stared out the window. His room in the west wing of One Enchanted Evening overlooked a crepe myrtle grove. Snow coated acres of AstroTurfed lawn like powdered sugar.

Despite his grumpy mood, he was grateful to Wesley for offering him a place to recuperate until he was ready to fly back to London. He just didn't know how to express his gratitude outside of the occasional grunts of thanks. More often than not, he was an absolute shit. He couldn't stop himself from being a shit. Long, endless days of boredom and pain nicked away at his psyche, transforming him into a monster. In a few short weeks, he had literally become one of those cantankerous old men in a nursing home, the one that nurses whisper about. His misery had taken a life of its own. He was a train wreck and he didn't know how to stop himself.

At long last, the door creaked open. Wesley and his pretty redheaded girlfriend with the annoying habit of saying 'Whaaa' tiptoed toward him as if they were walking on eggshells.

"Hey buddy," Wesley slapped him on the shoulder. "You're looking well."

Eames could sense Olive shooting Wesley a silent warning: *not what you say to a burn victim.*

Wesley cleared his throat. "Anything we can get you, buddy? Change of bandage? Something to read? Some company?"

Eames shot him a withering look. "No."

Olive set down a tray. The edge of her dinosaur-patterned skirt brushed against his hand. Eames glanced up and scowled at her dairy maid braids. Too fucking cheerful.

He eyed the tray. Minestrone soup. Orange juice. Antibiotics. Painkillers. A pink rectangle.

Wait.

What? That's new.

"What the fuck is that?" he asked.

Olive forced a nervous smile. "A cassette. The hospital packed it with your things."

"It's cool, isn't it?" Wesley asked, draping a protective arm around her shoulders. "Retro. We'd thought you'd want it back."

"And do what with it?" Eames asked.

"Listen to it?" Olive suggested.

"How do you propose I listen to it? Without. A. Bloody. Cassette. Player?"

"My dad used to have a Sony Walkman," Olive said. "I can find his if you want to use..."

He glanced up at her.

She gulped. "Well, enjoy your soup! Text us if you need anything!"

"We'll just..." Wesley scurried after Olive. "You know."

The door slammed.

Left alone again, Eames gave the pink cassette a scornful glance and returned to his favorite activity: staring out the window.

The hours passed. The sun dipped beyond the myrtle grove. Eames drifted into a fitful sleep. A burst of agony startled him awake.

He reached for his painkillers, swallowed them dry.

During his month-long recovery, pain loomed over his shoulder like a cloudburst. Eames clenched and unclenched his fists, waiting for the drugs to kick in.

Sweat beaded his forehead.

The seconds ticked by, a bottleneck of intense torture and then... *ahhh*... sweet release.

He slumped back in his wheelchair, exhausted, his eyes listlessly following the movement on the lawn below.

As owners of a wedding venue, Wesley and Olive were busy setting up for the winter season. They strung icicles-shaped lights across the stark oak branches and hung snowflake-shaped lanterns.

Eames watched them without interest, numbed to the surrounding beauty.

As evening settled into night, the venue's lights switched on.

Strings of icy blues glittered across fences, porch columns, and around the trunks of evergreens. Gigantic candy canes lined the walkway leading up to the stately mansion, each emitting a whimsical glow. There was even a glass tulip garden that flashed violet, green, and blue lights in sync with a never ending Christmas soundtrack.

One would think recovering in a place as magical as One Enchanted Evening would have lifted Eames' spirits.

His spirits were shit.

As beautiful as the world was outside, his world was muted

and devoid of color. The joyful atmosphere was an insult to his pain and hopelessness.

When he told Viola he couldn't hear shit, he wasn't bloody joking.

He literally *cannot* hear the music anymore. No, don't laugh. It was the truth.

He wasn't deaf. There was noise. Lots of noises. Living in the same house as Wesley and Olive had allowed him to put together a library of sounds. They were heavy gamers and there was always some audio disturbance to his peace.

At night, tossing and turning in the cocoon of his own misery, Eames could hear the happy jingles and melodies from their video games. Bleeps and bloops. Sirens and swirls. Computerized gunshots and ambient tones that transported him into a woodland quest.

There were brief sparks of inspiration. He was so close to putting it all together. He was on the bloody verge of arranging just one movement...

And then?

Poof.

Nothing.

Spark snuffed out.

Inspiration gone.

Before his accident, before his shitty second album, he could transform these sounds into music. Composing came as naturally to him as breathing. Now everything was just dull, garbled... noise.

In his darker moments (who was he kidding? All his moments were dark since the accident), he wondered if he was as talented as his fans said he was. He discovered he wasn't as talented as *he* thought he was. Everything that came out of him lately was the same old shit, the same old beats. Everything he created had been done before, either by him or some new face on the EDM scene.

The mouse girl was right. He was irrelevant. He was fucked.

The next day, when his hosts approached him for breakfast, he made an unusual request. "Wheel me outside."

Wesley and Olive looked at each other as if he'd delivered the most shocking request of the century. As their reactions dragged on, wasting precious seconds of his time, Eames snapped, "Bloody Hell, I'm asking to go outside not to the moon!"

Wesley grabbed the handles of his wheelchair. "Where would you like to go?"

"To the grove. Beneath the trees with all that shit on them?"

Olive brightened up. "You mean our electric icicle forest?"

"Yeah," he said. "The icicle forest—that place."

The next thing Eames knew, they'd parked him beneath a glittering canopy, a tartan throw draped over his lap, his hands mitten bound.

Yanking off the dumb mittens with his teeth, he twirled the pink cassette tape in his hand, his thumb and forefinger pinching a reel.

The icicles flashed in a pattern of pure whites and cool blues. The mouse girls' constructive criticism—No, strike that, they were accusations, weren't they? Insults. That fucking mouse girl's *insults* echoed through his head. He was a lazy musician, a hack trying to make a quick buck...

All true. Everything she said. The vault of his insecurities tossed in his face by a babbling git who couldn't even look him in the eye.

A tap on his shoulder. Eames ripped his eyes from the icicles.

"Can we get you anything else?" Wesley asked.

"Yes." Eames studied the cassette, a frown rippling his brow. He couldn't believe he'd resorted to this. "Where do I get my hands on a bloody Walkman?"

———

"Caleb? Conrad?" Viola poked her head into the twins' room. Crusty socks and boxers formed a laundry mountain between their unmade beds.

She wrinkled her nose and took a cautious step inside. "Guys?" she raised her voice over the sound of machine gun shots and stared down at two rustled strawberry blond heads.

Her seventeen-year-old brothers, Caleb and Conrad, were sitting cross-legged on the floor, an empty pizza box between them.

"Caleb? It's me. I'm home."

"Mmp," Caleb grunted, his freckled hands clutching his game controller, his eyes glued to the screen.

Fine reaction for someone who hadn't seen his sister in three weeks.

"Hey Viola," Conrad mumbled without turning around.

She smiled, expecting him to ask her how she'd been. Then she could tell them how she'd not only met Eames Fawkes but dared leave her demo by his hospital bedside. They'll never believe her.

Conrad never followed up his greeting. He jerked against his twin bed, his thumb smashing his controller. "Die motherfucker! Die!"

A pixelated soldier exploded like a watermelon.

"Conrad, where's Pa?" Viola asked.

"Oh hi Vi," Caleb glanced over his shoulder. "When did you come in?"

"Just a few minutes ago," she said.

"Mmph." Caleb had already returned to the game.

"Are you here to make dinner?" Conrad asked.

Viola sighed. "I guess."

"Mac and cheese casserole," Conrad said. "With hot dogs."

"And sprinkle some Doritos on top," Caleb said.

"Where's Pa?" Viola spoke to the back of their heads. "Guys? Guys... did you hear me?"

Viola propped a hand on her hip, her triumphant mood over-shadowed by a sense of invisibility. Who was she kidding? Of course they hadn't heard her. They never listen to a thing she said. She knew how the twins were when absorbed in their game. It would be hours before they emerged from their dark bedroom, squinting like voles in search of food.

Viola walked the narrow hallway of the double wide, picking up a discarded sock and shoving it into the laundry hamper. She got out a trash bag and began picking up Pa's empty beer cans from the floor around his tattered recliner and emptied his ashtray.

She pried open the curtains. A weak beam of morning light filtered into the dingy living room with its shoddy green shag carpet and peeling plasterwork. Without her care, the daisies she left by the windowsill had died. She dumped the wilted flower, pot and all, in the trash bag. Gathering her hair into a ponytail, Viola tackled the dirty dishes in the sink.

A bracing wind blew in from the back of the trailer, causing the screen door to flap on its hinges.

Peeling off her kitchen gloves, Viola ventured outside.

Beer cans littered the stoop.

Fresh leaves crunched under her boots. She spotted Pa snoozing on the ground, at the divide between their property and the spruce forest beyond. He had a knack for falling asleep in the most unusual places: the back pew of the Indigo Bay First Presbyterian Church being one of his most publicized hangover moments. By now, she was accustomed to fishing her father out of tricky and embarrassing situations, but as she knelt to rouse him, she never ceased to pity him.

Sprawled on his back, Pa snored like a hibernating grizzly bear, his gut rising and falling with every breath. A spool of spittle had dried on his patchy beard. Wet leaves coated his flannel shirt.

"Pa?" Viola tapped his cheek, jumping back when he tried to swat her away. "Wake up, it's me."

Groaning, he rubbed his eyes with his fingers. His nails were short and grimy. At last, he blinked up at her with bloodshot eyes. Those eyes could be as mean as a pit bull's, but today they crinkled at the corners at the sight of her face. "You came back, possum."

Viola smiled despite herself. He only called her 'Possum' when he was in a good mood.

"Come on, Pa," she said, draping his arm over her shoulder and helping him to his feet. She got a whiff of him and held her breath. He desperately needed a shower. "Let's get you home and cleaned up. I'm making dinner. Mac and cheese casserole."

"With those little mini Vienna sausages?"

She noticed that his hands were jittery. "And crushed Doritos."

"You moving back home, Possum?"

She bit her bottom lip, not daring to respond. Pa was silent as she helped him back to the trailer. Her decision to move out did not sit well with him. They'd had a huge, mostly one-sided argument which involved Pa shouting all manners of foul things at her. She was selfish. How could she think about moving to the city (Downtown Indigo Bay was only five miles away and hardly a bustling metropolis)? She was moving in with that 'scheming purple-haired liberal' who would surely lead Viola to ruination with her commie ways.

"I've got coffee on the pot," she said, purposefully ignoring his question. "And I reckon you'll want some aspirin for your head."

His thumb grazed her cheek. "You'll be staying awhile, Possum?" He sounded as hopeful as a child.

Viola hesitated. "Maybe overnight."

"Then everything's back to normal."

"Yes." A pang of resignation made her look away. She tilted

her head and gazed up at the winter sky. "Everything's back to normal."

———

EAMES STARED LISTLESSLY at the winter sky. The icicle lights were flashing a brilliant blue by the time Olive fished out her dad's old Sony Walkman and handed him the retro device.

Mumbling his thanks, he waited until he was alone before tucking on his headphones.

He didn't know what to expect. He didn't expect much.

Eames pressed play and sat through a long prelude of static.

"Typical."

The mouse couldn't even nail the technical basics of a demo recording. To his annoyance, he realized that the tape needed rewinding. He sank down in his wheelchair and pressed rewind, then play.

As her voice reached his ears, he jolted from his seat.

Eames fiddled with his headphones and pumped up the volume. The gray world melted away into a sheer explosion of the most vibrant colors.

"What the—" His hands dug into the arms of his wheelchair.

Her voice. That brilliant voice. Never in a million years would he match those vocals with that cowering girl. He shut his eyes. Perfect pitch. Untethered range. A soaring ethereal quality similar to an out of body experience. He saw the festivals, the manic pixie girls painted in neon, and her voice, serenading the desert night. She was the perfect instrument—pure and untrained—just waiting for him to play her.

By the time her demo finished, Eames had broken out into a cold sweat. With shaking hands, he rewound the cassette and played it again.

ABOUT THE AUTHOR

Teresa Yea is an awkward bean with a fondness for British period dramas and minimalism. In the grand scheme of romance novels, she likes dukes and viscounts, adorkable rom coms and spicy ebooks that blazes up her Kindle (you know the kind). She is obsessed with The Witch of Blackbird Pond, a book she has read over 15+ times and wrote about (lustfully) at her website teresayea.com

She seriously wants you to SIGN UP for her NEWSLETTER (https://teresayea.com/newsletter/) where she aims to entertain you... infrequently but with a lot of passion.

Follow her on Instagram @teresayea. She has never influenced anyone, unless you count book recs.

Follow her on Facebook @teresayeawriter for romance novel swooning and Benedict Cumberbatch ogling.

She also penned some broody fantasies about Victorian monster hunters and that gothic one about a cursed ruby. All have sexy times, spice level: Sriracha.

facebook.com/teresayeawriter

instagram.com/teresayea

ALSO BY TERESA YEA

Indigo Bay Series (Romantic Comedy)

Pixely Ever After (#1)

Once Upon a Photo Booth (#2) (coming soon!)

Symphony in the Snow (#3) (coming soon!)

Golden Age of Monsters (Dark Fantasy Romance)

Love in a Time of Monsters (#1)

Empire of Sand (prequel)

Gothic Horror

Black Heart, Red Ruby (standalone)

Printed in Great Britain
by Amazon